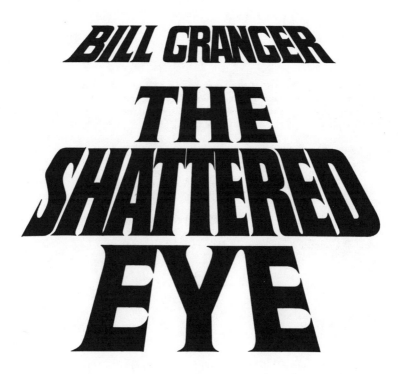

BILL GRANGER

THE SHATTERED EYE

CROWN PUBLISHERS, INC.
New York

Inquiries should be addressed to Crown Publishers, Inc., One Park Avenue, New York, New York 10016

Printed in the United States of America

Published simultaneously in Canada by General Publishing Company Limited

Library of Congress Cataloging in Publication Data

Granger, Bill.
The shattered eye.

I. Title
PS3557.R256S5 1982   813'.54   82-10043
ISBN 0-517-54742-2

The excerpt on page 1 is from *Rememberance of Things Past*, by Marcel Proust, translated by C. K. Scott Moncrieff. Copyright 1932 and renewed ©1969 by Random House, Inc. Reprinted by permission of Random House, Inc.

The excerpt on page 77 is from *The Second Coming* by William Butler Yeats. Copyright 1924 by Macmillan Publishing Co., Inc., and renewed 1952 by Bertha Georgie Yeats. Reprinted by permission of Michael and Anne Yeats and Macmillan Publishing Co., Inc.

10 9 8 7 6 5 4 3 2 1

First Edition

*For Larraine, who led me to Paris
and shared the adventures we found there.*

Note _____

Certain realities are reflected in this book.

In 1968, across Paris and in other parts of France, a fierce student-worker uprising against, among other things, the rigidity of the French educational system nearly toppled the government of Charles de Gaulle. The leftist revolt was eventually crushed, but reforms demanded by the students were enacted. The center of the revolt was in the Latin Quarter of the 5th arrondissement (or district) of Paris, which is one of the oldest neighborhoods in the ancient city. It is the site of the Sorbonne.

In spring 1981, thirteen years after those revolts, the French elected François Mitterand as the first leftist president of the Fifth Republic. In fact, the Mitterand government was the first leftist regime to control France since the Popular Front of Léon Blum in 1936.

Certain war games and "scenarios" developed by computer

programs speculate on the question of what the French armed response would be to an invasion of Western Europe by ground and air forces of the Warsaw Pact countries. This question was fully described in *A History of the Third World War* by General Sir John Hackett of the British army. At the present time, the question has not been resolved.

Computers are utilized by all the intelligence agencies of the United States.

The National Security Agency, as one of the intelligence services, is the hardware and software supplier of specialized goods to the various other services in the intelligence network.

British Intelligence has abandoned the old section names of MI-5 and MI-6. The new nomenclature is "secret."

The Frunze War College of the Soviet Union is located in the southwest district of Moscow.

Terror movements in Europe are many and widespread, operating chiefly in the Basque region of Spain, in Italy, in northern Ireland, and in principal cities, such as Paris. It is supposed by U.S. Intelligence authorities that some of these movements are controlled and/or supplied by the Soviet Union.

In spring 1982, terror threats were made against the life of François Mitterand and acts of assassination and sabotage were performed in Paris and in the region south of Paris.

By late 1982, the military and economic alliance of the United States and Western Europe (called NATO) had become very unstable. While the U.S. debated pulling its troops from the NATO line, Europeans from Germany and Sweden to Great Britain publicly protested the U.S. decision to deploy new nuclear weapons. Further jeopardizing this economic alliance was Europe's decision to participate in the building of a Soviet gas pipeline to the West, while, at the same time, the U.S. initiated various trade wars designed to punish European steel firms who were dealing with the USSR.

Each spring, the students of the Sorbonne in the Latin Quarter commemorate "the events" of 1968 with petty acts of vandalism and with marches in the narrow streets of the old district.

Finally, the agents portrayed in this book reveal that the Central Intelligence Agency faked certain reports to the American government during the Vietnam War. These charges have been publicly aired and debated.

Despite these realities, this book is a work of fiction.

The world has joked incessantly
for over fifty centuries
And every joke that's possible
has long ago been made.
—W.S. GILBERT

PART ONE
MEMENTO

*We passionately long that there may be another
life in which we shall be similar to what we are
here below. But we do pause to reflect that,
even without waiting for that other life, in
this life, after a few years we are unfaithful
to what we have been, to what we wished to
remain immortally.*

—Marcel Proust

1

Washington, D.C.

Mrs. Neumann did not knock at the door to Hanley's bare office before she entered, and she did not speak to him until she was settled on the government-issue metal chair in front of his desk. The temperature in the office hovered just about sixty degrees Fahrenheit, as always, and Mrs. Neumann, as always, wore the thick brown sweater she kept in her own office for her private meetings with the chief of operations of the R Section. It was just after nine-thirty in the morning on January 9, and Mrs. Neumann and her staff had been struggling with the knot of the problem for the past six days.

"Tinkertoy is puzzled," Mrs. Neumann said in her raspy whisper. For emphasis, she struck one large hand on the computer printout sheets that filled her generous lap. After the meeting with Hanley, a meeting without notes written or recordings made, the printouts would be shredded in the large machine in the central corridor.

"A computer cannot be puzzled. It is a machine." Hanley spoke precisely and waited for a reply, his clean, colorless fingers resting on the polished Formica top of the gun-metal-gray desk.

Mrs. Neumann had unlimited access to him because she never wasted his time, no matter how odd her manner or way of conveying information. It was pointless to ask her questions at the beginning of these conversations because she never arrived at her point sooner than she intended.

She was a large woman with big bones and a thickening waist; her bones seemed to stretch her healthy, leathery skin. She had expansive gestures and wore old-fashioned cotton dresses, like a farm woman from another century. Her massive head was crowned by thick, black, spiky hair, cut short, and she had once told Marge in the computer analysis section that her husband cut it for her twice a month. Despite years of practice, he had never become an expert barber.

She spoke at last. "It's in the raw data. The raw data we've been getting from the field in the past four months is the puzzler," she said. "Or rather . . ."

"Or rather what?"

Mrs. Neumann stared at Hanley for a moment, and Hanley tapped his fingers on the desk top. They both understood her look. She was about to bring up something he either would not understand or would not want to hear.

"It has to do with those created indices," she said finally.

Hanley sighed. He hated the words. He hated the computer called Tinkertoy. And he hated the nagging edge of this problem that would not be solved and would not become worse and would not go away.

"You're talking about the . : . indices . . . in your job file or memory bank or whatever you call it?"

"The additional ones, Hanley, the ones that weren't there before."

"That you believe weren't there before."

"Dammit, Hanley, the ones that make connections between entries that I know were never made."

"That you don't remember making," Hanley said.

"My memory is just fine," she said.

"Of course."

Three months ago, Mrs. Neumann had slammed into his office with a loud complaint: Someone in Section had tampered with her work files. She had been storing complicated variables in a separate memory file of the computer in order to relate certain types of data—to make cross-checks of minor bits of information. And now someone had tapped into her files and built up these false indices.

Hanley had called in the National Security Agency—the policeman of the intelligence services—to make a careful and routine check of personnel in computer analysis. They had found nothing, and Hanley had not been surprised. He had assumed that Mrs. Neumann had accidentally punched some incorrect entries into Tinkertoy and then gone back over them without remembering to erase them from the computer memory. Mrs. Neumann had not been mollified; her suspicions remained. "The trouble with all of you is that you don't know a damned thing about computers," she had said at the time. Everyone agreed with her on that.

"What's wrong now?" Hanley asked.

"All right. This new data—Tinkertoy has been giving me a correlation coefficient that—"

He held up his hand. "You've lost me again, Mrs. Neumann." He said it with a slight smile that was not pleasant, as though he were a teacher admonishing a child who skipped words in his reading.

"It's not that hard, Hanley. I wish you'd pay a little more attention to Tinkertoy."

"I am from another age, a noncomputer age. . . ."

"When spies were spies and men were men," she said. "Dammit, Hanley, I'm no older than you."

"Perhaps I am old-fashioned."

"Perhaps you can afford to be," she said in her raspy whisper.

"In any event," he said, "you are in charge of computer analysis, not me. So give me an analysis. In an approximation of plain English."

"Do you remember on 9 December when we picked up that flutter out of British intelligence through our London station?"

"From Auntie?" He used the British operation's slang term for itself. "That was about Auntie running a little operation at Mildenhall air force base?"

"Right. Our base in East Anglia."

"Actually, it is their base, I believe. They allow us to use it."

"What the hell are the British going to fly out there? Spitfires? The British air force is paper."

"No political commentary please, Mrs. Neumann."

"All right. We took all their garbage and fed it into Tinkertoy. All routine. Then on 14 December, Tinkertoy gets fed Quizon's crapola from Paris about new government postings and we dump it in. Nothing special from Quizon, but that doesn't surprise me—we never get anything but press clippings from the Paris papers from that old fool."

"Quizon has been with the Section for a long time."

"Too damned long." She paused and shifted her thoughts. "The point is that yesterday I was working from some of those indices. The ones that someone had put into my file when I complained before."

Another sigh. Hanley realized he wished he were out of this room, strolling down Fourteenth Street, away from this woman and her problem, which Hanley could not quite comprehend.

"So I entered one of those phony indices—"

"I thought you had cleared them from memory."

"I want to know who's been screwing around with my computer," Mrs. Neumann said. "Well, do you know what Tinkertoy gave me? The numbers were fantastic." She glanced at the look on Hanley's face and hurried ahead. "Anyway, I had this great idea right away. You know I was puzzled about the data those indices were throwing together because it didn't seem to mean anything to me. There were things in there like troop movements, but also odd things like indication codes on some individuals. It was like a bowl of popcorn with apples in it—I mean, what the hell do the apples have to do with popcorn?"

"Popcorn?"

"So I asked Tinkertoy to print out all the separate data items that had gone into those indices. And I worked a couple of hours last night going through all the stuff Tinkertoy threw at me, and then it hit me—"

"Overtime? Mrs. Neumann, we need authorization for overtime now. You know that."

"Damn overtime, listen to me. That index selected out—you can say related, if you want—only three names of individuals. Three goddamn names, Hanley."

Hanley stared at her.

"Two were British agents, the two agents at Lakenheath-Mildenhall. And one other. A French woman, an official in the Mitterand government. Madame Jeanne Clermont."

"But I don't really understand any—"

"Let me finish," she said sternly. "What do we have? We've

6

got someone who thinks Madame Clermont and this Lakenheath business are linked in some way important enough to make them want to enter my files—enter my files, Hanley—and play around inside Tinkertoy to find out how they relate to troop-movement figures or—"

"Troop movements. Mrs. Neumann, we have been through all this before. We've had the NSA run checks on everyone at the highest level. I thought we had agreed there is no evidence to support your idea that a mythical someone has tampered with Tinkertoy. Mrs. Neumann, we can't keep going back and forth over the same ground. We all become a little paranoid, it goes with the business, but you agreed that those 'created indices' you complained about must have been an accident."

"I said that you people didn't understand anything about computers."

"Mrs. Neumann, what is the importance of any of this, outside of your obviously firm-rooted paranoia?"

She made a face at him but continued: "Well, it struck me funny because you had talked to me about this Madame Clermont person. Before you sent Manning across. I don't know. I don't suppose it would have bothered me that much until we kept getting some other strange stuff coming out of Tinkertoy."

"Maybe it's a mistake."

"Tinkertoy doesn't make mistakes."

"Someone made a random entry sequence that coincidentally matched another entry sequence," Hanley said.

"Yes. I thought of that."

"Well? Who was it, if it wasn't you?"

"I don't know."

"You should know that."

"I know I should know that, but I don't. I went back over the entries, and there isn't any access code."

"Well, how did the stuff get into the machine?"

"Magic."

Hanley looked up with a sour expression pursing his lips.

Mrs. Neumann flashed him a broad smile. "I was kidding."

"There isn't anything funny."

"But there is. Someone can get into Tinkertoy. And now we're getting more of this crazy stuff. Troop strengths along the Czech corridor, you know, the spring games of the Warsaw Pact countries? They're doubled. I'm sure of it."

"What do you mean?"

"Hanley, I had a request from the Baltic desk for some figures on Polish armored strength in the northern sector, near Gdansk. So I punched it into Tinkertoy."

"Yes?" Hanley asked hurriedly.

"Well, when they came up with some of those troop strengths, something rang a bell up here." She touched her spiky hair.

"What bell?"

"About a year ago I had some reason to find out the strength of the Ninth Armored of the Polish army, and I remember distinctly the figure of two hundred forty-eight tank units."

"So?"

"Now Tinkertoy flashed it out four hundred ninety-six. Exactly double. In one year."

"Is that possible?"

"You tell me."

"Well, where did the new information come from?"

"That's it, Hanley." Her eyes were gleaming. "Tinkertoy said it was there all the time, made in the original report by Taurus in Krakow." Taurus was the Section R agent in Poland.

"Well, then it must be right."

"But it isn't, Hanley, I remember the number. It was two hundred forty-eight, not four hundred ninety-six. Exactly double."

"Your memory is fallible."

"Just as yours is, but I do remember some things, and I know I remembered that number, don't ask me why. And the number is wrong now. Then I went through all the troop strengths in Warsaw Pact, and the figures were incredible. If Tinkertoy is right, the Opposition is putting together a war machine for a hell of a lot more than some troop maneuvers or war games."

For the first time, Hanley felt a chill seeping through her words. He did not understand computers but he understood Mrs. Neumann's plain words: *a war machine.*

"Tell me," he said. His voice was quiet.

"Six hundred and fifty thousand troops," she said. "Two thousand six hundred and seventy-five tanks. Nineteen—that's one nine—armored divisions alone composed of mixed elements of the Czech, Polish, Hungarian, and Bulgarian forces, and—"

"Mrs. Neumann, that's impossible. There can't be so many troops for a war game."

"Right, Hanley, now you're getting it."

"But Tinkertoy can't be right."

8

"Every piece of data in Tinkertoy supports itself. Tinkertoy analyzes that the troop strengths indicate we should put NATO up on red alert status, code two. Now."

"But what do you think?" He realized his voice had assumed a pleading tone.

"Hanley, I'm in computers, you got other geniuses here to do the heavy thinking. I just give them the stuff to think with." She paused and looked across the government-issue desk at the middle-aged man with the pursed lips and dour expression. "I put in this name again, this Jeanne Clermont. I wanted all the readouts on her. Interesting woman, Hanley—a middle-class sort of background but she scored well in tests, went to the University of Paris at the Sorbonne. Became a revolutionary, of course—this was 1967. And in 1968, our William Manning uses her to get the stuff on the Reds there . . . And now she's in the Mitterand government."

"I know all this," Hanley said in his dry way.

"I'm just saying, Hanley, that a person like that could be hooked up with all kinds of funny business."

"Funny business?"

"She was with the Reds once, with those terror people, maybe she still loves them. The trouble with this business, I've told you before, is that you get people like that wandering in, making friends, and you never know what they're going to get into."

"I don't understand the point of this, Mrs. Neumann. Will you be clear? What do you suspect about Tinkertoy?"

"Garbage in, garbage out."

"Dammit, Mrs. Neumann. We always have had troop strength estimates for the Eastern Bloc. That's what we do." He let the sarcasm seep out. "We *are* in the business of intelligence."

"But what if it were changed?"

"But what if it wasn't changed?"

"Exactly."

"You are driving me mad. You are telling me that if there are changes in the data in Tinkertoy, it has something to do with this other change, the one where somebody allegedly and supposedly and all that—somebody somehow called up the names of Jeanne Clermont and these two British agents for some reason that even you don't understand."

"Now you've got it, Hanley," Mrs. Neumann said, smiling with a mother's pride written on her large face.

"But what do I have exactly?"

"I don't know, man. That's what the hell I've been trying to tell you and those idiots at NSA for the last four months—I just don't know. You think there's some answer in all this, that I should just pluck it out. Well, dammit, Hanley, I don't know any more."

And then Hanley realized the chill he felt had nothing to do with the temperature in the little room inside R Section. Tinkertoy could not be fixed. Tinkertoy could not be tapped. It had been set up that way.

But could Tinkertoy ever be wrong?

2 ___
Paris

William Manning put down *Le Monde* and dropped two ten-franc brass coins on the black tabletop to pay for the croissants and coffee. It was just after ten-thirty in the morning and business in the brasserie was slow. On the other side of the shop, two young men who might have been Sorbonne students were playing the electronic pinball machine with deadly seriousness.

The game involved an invasion of creatures from space who were destroyed systematically as the players fired rockets on a screen. Each "kill" was marked by an electronic sound like an explosion; the explosions reverberated in the brasserie, but no one seemed to notice them.

Behind the zinc counter, the proprietor polished the copper finish of the espresso machine while engaged in a long, ragging argument with a fat woman at the cash register who might have been his wife—they argued with intimacy. In front of the counter, the sole waiter lounged, reading the tables in the morning racing sheet.

Manning had entered the place twenty minutes earlier and cataloged all these elements of life there. Then he had selected the table by the rain-spattered window, even though it was chilly outside and the cold could be felt through the thin layer of glass. From his window he could watch the entrance to the English-language bookshop across the way. He knew there was no other exit from the shop; in any case, the woman he had followed for three weeks had no reason to think he was watching her or that she needed a way to escape his surveillance. In a few minutes, when she left the shop, it would be over in any case. One way or another.

Thirty-one days before, Manning had arrived in Paris on the Concorde flight from Dulles airport outside Washington. Time for an assignment was never unlimited in the Section; but this was a delicate matter, and even Hanley could provide no guidelines. "Be careful," he had said at last, as Manning prepared to fly to Paris; "Be careful," as though that would prepare Manning for everything.

He had surveyed the newspaper records for mention of her; he had talked long into the night with Herbert Quizon, the free-lance agent who had immersed himself in the details of her life for the past fifteen years. But no matter how much preparation there had been, nothing readied him for the first sight of her, emerging from the Métro station at the St. Michel entrance, bundled against the February cold in a black coat. None of it prepared him for the pain at seeing her again.

Manning had not spoken of the pain, even to Quizon. He was a thorough agent, a bit wearied by the work of the last fifteen years, but a "good man" in Hanley's patronizing evaluation. He had followed her to mass on Sunday at Notre-Dame. He would not have guessed that she practiced religion; he could not remember that she had taken part in Catholic rituals before. Not when he had first known her.

He had followed her with discretion, with a certain dogged skill that was noted in his records back in the Section. In fact, Manning had been code-named "Shadow" by the whimsical clerk in processing who had charge of such matters. Shadow had once observed at close hand, for sixteen months, the staff and cabinet of Ian Smith of the former country of Rhodesia. He never knew what use had been made of his information; he had never wanted to know. He was a man in perpetual shade, always at the edge of events, always the watcher and never the man watched. Until now, until he had to act against Jeanne Clermont again.

It was not difficult to perform surveillance on her. She had settled into a premature middle age that was as predictable as the hour of sunrise. Her habits were the crabbed habits of a spinster, but he refused to think of her by that ugly English word. She was Jeanne Clermont, as she had been to him fifteen years before; as she was now.

Twice in the past month he had broken into her apartment on the fourth floor of the old building at Number 12, rue Mazarine. He had carefully combed through the scattering of books and private papers and photographs that completed Manning's knowledge of her life in the past fifteen years. He had even found the little school-girl diary she still kept; the entries were without color, without use for him. Yet, slowly, with infinite care and patience, he broke into all the elements of her past life kept in the little apartment with the tall ceilings and the narrow windows. All her secrets were broken.

The second break-in had come less than three days before; it had shaken him, nearly to the point where Manning wanted to quit the assignment, to tell Hanley and Quizon that it was no use, to lie that she had a lover, that she knew he had once betrayed her, that the vague scheme would not work. The secret had been buried in an old schoolbook on the bottom shelf of the bookcase in her bedroom. It was a faded black-and-white photograph. Jeanne had forgotten it, no doubt, because the book was covered with dust. Manning had forgotten it as well, and it struck him like a blow.

In the photograph, she stood next to him as they had been fifteen years ago. Her hair was much longer than the way she wore it now. Her hands were in the pockets of her skirt. Her face was open and smiling, amused by the moment and by the chatter of the itinerant old photographer who had snared them at the entrance to the Tuileries that Saturday. It had been Saturday, he remembered it clearly. He remembered the photographer and his droll teasing of her: "Madame is too beautiful not to be photographed, even by someone like me." He had smiled, revealing yellow and broken teeth.

"Then you may photograph me, monsieur."

"Only fifty francs."

"But consider the honor, monsieur, to photograph someone so beautiful."

"Of course, of course, the honor is great, but unfortunately, I have not been a man of honor for some years. . . ."

How she had smiled, Manning thought again, holding the photograph in his hand in the dull afternoon light of her apartment. She had not only infected the moment with good feelings but she had somehow conveyed the warmth of it to memory, recalled again by the touch of the picture.

He had not wanted to be photographed, and in the picture he was shy and scowling. She had scolded him for his frown. "It could have been such a lovely picture, my keepsake," she had said.

12

"But you have me," he had said.

"How long, William?"

"As long as you want."

Of course, it had been a lie. Everything was a lie, everything he had said led to betrayal. He could not tell her that the agent who had recruited him had warned him, "You must not be photographed, that's elementary, at the demonstrations or at school. Remember, you don't know who's taking your picture and what he intends to do with it."

But Jeanne Clermont had twisted round him and had made him pay the fifty francs for the Polaroid photograph from the old photographer. What harm could there be in a Polaroid photograph?

"Please, William, don't be so sour, you are famous and wealthy, a correspondent from America, you have plenty of money."

"But the photograph won't last . . ."

"I swear, monsieur, on the grave of my mother, it will last forever."

And so it had. Here, in a page of a dusty schoolbook at the bottom of a bookcase in a Paris apartment. They had stood in the sunlight, facing the gardens, their backs to the Louvre. She held his arm and smiled. What would the Section have said?

He had felt a moment of loss so great that he thought he would die, that he was already dead. Three days ago, sitting on the floor of her bedroom, holding the photograph, hearing the voices of the past—Jeanne, the photographer, Verdun and the others at the university . . . What had their expectations of life been on that rare day fifteen years ago? She had shared her bed with him and, after a time, her love. And he had responded in a charade that would end only with terror and betrayal.

"I love you," he told Jeanne in the darkness of a spring night fifteen years ago. He had spoken the words over and over as they held each other in dreamlike embrace, sated by lovemaking, conscious of the feeling and the smells of the other commingled, breathing softly as one. He *had* loved her, in fact, which Hanley never knew, or Quizon, or anyone; he had loved her and betrayed her. Why hadn't he saved her? She might have escaped the net closing around them; she might have gone with him. But he had known, even as he held her, that she would not accept his love and the betrayal of the others. And so he had said nothing to her but that he loved her and would love her forever.

"Monsieur?"

Manning glanced up quickly at the waiter who suddenly hovered at his table.

The waiter had removed the cup of coffee and the plate that had contained the croissants and the ten-franc coins. In the rude way of brasserie waiters in Paris, he was unsubtly demanding further rent on the use of the table in the corner of the empty restaurant. Manning ordered a glass of beer. The waiter made a face that might have been disapproval or merely gas; he withdrew to the counter.

"I think I should arrange the matter on Saturday morning," Manning had told Hanley laconically on the safe phone thirty-six hours ago.

"Is it time?" The voice, scrambled by complex connectors at each end and flung across an ocean, was curiously tinny.

"I don't know. I've done all I can."

"But what if she turns you down?"

"Hanley, there are no certainties in the world."

"But it's important."

"I don't understand that; you've never explained that."

"We're not certain." Despite the flat tone, the voice from Washington was suddenly withdrawn into secrets. "We can't proceed on logical grounds."

"I don't know what you're talking about."

"Be careful." So Hanley had repeated the inane advice, the same he had given at the start of the assignment. He had said it might not work, that he could not predict the human factor. And Manning had not understood a word of it except that they wanted him to confront Jeanne Clermont after fifteen years and lie his way back into her confidence and, if possible, into her bed.

As he followed her, the scenes of the old city had made him ache with nostalgia. He had not been in Paris since 1968, since the night he fled the capital after giving the Section her name and the names of the others and the proofs and the locations of the secret houses. Three years later, after a tour in Vietnam, he had learned what had happened to her. A trade had been arranged between R Section and the French espionage agency, the Deuxième Bureau. It was not made clear to him what the Section had obtained. The French, teetering on the brink of revolution, had obtained time. And the names of those most likely to effect the revolution. And proof enough for a secret court and a secret state trial. Jeanne Clermont had simply disappeared for sixteen months.

Manning could not have returned to Paris on his own.

And then, on the first of February, Tinkertoy had turned up his name in a routine scan of names of personnel changes in the French government. Jeanne Clermont had linked William Manning.

"You might say this is a form of computer dating," Hanley had said flatly, unable to resist the joke but equally unable to make it funny.

"But she would know I betrayed her. How do I explain the absence of fifteen years?"

"You were a correspondent," Hanley said, consulting the file in front of him that day in February. "You told her you were pulling out for Saigon, that the war was heating up after Tet. . . ."

"And she was arrested three days later," Manning had argued.

"She expected it," Hanley said.

"And I never came back . . ."

"You were wounded in Saigon," Hanley had persisted. "We can make it seem to make sense to her."

But I had loved her, he thought then. I had made love to her, I had touched her, I had seen the hint of her soul behind her eyes.

"We need leverage," Hanley had said. "Inside the Mitterand government. These are uncertain times, I don't need to tell you that—"

"All times are uncertain."

"With the peace demonstrations and the Soviet disinformation program in West Germany—why, the West Germans are practically petrified, and—"

"Don't tell me politics. What do you want me to do?"

"I don't know," Hanley had said at last. And that was the way it had been left. Everything depended on Manning and Jeanne Clermont.

"Reestablish the relationship," Hanley had said.

"You're crazy."

"It may not be possible. You see, it is a reasonable risk. To take the chance . . ."

Chance. Risk. Logic. None of it made any sense and they knew it, but they had to cloud the nonsense in words that would mask their own doubts.

Manning put down the glass of beer in the bistro. The students had left the machines and were at the front door. And across the street, the door of the English bookstore opened. For a moment,

Jeanne Clermont stood framed in the opening, the thin light from the shop behind her. She glanced up at the leaden sky and felt the mist on her pale face. She looked up the street and down and seemed to consider; then she started across the shimmering street.

Manning watched her through the mist and the streaked window glass as though he saw her in a dream, through memory.

He had taken the photograph from her room that day. He had replaced all the books and the diaries and the papers, and he had made certain that she would find no trace of the intruder in her rooms. But he had taken the photograph; it was absurd, it broke all the rules, but he could not have left it.

She crossed to the walk in front of the brasserie, the book purchase tucked under the sleeve of her raincoat, and opened the door as though it were not a momentous act.

Manning could only look up at her as though he had been startled. His eyes were wide, and he felt a little afraid; he could not imagine being so close to her again.

Jeanne Clermont stopped in the doorway and stared at him. The door was partially open behind her, blocked by the frozen gesture of her hand. Then she dropped the book on the tiles; it made a loud sound, and the proprietor stopped in midargument, frowned, and glared at her.

Manning could not speak.

Jeanne picked up the book and let the door swing shut behind her.

She stood still for a moment. Her eyes were unchanging, large and calm and so blue that they made her pale skin seem even more pale by contrast. Perhaps there were little lines of age at the edge of her eyes, but perhaps they had always been there. Her mouth was still wide and handsome in the frame of her face. She did not speak.

"Jeanne." He half rose, pushing the chair screeching behind him.

Silence for a moment; they might have been the only people left alive in the city.

And then her eyes changed, her soul shifted behind the blue irises. Manning watched her eyes and thought he saw pain cross them. Or was it only a reflection of his own pain?

"William," she said. Her voice was low, as he had remembered it, but not young and not soft; it had acquired a burden with the years.

"I never expected, I never—" He began the lies and then

stopped; the words were not needed. He could only hope the deception of their meeting would be agreed to by her. Words would not mask it.

"No," Jeanne Clermont said. She stared at him the way one stares at an old photograph or recalls a memory. "Neither did I," she said.

And she took one hesitant step toward him.

3
Lakenheath, England

All things bright and beautiful,
All creatures great and small,
All things wise and wonderful;
The Lord God made them all . . .

Pim seemed to bounce up and down in the pew as he sang the familiar words with earnest feeling but without a decent regard for pitch or harmony. It did not really matter: his voice was lost with the others in the small congregation huddled at the back of the damp old church, and seemed nothing more than a surging whisper in the tide of the others, as though each word he spoke—however keenly felt—had to be hidden.

Next to him, Gaunt did not sing, but waited with ill-conceived impatience for the evensong service to be concluded. It was bizarre; nothing that had happened since Pim phoned him in London at noon and urgently asked to meet him in this rural village in the fens seemed real. And now, without saying anything to him by way of explanation, Pim had hurried Gaunt along into this ancient pile of church architecture to take part in evensong.

Gaunt looked down at Pim as the hymn progressed and saw that tears glistened in the small, deep hazel eyes. Gaunt, not for the first time that day, felt uncomfortable, as though Pim were embarrassing himself and Gaunt was helpless to do anything about it; it was akin to the feeling he sometimes had in the theater during a bad performance. Gaunt fancied himself a man of rare sympathies.

Gaunt—he was aptly named, for his dark face was cadaverous and his limbs seemed to hang as limply as rumpled clothes from his

17

trunk—turned his eyes away from Pim and his tears and fixed them on the young vicar enthusiastically leading the song. White alb and purple stole. Something stirred memory: Purple was the color of Lent, wasn't it? But it must be Lent, it was March; in any case, Easter would be late this year.

Not since childhood had Gaunt thought about matters such as Lent or the color of liturgical vestments in the Anglican Church. Why had Pim dragged him to this place on a dull, foggy Sunday afternoon?

"But you must come," Pim had said. "Something has transpired."

Gaunt, comfortable in his library in the elegant flat he owned off the Marylebone Road, had not wanted to respond to Pim's telephone call. In the first place, he did not want to be connected to Pim's strange little network at all, but circumstances and politics inside Auntie had conspired against him. There were always conspiracies in the intelligence branch, and Gaunt felt, with some justification, that he was often made the victim of them.

"I'm sorry I had to call you," Pim had said at the remote Lakenheath train station.

"Had to change trains at Ely," Gaunt complained.

"I know, I know. Back of beyond here, only sixty-five miles from London. Difficult to believe, isn't it?"

"What dreadful thing has transpired—"

"Not now, wait till we get into the village." He had pushed the little Ford Escort down the narrow A highway to the winding high street of Lakenheath, two miles away. As he talked, his breath rose in steamy puffs from his thick red lips. Gaunt could almost read his words like the smoke signals of red Indians.

"Is the heater broken?"

"Yes, I'm afraid so, meant to have it repaired but there are too many—"

"My God, I'm certain Auntie can come up with the necessary funds to finance it if—"

"Not that," Pim had said. The words had tumbled out of the roly-poly mouth like clowns on a mat. "Actually, just have time to go up to the church in the village, got myself in a bit of a bind, I'm afraid, you see. I've been studying this particular church for weeks now, wanted to get around the vicar. The old vicar was a bit of a curmudgeon, this new one is much better. Really fascinating church, you see, I told the vicar I would attend evensong and he let me have an hour with the brasses."

"What are you talking about?"

"Brasses. Brass of the De Lacey knight, really superb, though a bit small. Fourteenth-century, been closed for years and—"

"Brass? Are you speaking of brass rubbings? Is that what this is all about?"

The irritation had startled Pim, and he had turned to his companion in the cold little car as it chugged into Lakenheath. Pim's eyes had widened, and his mouth dropped. "Why, of course not. I wouldn't have called you up here about brass rubbings, Gaunt. That's just my little hobby, you might say. What do you think this is about, anyway?"

The response irritated Gaunt into temporary silence. The irritation had begun with the phone call and been compounded by the race across London to the train to Anglia leaving from Liverpool Street Station, and heightened by the five-minute wait at Lakenheath platform.

The silence encouraged Pim:

"London doesn't understand the difficulties in this sort of operation. These people are worse than Russians when it comes to gossip and suspicion; in fact, they're worse than the Irish . . . London gave me no methodology on this, only the target. I had to take Felker, for instance, I told you from the first that Med Section had fobbed off Felker onto us . . ."

On and on, a mosaic of words that made a crazy-quilt pattern. Until he mentioned Felker a second time, and Gaunt was compelled to interrupt.

"This is about Felker then?"

For the second time, Pim turned in the little car and looked at his companion with something like astonishment pasted on the porcine features.

"Of course, who do you suppose it would be about? I never wanted Felker, I want you to note that. Later, I mean, when we make the report."

Felker. The weak link in the whole strange pattern of the operation that had gone on all that winter at Mildenhall, where the American air force maintained its strong operations.

"Why can't you tell me now?" Gaunt had pleaded, following the little man into the churchyard and around the broken path to the side door of the Norman edifice, with its squat tower and bleak yet eloquent walls and windows.

"I saw the pastor. In the high street, I had to agree . . . he remembered that I had promised . . . this is such a mess, but it will

19

all be straightened out . . ." The words had trailed off as Pim led Gaunt into the church and they were made silent by the presence of the others in the little congregation.

Something had gone terribly wrong. Gaunt knew Pim, and for all the little man's distracted speech and fluttering ways, he was not a fool. Something had gone terribly wrong with the assignment.

"And I must say what comfort there is to be found in the words of the Twenty-third Psalm. Because it is not only the boasting of David in the power and majesty of God and in David's belief that God will uphold the faithful; it is in the certainty that God will surely comfort us in our moment of trouble, as we walk 'through the valley of the shadow of death.' What shall we fear? Nothing but our fear of God. Comfort is what He brings us in that terrible hour. Such a cozy word, 'comfort'; it conjures up the image of a friendly fire at the end of a long and damp day in the fields . . ."

Gaunt frowned at the words of the vicar, but none would have noticed the frown; his face had few emotional ranges that were not dominated by his thin lips and narrow eyes. If he were to smile, it might be mistaken for a frown. He had large teeth and they were bared—at smile or frown—by the thin layer of lips.

Rubbish, thought Gaunt. He felt the service would never end. He felt as he had as a child, trapped by the adult conventions of service and worship and meaningless rituals and words that lied. Shall I fear no evil? Of course I shall fear it; it cloaks every step I make in the service; it cloaks the silly chatter of Pim, who prattles about brass rubbings when all he means is that he cannot tell me yet about Felker. What is he waiting for?

Gaunt looked at Pim in the pew next to him and saw that the porcine features were in repose; the words of the vicar, however hoary, rolled over Pim like comforting waves of heat from that fire crackling in the metaphorical fireplace, waiting for him at the end of a gray, wet day in the fields.

A day like this Sunday, Gaunt thought.

"And remember always that the Lord shall be with you, all of you, each in your secret hearts, all the days of your life, and let this comfort you. . . ."

But there was no comfort, Gaunt would argue. Accept that there is no comfort and the end of the long gray day in the fields is only darkness and the peace of oblivion.

Rain began to beat again at the windows, gently, like a stranger knocking at the back door. Cold, mist, rain, wind; there was no comfort in nature or in words or priests. Especially in thoughts of God.

They rose and sang another hymn, and Gaunt groaned another "My God, Pim" under his breath, but the little man ignored him and sang the hymn in the same surging flat voice as before, rolling like the cold waters in the canals that cut through the farm fields in Anglia. Gaunt had studied the countryside from the window of the first-class compartment of the train up from London. Flat and timeless and dismal, with the flat sky pressing down on the flat earth as though all things had lost a dimension. The fields were turned for spring planting and were black, held down by leaden unmoving clouds that stretched from the Wash down to London and beyond.

Pim touched his shoulder. He realized he had been daydreaming and the service was over. He moved out of the pew, holding his trilby in hand. The young vicar had moved down to the side door that faced the graveyard. Darkness had fallen. The vicar's youthful face was bright with good-fellowship and a smile that bespoke gratitude to the congregation; at least they had come to be comforted.

"Thank you for attending, thank you, Mr. Pim."

"It was a wonderful service, Vicar."

"And for bringing your friend . . ."

The vicar wanted to talk, to pin them in conversation, but behind them a large woman in a gray coat shoved up to gush at the young minister. "What a beautiful sentiment," she began.

Pim escaped with Gaunt into the mist of the graveyard. They stood for a moment and felt the chill seep into their clothing.

"What now, Pim? Tea at the vicarage?"

The little man huddled into his mackintosh; his piggish eyes darted up and showed a trace of annoyance. "Yes, Gaunt, that's all very well. In fact, I met the vicar on the high street scarcely two hours ago, he reminded me about the service, and I *had* promised him. You don't seem to appreciate the difficulties in operating—in running any decent sort of operation—in this country. Especially in Suffolk. My God, Gaunt, these people consider a stranger someone who has lived here less than thirty years. We have constrictions in this sort of society, you simply don't understand, no one at Auntie understands—"

"All right, all right, what now? What about Felker?"

"Yes. What about Felker?" The voice was solemn, dirgelike. The rain and darkness closed around them; they were beyond the pale of light coming from the church door, beyond the gaggle of women and elderly men gathered around the young priest.

"Leave the car, let's go up to the Half Moon for a warm pint."

"Pim . . ."

But the little man led the way without words. Again, Gaunt followed him around the bulk of the Norman spire and up the high street, which was merely an extension of the A highway. At the end of the strip of shops squatted the Half Moon with its dark, flinty stone glistening in the damp. To the side of the structure were the outside toilet facilities. The stink of centuries was in the stones and in the damp wood. The green door beckoned with a single lamp above it and a wooden sign that said the proprietor had license to sell beverages on or off premises.

"Saloon bar," Pim said, nodding toward the dark inner entrance. They climbed the steps and waited at the bar.

The proprietor was a middle-aged man with a round bald head and sly blue eyes. The public bar on the other side of the pub was bright and cozy; the saloon bar, albeit more elegant, was cold and empty and dark.

"Evening," the publican said.

"Two pints bitter," Pim ordered.

Gaunt interrupted with a stubborn tone. "Large Grant's, I think, if you have it."

"We have it, sur," the publican said, immediately adopting an air of hostile subservience. His accent was pure Suffolk, the words uttered with a slurred reluctance, each sound born like a breech calf, half strangled through the clenched lips.

The publican drew the bitter and placed the pint on the bar and then measured a portion of smoky Scotch into the snifter glass.

"Ice, sur?" the publican said.

"No thank you."

"Americans," he said.

Gaunt said, "I beg your pardon?"

"The American base, sur. Not far from here. At Mildenhall? We get Americans sometimes, not often, they don't patronize the village shops, have all their goods brought to them in the PX. Even flour. Don't like our flour, they say. Everything has to be made with ice. And vodka. They don't fancy whiskey; everything must be vodka."

"Yes, isn't it so?" Pim said brightly. "Ah, well; we have to put up with them."

"I don't mind the ones drink quiet and don't make a fuss." The publican furrowed his brow. "The local girls. That's what I can't stand. They hitch up to the base every Saturday night, want to get themselves a rich American, I suppose. England isn't good enough—"

"Ah, well, just so," said Pim.

Gaunt withdrew from the circle of light at the bar. Why did Pim indulge these people? The conversations of rustics were endless, pointless, circles in circles.

"Mind, I don't have a prejudice against them. Except the blacks, I can't abide them in my place."

"Yes, yes, feel just the same."

"Nothing I like less than to see a black one with one of the local girls. They have no shame."

"Who? The blacks?" Gaunt could not resist it; the frustrations of the day were piled in his remark.

The publican gave him an angry look and turned away, back to the public bar on the far side of the old house. A game of darts was in progress there, and they could hear the steady *thunk thunk* as the darts embedded themselves in the board.

"You didn't have to say that."

"My God, sit down, Pim, and give a fill and stop this bucolic tour."

"This is my territory, Gaunt; this is my operation. You can't come la-de-da from Auntie and queer it for me." The uninflected voice suddenly found its roots in the East End; it was rough, threatening. The little man who had seemed so ridiculous weeping at church seemed dangerous now.

"Pim, I have been waiting two hours for your fill, and I have endured being prayed over, sung at, and now been the unwilling participant in a blatantly racist conversation that has absolutely no point except to endear you to a half-wit publican and—"

"Careful. Careful." Softly, dangerously.

Gaunt thought of something more to say and then thought not to say it. The two men sat down at a table removed from the bar in the half-darkness and sipped their beverages for a moment. Gaunt tasted the smoky whisky and felt it warm him.

"Yesterday," Pim began. "We were supposed to meet at Ely. You see, I had arranged to take some rubbings from the tombs in the cathedral and—"

Gaunt put down his glass heavily. "Damn your brass rubbings and damn your churches. I want to know about Felker."

"As I was saying." Pim paused. His voice had resumed its toneless quality. Each word was important because it was half hidden, even as it was uttered; each word counted now. "Ely was safe, I could watch his coming and cover him. Felker didn't arrive. I waited first at the cathedral and then at the fallback in Ely. Then I went to the third fallback, to the safe house. Felker wasn't coming; something had gone wrong. You see, we were very close to the Opposition man; very close. Much closer than I could signal you in the reports."

"Dammit, Pim, I was your control officer."

"Yes. But you have to have a feeling for this sort of thing. In the field."

"I've been in the field."

"But you've been at Auntie too long. Too long. There was nothing I could explain to you. Not until it happened."

Auntie. Contempt was mingled in the utterance of the common, ragging nickname adopted by all the field agents for headquarters of the Ministry for External Affairs (Extraordinary). "Auntie" was so widespread that the word had shown up from time to time in official correspondences between the minister and department heads; naturally, the minister initiated the use of the word in such exchanges. At one time, the intelligence units for internal and external espionage had been coded MI-5 and MI-6 respectively. After the embarrassment of the Philby spy network inside British intelligence and subsequent revelations of other traitors, a housecleaning had thrown out both bathwater and baby in an attempt to restore the prestige of British intelligence. And so the old MI-5 became Ministry for Internal Affairs (Extraordinary) and foreign intelligence became the preserve of Auntie. No one quite knew why "Auntie" was chosen as a nickname; like all nicknames, it came about spontaneously and it was kept because it seemed to fit perfectly.

"And so? Pim? What happened?"

"To Felker, you mean? Why, that's obvious."

"Not to me."

"He bolted."

There was a long moment of silence. Gaunt felt failure creep around his neck like the chill of the wetlands all around. He brushed at it with his hand and realized he felt choked. It had been his operation, he had been control officer, and yet, at the critical moment he had not been in control at all.

"I ran the checks all night."

24

"Through Auntie? Wasn't that indiscreet? I mean—"

"No, no. I'm not such a fool. He simply took the ferry at Harwich to the Hook of Holland. Somewhere in the Low Countries now, I should guess. Unless he's made it to Germany. The funny thing is that he did so little to cover his trail. Do you suppose he wants someone to know he's gone?"

"We know."

"Not us, Gaunt."

Another silence. Speech seemed so difficult now, as though both were learning a foreign language.

"You should have notified me right away, it was your—"

"Don't become tedious." Again the piggish eyes darted up a warning glance. "By the time I was certain, absolutely rock certain, there was nothing to be done. You see, I thought perhaps Reed had done him in."

The Soviet agent. The watcher at Mildenhall who had been the object of the operation. The Soviet agent who seemed so in love with the lifestyle of England. The Soviet agent who whored in Piccadilly with the Soho boys; the Soviet agent who liked fast cars and Seville Row clothes. He had been utterly corruptible. They had meant to turn him, and now Felker, their agent at the point of contact, was gone.

"And Reed did not?"

"No. I was certain of that. At the end, I mean. You see, I saw the problem in two ways. If Felker had bolted, there was nothing to be done except to cover the trail. For Auntie and for our Soviet friends. I mean, it would hardly do for the Opposition to think that one of ours could prove less than trustworthy. We're all done with traitors, ever since the reforms. Auntie says so."

"Your sarcasm is misplaced. This is so fantastic, I scarcely believe what I'm hearing."

" 'More things in heaven and earth . . .' "

"Didn't you have a clue? I mean, you were the network man. You saw Felker every day."

"Not every day, but no, I didn't. Not a flutter, all this time wasted," Pim said. For the first time, he sounded tired and a trifle sad.

"You should have alerted me."

"And what would you have done, Gaunt? Raised the hue and cry? Alerted the countryside? 'Find this man.' I did what had to be done. I had to be certain."

Gaunt picked up the glass and sipped. The whisky slid

smoothly over his palate and throat, but it did not warm him. He felt the chill of the old building, of the bare flat countryside, of the darkness without.

"I had to be certain about Felker. Why did he leave a trail? And why did he leave at all?" Pim seemed to ask the questions of himself.

"Turned. He was turned."

"Not at all. Reed was a weak man."

"It was a trap."

"A strange trap, then. No. I wanted to understand what Reed had said to Felker or what Felker had picked up from Reed or what Felker had that was suddenly worth what he did. Yes. Something of value had been obtained."

"How can you be certain Reed didn't kill him or threaten him?"

"That is not a possibility, I'm afraid."

"How can you be certain?"

"I can be certain. It is not a possibility."

"Dammit, Pim."

"Consider the problem I faced last night." Pim started to pick up his glass of beer and then paused; he let his hand, a delicate hand with finely formed fingers, rest around the glass.

"Felker bolted. What was the reason? And what would follow? By bolting, Felker revealed the operation here. It was a matter of damage control—what would the Soviets think once they learned that Felker had skipped our control? They'd go after him. They'd contact their agent in place at Mildenhall. They would send investigators. They would be very thorough. And what about Reed? He could return to Moscow and lay out Felker's defection for his masters and get back in the club. In any case, he would be transferred out of Mildenhall. The Soviets aren't stupid. They would know we were after Reed."

Gaunt waited. In the half-light, his drawn features made his face a skull.

"The problem of Felker could wait until I resolved the problem of the Soviet agent in place here. It was a field decision."

"You should have consulted me."

"I knew what you would have advised, and you would have been wrong. I didn't have time to persuade you."

"Dammit."

"Felker had been your recommendation, after all. To the network. When I first proposed the scheme."

"Felker came to our little operation from Med Section. He was recommended," Gaunt said. The bureaucrat surfaced suddenly as a shark. "I knew nothing of him except the recommendations I received. He did good work on Malta for Med Section."

"And what did Felker learn?" Crooned softly by Pim, his hands immobile on the table.

"You might have thought to ask the Soviet agent," Gaunt said with sarcasm.

"Yes. I thought of that. Right away."

Suddenly, the door to the saloon section opened and an American in cheap civilian clothing and a girl who was heavy in the hips entered. The American appeared to be a little drunk. He asked for the publican in a loud voice. She was English; she spoke with the same Suffolk accent as the publican.

"Vodka, vodka on the rocks. With a twist. You got a lemon?"

"Lemon juice. Lemons are very hard to come by at this time of—"

"Yeah, yeah, you guys haven't heard of Florida. Jenny? Whaddaya having?"

"Shandy, please, not too bitter."

The publican ducked his head with subservience intended as a reprimand to both of them. He placed an ancient plastic ice bucket on the bar in front of the American and then served the drinks. Gaunt and Pim were silent, staring at the bar, staring at nothing. Pim's last weary words were slowly sinking in.

Yes. I thought of that. Right away.

"I'm gonna take three ice cubes, if that's okay," the American said.

"Certainly. Sur." The publican spoke without pleasantness; the veneer of servility had been stripped back to bone-chilling politeness.

"Ought to be," the American grumbled, dropping the cubes in his drink.

"One pound twenty p then," the publican said, and the American pulled a pile of mixed American dollars and English notes out of his pocket and handed over two soiled bills.

"And you made contact," Gaunt said, turning back from the tableau at the bar.

"Yes. It was the only way, I saw that. I had to determine what made Felker bolt."

27

"But you broke cover . . ."

"Of course. I made it perfectly clear to Reed that the game was up."

"We had no scenario for that."

Pim pulled a face at Gaunt's use of the Americanism. "We cannot anticipate every eventuality. It was important to act quickly, in the event of Reed wanting to break as well. I got hold of Reed as soon as I was certain that Felker was really blown. Reed broke down, hadn't known Felker was an agent."

"Is that true?"

"No. Naturally not. We were seeking to turn Reed, Reed had some inkling of Felker's identity. I told him as much. Reed was not an accomplished liar, in any case. I think the Soviets decided to use him because he appeared so Anglo and because he had a certain physical attraction. And inclination. For the younger men at the base."

"Spare me the details."

"Reed." Pim seemed lost in reverie. "He claimed his great-grandfather was John Reed, he was half American, he claimed. Y'recall, John Reed, the journalist who recorded the Russian Revolution? Buried in the Kremlin. Great hero over there. 'I have seen the future and it works.' "

"Pim, what are you talking about?"

"Reed. He was weak in the end. I think I mentioned that in one of the interim reports. Led to the operation in the first place. Spotted him the second week he was here, I said he was a Soviet agent, and then I was certain we could turn him. Weak. Would have been useful to us." Spoken sadly.

"Where is Reed now?"

"Broke down completely at last and requested asylum. Of course I said we would take him in—if he cooperated. So he filled me in a bit and then a bit more. Felker took a cipher book, you see. What was the cipher? Well, it was coded out of a Graham Greene novel—what do you think of that?"

"Absurd."

"Well, code books tend to be. Such an old-fashioned device. *England Made Me.*"

"What did you say?"

"The name of the book. By Greene."

"It sounds like you and Reed had a lovely chat. Just where is he by now? Halfway to Moscow?"

Pim looked earnestly at the cadaverous figure on his left. His hands rested on the table. "You do see that this is a mutual problem, don't you? I can't be left here all alone in this."

"You should have notified me right away."

"But you sent me Felker. You told me that Felker was reliable."

"I received Felker from Med Section with the highest recommendations."

"Med Section is a fairy farm," Pim snapped. "La-de-da boys, traipsing around Auntie in drag . . ."

"Dammit, Pim, that's the second time tonight you've been offensive. I'm treated to racist jokes and now—"

"Our problem," Pim said softly. "We can't indulge in the luxury of mutual recriminations. Not now. I talked to Reed about the book and then about messages. Received a request from Moscow ten days ago to determine the date of the next NATO exercise, something about airlifting hospital supplies and personnel to a mock battlefield. I mean, hardly high priority, it will be in the papers before long . . ."

"Where is Reed?"

Pim stared at him for a moment and then rose, resting his hand on Gaunt's sleeve. The sleeve of the raincoat was still damp beneath his touch. At the bar, the American and his girl friend were talking softly. The American had rested his hand on the thigh of the heavy girl; she had rested her hand on his lap. She was kneading the folds of his trousers across his lap. For a moment, Gaunt stared at them. Then he felt the tug on his sleeve and rose noisily.

"Outside," Pim said.

They pushed open the saloon bar door. The American laughed suddenly, and Gaunt thought he heard the English girl say "fags."

The outside door slammed behind them. The wind slapped their faces. It was much colder now, much wetter. Pim led the way across to the lavatory building, erected from the same sharp black stone as the public house.

"We better use the facilities now, while we have the chance," Pim said.

Gaunt followed; it all seemed like an absurd dream to him. The two men unzipped their flies and aimed at the ancient trough built into the base of the dark, damp wall.

"You see, I had to save us," Pim said. "The mission was blown when Felker took off. Reed was no use to us. You see that, don't you?"

In the trough, their mingled urine steamed in the cold. They zipped their trousers and stood still for a moment, staring at the wall of the lavatory.

Gaunt thought now that he understood. The thought came as a weight to him; it pressed on his chest. Now the whole trip to Anglia took on a different shading, as though the melancholy premonitions of the black fields viewed from the train window had been directed to prepare him for this moment.

He followed Pim outside into the cold wind.

"Where is Reed, then?"

Pim looked at him. "Do you understand?"

Gaunt nodded.

"In the boot."

"My God. How long?"

"This afternoon. I didn't want to leave him. I thought it best if the body wasn't discovered for a couple of days. It will give us a chance to act. To put out a net for Felker in a quiet way. Obviously, we know more about him than the Americans. Or the Russians."

"Was it necessary?" Gaunt's face was bloodless, and he realized his hands were cold.

"Felker must be seen to have been the beginning and end of the network. The Soviets can't get wind that a whole damned section of Auntie is involved in spying on our American friends on a continuing basis. This had to be a one-time encounter, Felker to Reed. And Felker killed Reed and then decided to resume his previous status as an . . . independent agent."

"Felker had been with us for seven years."

"He wasn't even British," Pim said, as though that explained everything.

"What are you going to do with . . . with . . ."

"Our friend? In the boot? I wanted to wait until evensong was over and traffic was light. Everyone abroad is in the pubs now. I think it's the best time for this sort of thing."

"How can you talk about this? You had no sanction to eliminate Reed. And on home soil, yet."

"Don't go on about that," Pim said. "It's in your interest as much as mine to arrange a convenient story for the death of Reed. It explains Felker, it shifts the burden back to Med Section, they fobbed the fairy onto us in the first place, they assured us Felker was absolutely reliable. You and I, Gaunt, we never completely trusted him, did we? But our hands were tied."

"This is madness. Auntie will never accept such thin lies."

30

Pim was now leading the way up the high street back to the black Ford Escort. Despite his longer legs, Gaunt felt like a schoolboy trying to keep up with the older children.

"Auntie accepts such lies all the time; Auntie will believe whatever she wants. It will be convenient for Q to think that Med Section bollixed the matter. Q has been down on Med and their work, especially in Malta."

"You know so damned much about the politics at Auntie . . ."

Pim permitted the briefest of smiles. "After all, I *am* an intelligence agent."

"And why am I here? Why couldn't you have done what needed to be done and then come down to London and given me a fill?"

"That's obvious, isn't it, Gaunt?"

"Dammit, Pim, you had no sanctions."

"What's done is done."

They entered the car, and Pim quickly pulled out of the quiet village and followed the meandering A highway past the cricket grounds and toward the American air force facilities. As they neared the top of a small hill, Pim switched off the lights and the automobile plunged into the blackness of a side road that Gaunt had not even seen. In the distance, the faintest rim of half-light marked the horizon and indicated there was still a sun somewhere in the world; that there was still light.

"Here," Pim said. He stopped the car but did not shut off the engine. The motor purred quietly.

Pim got out of the car. Gaunt hesitated for a moment and then opened his side. "Don't you have a torch?"

"Do you want to advertise?"

"But how can we see?"

"Your eyes will adjust in a moment."

"Where are we?"

"At the edge of a farmer's field. He plowed last week, I don't fancy he'll be down this way for a while. There's always the chance, I suppose, but I think we should have three or four days at least until the body is discovered."

"This is horrible."

"It's been a long time since you were in the field, Gaunt."

"My God, I never did anything like this."

"The occasion never demanded it," Pim said. "There. I've got my night vision."

He opened the boot of the car. Reed had been a tall man with

31

fair hair. His head was twisted down unnaturally and the whole body bent double. One of his hands was bloody, but the blood was congealed. Gaunt looked closely and felt sick.

"Banged his hand when I slammed the lid of the boot down against it. Had to sort of wedge him in," Pim said, like a clerk explaining the packaging of a new product.

"I'm going to be ill," Gaunt said.

"No." The voice was small and mean again. "You're gonna do what you got to do. Help me."

Pim reached around the middle of the bent corpse and tugged. For a terrible moment it seemed the body would not be moved, but then it came squeezing out of the narrow opening, gradually, the head lolling like a broken doll's head.

"Damn you, pick up his head, I don't want blood on the padding."

Gaunt moved in a dream. He felt the cold burden of the head in his hands. He pulled. He had touched a skull once, as a child, a skull in a display at the British Museum. Columbian Art or something; a horrible thing. It had not frightened him in the museum, but later, in dreams in his own bed in the house off Bloomsbury Square, he had been seized by the most horrible nightmares. The bad dreams had lasted for years. The nightmares concerned the faces of the dead, and as he had grown older, he had seen the death mask in his own features.

He was not afraid now. He helped the little man carry the burden up the grassy incline. Once he almost fell when his foot stumbled into a rabbit hole.

The nightmares would come later, in his own bed again in London, in the darkness.

"Now push him over," said Pim.

The body of the dead agent tumbled cleanly over the precipice and splashed into the waters channeled at the edge of the plowed field.

"That should do it," Pim said, a shopkeeper closing for the day. "Don't linger now."

Pim touched the damp sleeve of Gaunt's coat. Gaunt was pulled out of his reverie. He hurried after the little man down the incline to the waiting car.

Pim closed the boot lid softly, and the two men got inside. Slowly, he started off down the one-lane road.

"Lights," Gaunt said nervously.

"Wait till we get back to the highway. I can see well enough."

"What if you go into a ditch?"

"I told you, this is my territory—my area of expertise, you might say."

Gaunt closed his eyes.

He felt the burden of the skull beneath his hands. He opened his eyes and blackness remained, dead and formless as oblivion must be. Pim's territory. But the nightmare would be his own.

4

Bethesda, Maryland

"Devereaux resigned."

The Old Man took the news without visible sign. He picked up the black briar pipe from the rosewood pipe stand on his desk and slowly began to tamp shreds of rough-cut tobacco into the stained bowl. He worked smoothly, his fingers darting into the bowl and around its rim like spiders fixing webs.

Hanley waited for him to speak. He did not look at the Old Man directly nor at the activity of his spider fingers. He fixed his gaze at a place on the teak desk where there was nothing at all and the gloss of the dark wood provided a partial reflection of himself. He felt aged; he looked old, in fact; but the lines of age had been most pronounced since the Old Man decided nine days before to suddenly pull Devereaux back into headquarters. The Old Man knew what the result would be. It was as though each had taken a speaking part in a tattered melodrama where the lines were hoary and inevitable and the denouement long expected; yet these players were expected to proceed to the end of the act as though none of them knew how it would all turn out.

"I really didn't expect that," the Old Man said. He was done with tamping and filling at last. Now he selected a large wooden match from another rosewood holder and struck it against a flint and let the flame be sucked into the pipe bowl three times. The air in the small room was suddenly filled with the acrid, sickly sweet odor of burning tobacco. "This morning all this happened?"

"Last night. He dropped into the Section after closing time.

He said he wasn't going to come at all but then decided he should do that. At least that."

"What did he say to you?"

"Nothing more."

"No fond farewells?" The Old Man stared at the puffs of smoke rising from the pipe; only the tone of his voice indicated a gossip's interest in what had happened.

"Did you expect any?" Hanley let the bitterness creep into his voice. Devereaux had been useful to the Section.

The Old Man continued to study the clouds of smoke for a moment as though they contained certain visions reserved for him.

"He wasn't independent, you know, Hanley. You of all people should know that."

"That was never at issue."

"Of course it was. He was just an agent, Hanley. I think he should have appreciated the promotion."

Hanley did not speak. He continued to stare at the balding image of himself reflected in the gleam of the desk top.

"Too much arrogance," the Old Man said.

"What?"

"Insolence, arrogance—whatever you call it. From the beginning. I suspected he was out of control. He was going out of control. It's happened before, with the Langley Firm, with us. These people operate alone, they begin to think they *are* the Section. That fellow at Langley . . ."

"Agee."

"Damn. He blew the whistle, and by God, he got away with it. I would have taken care of him."

"Devereaux won't write a book."

Hanley felt cold and sickened. He glanced down at his colorless fingers, pressed on the crease of his trousers. Devereaux was gone; Devereaux had been useful. In a strange way, Hanley felt he would miss him, and Hanley always prided himself on his lack of emotion. Well, it was done with. After all, Devereaux was only an agent.

"What about this Paris adventure?"

The Old Man's voice shook Hanley out of his reverie.

"We've got Manning in place, at least. No slipups yet."

Hanley did not carry notes or papers; everything in the meeting was official but off-the-record between them. Later, summaries of the minutes would be typed and filed in cardboard holders marked "TS—Priority One." It was the regular weekly meeting between Rear Admiral Thomas M. Galloway (USN Ret), director of R Section, and his chief of operations. For the convenience of the Old Man, it was held in the library of Galloway's Bethesda house, at the rear of the two-story brick colonial off the Old Georgetown Road in the northwest suburb of Washington.

Outside the sliding patio windows was a tangle of private forest land. March had stolen in quietly, and green shoots of garlic and wild onion and wild asparagus were pushing through the brown, muddy earth between the thin trees. Damp southern breezes from Virginia caressed the capital city and made life in government seem suddenly vague and unimportant. Hanley had grumped that it was spring fever, and like all his mundane announcements, it had circulated within the Section among the clerks and cipher personnel who were amused by all that Hanley said.

"But has he made any move?"

"Of course." Hanley looked up. "He's there, he's made contact, the . . . liaison."

"Is he in her pants yet?"

Hanley was offended. He frowned, but the Old Man smiled at the crudity; something in the mission had struck a ribald note from the beginning. The Old man sometimes fancied himself a rough old sea dog given to bawdy talk and hard language; in fact, the Old Man had spent his dull naval career sailing a desk in the intelligence division of the Office of Naval Operations, deciphering stolen cables and suggesting impractical new ways to gauge Soviet naval strength. He had been made director of R Section after his family gave a large contribution to the 1972 reelection campaign of Richard Nixon.

"I don't know . . . details of the relationship," Hanley continued in his prim, flat Nebraska accent. "I thought we were more concerned with the initial contact, whether it would come off. The human factor here—"

"The human factor is if Manning can cut the mustard twice with the same goddamn Communist French whore," the Old Man said.

Hanley winced. He felt aged; the winter had aged him, Devereaux's leaving had aged him. Sending Manning back into the same assignment after fifteen years had aged him. And Tinkertoy. Always the thought of Tinkertoy, casting a shadow in the past months on all other matters inside the Section.

"Tinkertoy," Hanley said.

"What about the damned thing now? Are we finished with the Paris briefing?"

"We put Manning in place because of the initial cross-reference," Hanley began, as though in a dream. He was not so much informing the Old Man as recalling his own memory, trying to put a special link between all the disparate events of the past few months.

"Tinkertoy coughed up Manning's name when we ran a routine comp search for some appointments announced by the Mitterand government. I vaguely remembered the whole business—he was freshly recruited, a journalist initially, and we had trained Manning and sent him back to Paris under Quizon's control. He had made contact with this woman in the first place—"

"I knew all that, dammit," the Old Man said, picking a quarrel.

"Yes. We knew that," Hanley said in the same vague way. "Mrs. Neumann was scanning Tinkertoy again this week. She's convinced something is wrong." He paused and chose a rare adjective: "Terribly wrong."

"What happened?"

"Tinkertoy. Mrs. Neumann ran a comp search on the name of that Soviet agent, the one who was killed near our air force base in England. Reed. And Reed linked with Mme Clermont."

"That's ridiculous."

"Machines don't make jokes," Hanley said. "If Tinkertoy is having a joke, no one understands what it is. The link had not been there before, Mrs. Neumann is certain of that. Someone has entered Tinkertoy and linked Reed with Clermont."

"Mrs. Neumann is the human factor here, you're always talking about the human factor—how can she be sure that she didn't—"

"Dammit, no one can be sure of anything except Tinkertoy," Hanley said. The outburst was unusual. It reflected his frustrations. "But if someone did tamper with the computer, if someone marked the machine to turn up Reed with Clermont, then why did they do it?"

"What was the similarity?"

"Tinkertoy had nothing to say. Nothing. That's why it had to be tampered with. It was like a card-sorting machine: We put in Reed's name to see what links would come up. Madame Clermont. But it just turned up. There's no attachment to it. Just a name, sitting naked there in the middle of Tinkertoy's memory."

"I don't understand this."

"Neither do I."

"I can't use crap like this, a bunch of crap out of the computer that even you people don't understand."

"Use?"

"For stroking, goddammit, what do you think this is all about? That goddamn character over at Office of Budget has got us taking a six-million-dollar cut in operations this year so he can give it to his pals in Langley. Where the hell do we make a cut like that? And when I go up to the Hill to do some politicking, those boys don't want to hear a bunch of crap about a rogue computer."

Budget. Always the Old Man's prime concern. Budget was power, power to balance the interest of R Section against the interests of Langley—the Central Intelligence Agency. The Old Man had played a dangerous game for the past two years. He had judiciously begun to leak secrets of the Section to members of the oversight subcommittee that watched Section's operations. And, as the Old Man said, he couldn't give them crap about a computer search, because he didn't even understand it.

"Reed had one other link as well," Hanley said.

"Damn."

"The Rome business."

"Damn. That doesn't make any goddamn sense."

Hanley closed his eyes for a moment; when he opened them, everything remained—the room, the silence, the polished desk in front of him.

Four days earlier, there had been a foul-up at the embassy in Rome.

The embassy, at the end of Via Veneto, had received a routine transmission and passed it along to the R Section station chief, who worked out of an apartment at number 7, Via Icilio, on the Monte Aventino in a fashionable neighborhood just across the Tiber from the Vatican.

The Section did not share quarters in any of the American embassies. That space was reserved for the CIA. The Section, as a relative newcomer to the intelligence services of the United States, maintained the elaborate fiction that it did not, in fact, exist. The peculiar arrangement in Rome was typical: Embassy personnel separated cables for the two intelligence sections, sending one set to the first-floor CIA offices in the embassy and the second group to the R Section man across the city.

This time, a bored cipher clerk (GS 11) in the basement of the embassy, thinking of his planned assignation that night with the younger daughter of the American ambassador (who had a reputation for such things), did not listen carefully to the open-code message he received. While he enciphered it, his daydreaming eyes saw the word "Alphabet," which was code for R Section, and he routed it to the apartment on Via Icilio.

And not to the operations chief of the Central Intelligence Agency in Rome, for whom it was intended.

The missent message was simple: "Felker probe double X priority. Alphabetman placed at Frog."

R Section agent at Paris on operation. The search for Felker assumes a double X priority.

And now Mrs. Neumann saw the incident at Rome link up to the computer search for the name of Reed, the dead Soviet agent found in England.

"Maddening," Hanley said.

"But did this link just hang there dangling in the wind?" the Old Man asked.

"In the computer. Yes. No marking link, no reason to relate them . . ."

"Well, the business of us sending someone to Paris, that might have explained the linkup."

"No. We could eliminate the part of the message and the link still turned up. You see, it isn't a link per se, but a sorting mechanism. The way you would mark some cards red and some cards black. Press black and all the black cards turn up, whether they're linked or not—the similarity between them is in the actual sorting category."

"I don't understand that."

"Someone—someone or some group or something—with access to Tinkertoy wants us to make these connections. Mme Clermont and the business at Lakenheath and this business with Felker and that bit of news we got out of the Helsinki door in the winter—about the Warsaw Pact games against Western Europe . . ."

"That linked as well?"

"Yes. You see, it has all the elements of separate chords in a conspiracy. Are the Soviets going to move to the West? Are they going to threaten to do so? And why should we be informed of it in this roundabout way through these tricks of Tinkertoy?"

"The Soviets?"

"Why would the Opposition want us to be on guard against them?"

"Well, what do your geniuses in computer analysis say?"

"We haven't told them yet. Mrs. Neumann told me all this yesterday afternoon."

"What are you going to do with it?"

"I don't know. I thought you might have an idea."

"I don't know a damned thing about computers."

"Yes. And I know so little. Mrs. Neumann says there are very few possibilities and each raises new questions. And if they are really links, why wasn't the supporting information entered into Tinkertoy? And if the computer has been fouled, who fouled it? One of us? Or has the tap come from outside?"

"Is that possible?"

"A boy in Chicago tapped into a university computer. Industrial spies tap into competitors' computers all the time. Security is not secure. We construct the most elaborate security systems and then man them with GS 5s who make less than eighteen thousand dollars a year. In theory, Tinkertoy is untappable. But that is theory."

"What if we shut it down?"

"What would that do, except to hobble ourselves because of a theory that the computer is tapped?"

"The computer has got us by the nuts, is that it?"

Hanley considered the observation. After a pause, he said, "Yes. That's it. We don't know the difference between good information and bad without Tinkertoy. And perhaps we cannot trust Tinkertoy."

"What do you want to do?" He said this quietly. The Old Man relit his pipe.

"I thought we ought to warn Manning. If there is danger."

"Danger? From what? That French whore? Danger of the clap is all."

"It's a delicate matter."

"Getting her into the sack again after fifteen years of *adiós* is always delicate."

Hanley waited while the Old Man chuckled. Joke, Hanley thought sadly; it is just a joke.

"I had thought about Devereaux," Hanley said at last, scarcely aware he was speaking aloud.

"About what?"

"Paris. Manning. As a backup. After the first time we used Manning, we sent him to Vietnam and Devereaux broke him in there. They both spoke French. Quizon—"

"Quizon is our stringer at Paris."

"—is an old man. I don't know. I had a premonition."

"Premonition? You're talking like an old woman, Hanley. Devereaux was just a fucking agent, just one fucking man."

"The human factor," Hanley said. "I thought it would have been . . . worth the effort."

"You're jumping from one to another. You're talking about Devereaux and then about Tinkertoy and this Paris business. There's no connection."

"That's because I'm not logical like Tinkertoy," Hanley said.

"Why should Manning be warned? And how the hell can you warn him without bringing up all this other stuff about Tinkertoy? He doesn't have a need-to-know on that."

"It was a thought."

"Are you going to say 'be careful'? "

It was exactly what Hanley had said the last night he saw Manning. Be careful. Poor old Hanley, poor mundane Hanley. Devereaux would have been amused by his old-maid caution.

"Look, Hanley, you've got this Devereaux business too much on your mind. He's the one who resigned."

"He would never come into the Section."

"It was his choice."

"It was no choice at all."

"He was part of the team, he had to do the best thing for the Section."

"We pulled him out of Vietnam fifteen years ago. Sent Manning in. Before your time, Admiral. He sent back an evaluation predicting the Tet offensive by the North. Sent it nine months before Tet. Naturally, it was shot down by Langley. We didn't know then that Langley was building up its own case, faking the evidence of our 'victories' in Vietnam."

"That's under the bridge, that's a long time ago," the Old Man said. ·

Hanley talked on softly, as though still in a sort of reverie. "The national security adviser ordered us to bring him back. He said we didn't need defeatists in the field. Defeatists. November gave us the truth and we killed the messenger. He only wanted to go back to Vietnam. I knew it, but we had a standing flag in his file, always: No Eastern duty. Exile. I think he felt he was an exile in the West."

The Old Man sucked the dry stem of his pipe for a moment and stared shrewdly at the other man. "You knew him better than anyone," the Old Man said finally.

Hanley blinked and came out of the fog of remembrance. He realized, with something like regret, that it was perfectly true. He knew Devereaux as well as anyone had known him. And he didn't know him at all.

5
Venice

The pigeons outside the second-floor window fluttered noisily on the droppings-splattered ledge, and Felker, listening to the cooing and rustling feathers, realized it was not a dream. He had dreamed of the pigeons all during the restless night after the boy from the front desk brought him the message; the pigeons settled around him in the dream and then on him, the air filled with feathers and their small amazed eyes, the stench of them smothering him in the dream. There had been a woman in Hamburg, long ago, who fed the pigeons and let them settle on her, on her arms and even her hat. She was a filthy beast, as filthy as the pigeons themselves. In the morning, now, the pigeons always seemed angry, with the sunlight or with each other; their cooing took on an air of challenge.

Felker realized he was sweating, though the room was not warm.

No. He wouldn't lose his nerve just yet.

He grasped the package of Senior Service on the scarred pine table next to the double bed and shook out a cigarette. He sat on the edge of the bed and lit it and blew the smoke against the shuttered windows. His body was small, powerful, and he was naked. He had black hair on his back and chest, and wiry hair spiking his scalp. His eyes were deep and suspicious and black. There was a long, livid scar down the left side of his chest where they had removed part of one lung. Don't smoke, the doctors had said, it is dangerous. He had been amused by that, as though everything in his life were not fraught with the sense of impending death.

He had waited for contact for twenty-one days.

Waiting was more difficult to face than terror. Waiting crawled around him, made him itch.

Felker had not expected it to be so difficult to contact the Americans.

He had a story for them. It would pay good money. The Americans always paid, unlike the parsimonious English, who wanted every account line filled in.

He would tell them about English spies at the American base and about Soviet spies as well. And about the code book he had taken from Reed—book and encoded messages as well.

He inhaled again and let the smoke trail out of his nostrils.

California. He would live in California. It sounded like a good place to live, like Venice, warm and with water. He wanted to be warm.

Three days ago, the Americans had made contact at last; their agent met him on the Rialto bridge over the Grand Canal.

The American looked like an Italian; he wore a bow tie. His eyes were cynical, even contemptuous. Felker had been amazed by all he knew. Felker had tried to tempt him with the code book; they knew about that. And the American had told him that Reed was dead and that Felker had killed him.

Felker had realized the English double-crossed him, even at the end. Pim. Pim had killed Reed and laid the blame on Felker. So all of Felker's caution had been justified. The Soviets would think Felker had killed Reed, and the Americans thought so as well.

"So what is it that you have to sell us?" the American agent, Cacciato, had finally asked.

"Messages. Dozens of them. Encoded. And you can break them with the book code. Simple stuff."

"And what do the messages say?"

"Are you crazy? First we make a deal."

They had bargained on the Rialto bridge, where centuries of traders had bargained before them. Around them old women hustled to morning shops; below, the Grand Canal was full of mid-morning traffic: barges and the water buses called vaporettas and gondolas and motor cruisers.

"We know about you, Felker," the American had said and smiled. "You were a terrorist, in Munich."

"Arms dealer, please," Felker had protested.

"A terrorist. Moving Czech arms to the Irish Republican Army, cash on demand, very profitable until our British friends at Auntie tumbled to you."

"Businessman, just like American businessmen. You sell to the highest bidder, and a hell of a lot worse than Czech machine guns."

"The English found you and turned you."

"The English took me to their house in Heidelberg and they did things."

"Torture? Are you delicate now?"

Felker had not been angry. It was part of the bargaining. Yes, he had thought, they tortured me and I never forgot it.

"You worked Malta for them."

"And Marseilles. I lost part of my lung at Marseilles, it was a trap. The English were watching the heroin trade."

Cacciato had frowned at last. "To make sure it only went to America."

"Something like that," Felker had said. "I've got stories and stories for you."

And so they had talked and bargained and played the game, and when the American left the bridge, they thought they understood each other.

Felker had waited two more days and then the second message had come, the night before. It had robbed him of sleep, along with the cooing pigeons beyond the shuttered windows.

Felker now rose from his bed in the darkened morning room and went to the dresser. He began to pull his clothing out of the drawers. He had bathed the night before, paying 1,500 lire for the bathtub hot water faucet, which was kept behind the front desk. The faucet was returned upon completion of the bath.

The American response had been firm. They would go along with Felker's requests for asylum and money. He would take the third charter boat at the San Marco piazza dock at seven and go to the island of the Lido beyond the tight cluster of islands that is central Venice. He would walk across the Lido to the deserted beach, and there he would be met and picked up by a fast boat for Corfu. Felker would simply disappear from the face of the earth, and neither the British nor the Soviets would know who held him.

Pim, Felker thought suddenly, seeing the face of the fat Englishman. He had killed Reed and nearly done in Felker. He had always had contempt for Pim, but at the moment of crisis Pim had done the right thing exactly in killing Reed. Exactly what Felker would have done.

6
Paris

"I'm sorry to be late."

"I was early."

"There were so many distractions at the last minute, I had to just leave them."

"I was watching the old man playing the accordion."

Manning half rose as Jeanne Clermont came to the table, but she sat down quickly across from him and he sank back into his chair. It was the first springlike day, and Henri had placed tables on the sidewalk in front of his restaurant, the Rose de France. Manning had chosen the table farthest from the open door of the brasserie, across the walk from the stately elms in the place Dauphine.

Jeanne knew he was watching her, but she assumed the distracted air of a woman who had been too busy all day to attend to herself and was now attempting to settle into a mood of relaxation.

For a moment, she touched things: the table, her purse; she touched her sleeve, touched the glass of red wine that he had poured for her.

But she knew he watched her gestures and that pleased her. So she was smiling at him when she finally looked up.

Manning merely stared in return. Her eyes, he thought; they were really wonderful. He had tried to recall them exactly at night, alone, sleeping in the darkness of his hotel room. Her eyes were light blue and yet deep and yet not always blue at all; sometimes there were elements of green in them, and they seemed to change colors in the changing light of day and evening like colors in a clear pool or colors in a storm at sea. Her pale face was wide, calm, even peaceful, even at moments when she was hurried or distracted; her eyes arbitrated her moods as though her soul, hidden by the gentle reserve of her face, flashed to life only in her eyes.

She suddenly reached across the table and let her red-tipped nails touch his hand. He opened his hand and received hers.

44

"William. This is so nice, I'm glad you thought of it. You came early to take the table by the walk."

Now he smiled in return. "Yes. Do you remember when we were first here?"

For a moment, her eyes seemed sad, as though all memories were tinged with bitterness. But it was only a moment. "We had a glass of wine, wasn't it? We really couldn't afford to eat here, but the owner understood; he thought we were in love."

"Even radicals like us," Manning said.

"Oh, not you, William." She removed her hand from his and picked up the glass of red wine and tasted it. "You were never a radical; you only loved me, and you put up with my friends and my little speeches to you."

Manning shook his head. "Everyone is a radical when they're young."

"Are we so old?"

"Not you, Jeanne. Not you, ever."

"Are you so old, William, then?"

He saw her smile, but the question bothered him; he wanted to turn it away. "No. Not now. Every moment I see you, I am young."

"But when you go away, are you old then?"

Manning didn't understand her. Silence lay between them for a moment. Then she put down her glass and touched his hand again across the white tablecloth.

"Don't be solemn, William. It is spring and we're together and that's enough. You have too much romance in you."

"And you, Jeanne?"

"This is enough for me," she said.

But the puzzled look remained on his face. He thought to speak, but Henri came to the table. Henri was a large man with a white shirt and tie and a large, round face like a harvest moon, fringed with yellow clouds of hair.

"Madame," he said.

"Monsieur," she replied in the formal manner of Parisians greeting each other. "I don't want very much tonight, Henri. William? Will you order?"

"Trout. Fresh and the best I've seen for months, it must be a harbinger of the new season."

"And lemon sauce?" she said.

"With shallots this time."

"That sounds wonderful. What do you think, William?"

He gave in and smiled and joined her in ordering. She ordered food with a sensualist's delight, always starting with a *pro forma* "not too much" and ending with special orders of potatoes and salads.

It had been warm all day. The sky was filled with fast-moving cumulus clouds that made the sun dart in and out like a schoolboy playing a game.

"Oh, there he is, William," he said, pointing one elegant finger at the old man who was now returning to the restaurant across the park. "He'll play for us."

The old man began a sentimental song, playing the melody with nimble fingers but dragging out the chords to wring the last bit of nostalgia from them. It was a melancholy song, like the last gay song of an evening or the last music of Christmas, fading in the new year. The sweet notes carried clearly on the little breeze that rippled through the trees in the oasis of quiet formed by the phalanx of apartment buildings along two sides of the triangular park. The place Dauphine was baffled against the city's evening roar; here, on the Ile de la Cité, in the middle of the Seine, they might have been at a country inn or picnicking on Sunday afternoon in the gardens of Versailles.

"After all these years," he said. "I didn't expect to share the first day of spring with you again."

She glanced up quickly to see his eyes, and they were waiting for her. She looked away, at the old man playing in the park.

"Your romance, William," she said softly, not looking at him, gazing at the old man and gazing at something in memory. "It has lasted now into our middle age."

"Each moment now is only a reflection of the past."

She turned to him. "Is that Proust?"

"No. Only William Manning."

She laughed then and it was all right, he realized. For a moment, he felt he had gone too far, that he had betrayed something to her. Or she had warned him away from her.

He could not explain it to anyone, not to Quizon or Hanley; it could not be put in a report back to Section. He had been successful. He had reestablished contact with her. He had lied successfully to her. He had let the liaison progress as Hanley had wanted. What he could not say was that he had found he still loved her; but then, love was not the province of an intelligence agency.

Yet this second loving had brought guilt, etched so deeply by what he had done to her and by what he would do again that the love seemed more intense, in the way a picture will be intensified in the eye of the beholder by a dark border. He did not love Jeanne now out of pity for what he had done or would do again; he did not sentimentalize his longing for her; and yet this love was much more terrifying to him than anything that had happened to him in his fifteen years in the Section. Perhaps it was because they had grown older; perhaps all the winters apart made this spring seem so fragile.

"William? What did you do today?"

He was startled; the music had ended. She stared at him.

"Not much. It's been slow; I went around to the palace to see what your leader had nationalized today, but he had rested from his labors."

She frowned. "You don't understand."

"I'm sorry, I don't want to fight with you about Mitterand. I'm in the habit of being too cynical. I got a telex from the editor, he said he wants an assessment of the peace movement. It'll be the second in two years." He made a face. "Same peace movement, same dreary leaders, same—"

"Yes," she said. "The same dreary subject. Peace is such a bore, isn't it?"

"Tedious, I think; at best, it's tedious." He smiled, but she would not return it.

"Nothing excites like war," she said. "Nothing makes one so alive as the thought of killing."

"Death makes life seem more precious." He kept smiling, but her look was bitter, and he realized he had stumbled.

"Anyone's death. Vicarious thrills are not enough for you."

"Jeanne. The peace movement is a sham, a coward's way."

"People are cowards if they do not want to die?"

"Everyone dies," Manning said.

"Yes. But to be burned or bombed. Or I forget, William, you are an American, you have not suffered occupation or death from planes or heard the sound of cannons beyond your own building."

"I saw death enough."

"Yes. Correspondent in Vietnam. But then, they were not your people, your home."

"My friends died as well as my enemies," he said.

"So, William, it is more terrible then that you cannot raise peace to any place in your mind higher than an annoyance visited upon you by an editor at your news service."

47

"Dammit." She had drawn him this far and he realized he wanted to fight with her, that she had stirred some bit of him that rekindled memory. "What do death masks worn in parades and bonfires and flag-burning and 'Down with the U.S.A.' have to do with peace?"

"Who has the bombs if not the Americans?"

"The French for one. And the Soviets."

"Yes. The revolution should begin here as well."

"Revolution. You mean Europe now turns to peace after exhausting the world with a century of wars."

"This is not 1914 and not 1939. This is not the Europe in your history books anymore. These children in the streets wear masks of death but they have no illusions, William. Not about war. Not about nations."

"I can't believe I'm talking to a woman who works for the most chauvinist government in the world about peace, the end of nations, mere anarchy." He leaned forward so that the words, delivered in a low voice, would slap her, would hurt her. "No parades on the Champs-Elysées anymore? No memorials beneath the Arc de Triomphe? Will the president of France give up his memorial walks through Normandy to salute the war dead? Or not lay red roses at the Pantheon?"

"Mitterand is of another time. He cannot help his own history, any more than I, but he can have sympathy with a new time."

"You're too old to take this nonsense seriously."

"Because, as you say, William, I am 'too old,' I must take it more seriously. Only children have time for games; only fools, William, have time for patriotism."

"Does Mitterand know he has an anarchist working for him?"

"Mitterand knows my history." And now a bitter tinge dulled each word. "I told them the truth. I do not join a government by masking myself. I am not so important to them, but what I think or do or say is more important to me than any position in the regime."

"I don't want to fight with you." It was true, in fact, but the words had carried a force beyond his control.

"But it is noble to fight, isn't it? War makes one alive."

"Jeanne."

"No, William. Let us not have peace between us."

"Jeanne."

"No." For a moment he thought he saw a hint of tears in her eyes, but she did not cry. "No," she repeated, shaking her head.

48

"You have made me too angry because you are too cynical. You were not cynical; that is the difficulty in remembering when we were young. You must always compare what you have become to what you once were."

What was I? Manning wondered suddenly. But he spoke lies. "I am what I was. I was young and gallant."

"You were never that young, William; even when—even in those days—you had a reserve. You had no passion. You seemed never to have had a youth."

"I had passion," he said. "For you."

"Yes." She gazed at him for a long moment. "I wondered what that reserve was in you. I was fascinated by you. You seem so cool, so distant."

"Never to you."

"Yes. Even to me."

"That's not true."

"I loved you," she said.

"I told you, I loved you," he said.

"Yes." Softly. "You told me."

The old man with the accordion came across the little street to them. Manning pulled a twenty-franc note out his pocket and gave it to him. The old man bowed and smiled. "Spring," the old man said to her. "Would you like a song?"

She was distracted. She looked at the old man and her mood shifted again; he could see it in her eyes, in the way they caught the light of the dying afternoon.

"Thank you."

"What would you wish?"

"Anything."

The old man began to play again, sweetly, reaching for a soul through the chords. The song was not beautiful but it suited the moment.

"I'm sorry, Jeanne," she said.

"We won't talk about it."

They ate quietly as though the argument had exhausted them; but it wasn't the fight, it was the memory of fifteen years before that had been stirred to life.

Jeanne Clermont, he thought, what have you become? What did I do to you? But as soon as he thought it, he realized the thought pleased him. The act of betrayal had somehow made the memory of their affair final and quite beautiful. How would it have ended oth-

49

erwise? Would they have gone on and on until it ended in recriminations and acts of hatred, in nagging days and nights of growing loathing?

She had no lovers now, that was certain.

Three years before, her husband, Giscard, had died of leukemia. His death had not grieved her greatly and she resumed her maiden name, which did not shock anyone who knew her. She had been a good wife to Giscard, her friends agreed, and she had not caused any scandal in the four years of their marriage. Giscard. She had married him out of pity, they said; he had followed her like a dog for years. And she had married him without love but with a certain kindness that was apparent to all but Giscard.

He sipped the last of the wine and contemplated her in the lights of the restaurant that stabbed at the gentle darkness falling over the city. They had sat together in this restaurant fifteen years ago. He had loved her and he had wanted to betray her; did he love her now, even as he sought to use her again?

Yes.

The thought pursued him as they left the restaurant and crossed the Pont Neuf to the Left Bank. Below, the darkened, turgid waters of the Seine surged stubbornly against the ancient piers. She took his arm without a word, and he felt her shiver.

"It's going to rain," she said. "I can always feel it in the breeze at night, after the first warm day. It always rains at the end."

Rue Mazarine was narrow and winding, a dirty street despite the daily washing of the street cleaners who came out with their old, long brooms.

He felt the slight weight of her next to him, felt the warmth of her press against him; so they had walked before through the unchanging streets of the city. What was the use of memory, except to cause pain?

She wore the same perfume, he thought; but was that true or only a trick of mind? He had once called her the revolutionary in silk; he had mocked her and she had laughed because that was what he had intended.

"Why are you laughing?"

"I'm remembering," Manning said. "You were so radical but you always wore makeup, always wore perfume."

"I'm a woman," Jeanne said, explaining everything. "Are there no contradictions in your nature?"

"Do you see any?"

"I remembered you were so solemn and yet you would sud-

50

denly be a child. Remember when you wanted to fight Verdun over that incident?"

"Verdun wanted you."

"You do remember."

"He goaded me. I didn't mind that; I minded that he was using you."

"But you used me," Jeanne said.

He stopped and looked at her. "I loved you."

"Perhaps Verdun loved me as well."

"Not the way I loved you."

"William," she said as though beginning something. But then she paused. Was there something she didn't want to tell him?

"Good night," he said at last. They were at the double doors at the entrance to her apartment building. The building was old and out of fashion, crowned with gargoyles.

He kissed her then, gently. It had been six weeks since he arranged to meet her. It was a difficult matter, he had explained in a report to Hanley; Jeanne was not a fool but she must be made to believe him. He built the lie of his relationship with her carefully.

Unexpectedly now, she held him close and let the kiss linger between them. When they pulled apart from each other, they were breathless, a little surprised, lost. She would not let him go; she held his arm.

"Storm," she said at last. "Can you feel it coming up in the wind?"

"It's spring," he said. "Do you remember the night we slept on the couch in Verdun's flat and watched the rain? The windows were open, we could smell the rain falling."

"I cannot let you go," Jeanne said.

He did not speak.

"You see, I betray myself; when I saw you that morning in the brasserie across from the bookstore, I thought this would not happen to me. I did not hate you; it had been so long ago and so many memories intervened. But I did not think I would be reminded of loving you. Memory was dead ashes, cold, useless, incapable of heat."

He put his finger to her lips, but she turned her head away from him. When she looked back at him, her eyes were wet.

"Curiosity—I thought I would see you once, just to hear you speak again, to watch your eyes as you looked at me, to hear you laugh. Once only and I would let you go and never see you again. And perhaps just a second time, then I would permit myself to be with you, just to feel your arm in mine again; to walk with you on the rue des Ecoles again, as we had been. Do you remember it?"

"But I remember," he said. "Everything."

"Oh, William." It was not loud. Low and haunting, and he felt ripped by her voice.

"So I said I would see you each time for the last time, again and again, to see if you remembered all that I remembered, to make certain that I had not dreamed you. I wanted to see your flaws, to see how you had become twisted, to see that you were not the ideal I had carried in my memory. . . ."

He realized at last then: She was crying. Not weeping loudly, but there were tears in her voice. In a moment, her soul behind the eyes shifted and she was naked to face her own pain.

He could only hold her.

After a long moment she led him through the outer door into the old building and across the corridor past the room of the sleeping concierge. She looked in at the window of the concierge's station and spoke the perfunctory "Good evening, madame" and continued up the stairs. He followed her up the winding flights in the dim-lit hallways to her own rooms, to the door with double locks.

The rooms were dark. They went from room to room and she did not light them. At the front room, she opened the windows to the balcony and stood on it. Below, the snaking length of rue Mazarine was still full of street life; above, across the rooftops of the city, they could see the clouds reflected red against the city lights. The spires of Notre-Dame were bright on the island. The gauzy drapes billowed into the room. The approaching storm smelled fresh to them; lightning broke the sky into pieces, and low, certain thunder rumbled across the roofs.

In that moment, he wanted to leave her. I could not use you again, he thought; I could not betray you.

But he joined her on the balcony. The wind plucked at their clothing. They stood very close, their hands on the wrought iron railing. He felt giddy, unaccustomed to naked heights, to her so close to him.

She did not look at him for a long time but looked at the city. He watched her face reflected in the lightning.

And then she turned to him. "I will not ask you again why you left me, William," she began slowly, the voice strange, remote, and yet almost a whisper.

"Jeanne, you knew I was transferred out and—"

"No." She placed her fingertip to his lips. "Don't tell me any-thing, only this—why did you come back to me, William?"

"An accident," he said.

She searched his eyes before she spoke again. "Memory might have lasted me all my life. It did not pain me anymore, to remember you. But you came back. I feel all the wounds again."

"I saw you," he said. "I could not have spoken to you. I knew you were here when I was sent back. I saw your name in the directory. I knew you were here."

"You followed me," she said.

"Yes. I wanted just to see you first." It was true, of course, most of it. He touched her hand. "Like you, I wanted to see you. Once. And then I thought to speak to you."

She closed her eyes as though in pain. In a moment, she opened them. The room was still, but the wind shattered the calm of it. Suddenly, papers on a table were flying across the room, splattering on the far wall. Neither moved or seemed to notice it.

"Come," Jeanne Clermont said. "We will lie together on the couch and watch the storm. As we had."

And when they were naked and she had pulled a coverlet over them, Manning felt her body move beneath him, the pale body he remembered, which he now saw again; he felt her hand upon his neck pulling him close to her. The warmth of her rushed at him; he did not know until that moment how cold he had become. They heard the raindrops on the little balcony beyond the tall windows. The drapes blew about like ghosts.

He felt himself falling; he closed his eyes so that he would not see the fall.

He felt her and touched her and she touched him. Lips, soft-ness, wetness; a yielding and lostness; it seemed a vacuum had exploded in time and shattered him with a thousand shards of mem-ory, cutting his flesh and piercing him.

7

Venice

The ancient clock in the Clock Tower tolled seven, and the pigeons, as though they had not heard the sound a thousand times before, suddenly rose in the great square in front of St. Mark's Cathedral and pirouetted in formation around the façade of buildings.

Time.

Felker rose from the table in the restaurant where he had been watching the square for any sign that the plan would not proceed. The American's message had told him to be exactly on time, but Felker knew that it was much safer to be late.

The third motorboat was painted white. Behind the wheel was a young, sullen Italian with a white and blue striped sailor's shirt made of heavy cotton. He wore a dirty beret, and he had not shaved for days. His face was defiant and the eyes seemed to sulk as they watched him approach.

"Are you for hire?" Felker began in his harsh rendition of Italian.

"Why do you suppose I'm sitting here? Do I look like a tourist?"

"Will you take me across to the Lido?"

"Why do you want to go to the Lido at this hour? You could take a vaporetto."

"I want this boat.'

The young man smiled then, unexpectedly, but the smile had nothing to do with mirth. "It'll cost you double. I can't be certain I'll get any fares tonight from the island."

"I don't care about the cost."

"It's your money. Thirty thousand lire."

"It's too much."

"Hire another boat then."

But Felker climbed aboard. He sat on the red cushions in the rear of the boat.

"In advance."

"All right." He pulled soiled ten-thousand-lire notes out of his pocket. They made the transaction, and the young man turned back to the dash of the boat. He turned the key in the ignition and the motor roared to life. He reached forward and aft and threw off the lines and swung the boat out into the canal expertly, careful not to bump the pilings.

Across the expanse of dark Adriatic, the Lido waited in the faded light scarcely two miles from the Piazza San Marco.

Felker stared out into the blackness; the sea breeze washed his blank face. The waters were pitch-dark; lights from the Lido were

54

the only signs the island existed at all. The boat plowed slowly through the swells of the quiet sea; the swells lifted the boat, and the bottom shook each time it settled into the troughs.

"Lights," Felker said.

"What did you say?"

"Lights."

"The Lido?"

"Running lights. Don't you have running lights on this boat?"

"I don't like to use them. They're expensive to replace. I can see well enough; that's all that counts."

"But what if you hit something?"

There was silence.

"Are you trying to tell me how to run my boat?"

Felker spoke to the back of the Italian's head. "You could hit something in the dark."

"I never hit anything I don't intend to hit."

For a moment, the remark made no impression on Felker; but he was trained, he had reacted quickly before.

He looked up.

The sullen man at the wheel had turned even as the boat surged over the swells to the Lido. He had a large black pistol in his hand.

The first shot struck Felker in the right shoulder and spun him half around, slamming him back into the red vinyl seats.

Silencer.

For a dazed moment, before the pain began, Felker did not even know he had been shot.

In the next moment, he leaped over the side and fell into the turgid waters of the Adriatic.

The water closed over his head and he held his breath as he sank, saving his strength for the struggle back to the surface. In the inky depth, his shoes felt like weights on his feet. He allowed himself a moment to sink farther while pushing them off with first his heel and then his bare toes. Then he kicked upward and broke the surface after an agonizing moment.

He saw nothing.

Then he heard the purr of the motorboat in the darkness. The young man was looking for him.

Carefully, he treaded water; he felt the throbbing pain of his shoulder begin to overwhelm him. He would not accept the pain; he had been given pain before. He closed his eyes a moment and felt the saltwater scratching at the lids. He endured the pain, and when the wave of hurt passed, he felt nausea rise in him. The water was cold and his belly felt rigid; the cold, after a moment, numbed the pain. His right arm was growing stiffer by the minute in the still-icy spring waters.

Felker did not panic; he turned slowly in the water and looked for bearings. It appeared that the Piazza San Marco and the Lido were about the same distance from him, each about a mile. The young man in the boat had chosen the spot carefully.

Suddenly, he saw a flash of white in the water.

The boat had turned, was bearing down on him, this time with the running lights on and a spotlight probing at the black swells.

Again, he let his body sink in the water. The clothing dragged him down, and he unfastened his belt while submerged and pushed out of the wet, clinging material of his trousers. His pistol sank beneath him into the icy blackness. The water pressed at his chest and face, but he swam carefully beneath the surface for as long as he could.

He saw the white underbelly of the boat pass over him. He couldn't stand it anymore. He inhaled, and the water rushed into his nose and lung and mouth; frantically, he broke the surface, coughing for air. The panic had seized him that time; it was the panic he had felt when the British agents had tortured him in the safehouse in Germany.

His right arm was completely stiff, detached now in mind, merely a memory of an arm. It was difficult to tread the swells in the wake of the white boat. The waters lifted him, the waves slapped him. The sea had roughened. Again he swallowed water and shivered. The coldness pressed from without and within.

He listened for the white boat, but there was only silence now. Slowly, with pain, he began to swim awkwardly with one good arm for the lights of San Marco piazza; maybe it wasn't a mile, as it seemed; distances deceived in the water.

He struggled for ten minutes, but the lights of the island of Venice seemed no closer. The water seemed to drag at him, plucking at the bared skin of his legs, numbing his feet, numbing his hands reaching out in the darkness.

And then he saw it.

Bearing down from the Lido was the great, gray shape of a bulky vaporetto, its lights blazing. Felker began to wave frantically with his good arm, but each time he lifted his hand, he sank a little beneath the surface. He shouted to the boat.

And then the large, slow-moving water bus changed direction slightly.

They saw him! Felker wanted to laugh. They were coming for him.

Survive, survive!

Survived Malta and the ambush, survived the British torture, survived in Lakenheath; again and again, and now he would survive this, get back to his rooms, take a warm bath and get into dry clothing and take the midnight train to the mainland and go to Bremen, find his friends, find what went wrong—

The boat struck him and churned over his body and slid on; the remains were mangled in the screws at the back of the old craft propelling it on.

8

Washington

Anyone who had followed Hanley this morning—and who knew his habits—would have been surprised.

Each day, at precisely 11:45 A.M., he would leave his cold, bare office hidden in the rocklike edifice of the Department of Agriculture building on Fourteenth Street and walk two blocks to the little bar and grill that still survived the encroachment of a more fashionable Washington around it. Each day, he would order exactly the same lunch—one cheeseburger and one dry martini straight up—and he would sit in the same booth in the back of the narrow diner and leave the same tip at the conclusion of the meal.

But this morning, though he left at the usual time and started up the same street, he turned at K Street and walked two blocks west to Sixteenth, turned again, walked across the street against the lights, and entered a large office complex on L Street, just two blocks from the *Washington Post* building.

The telephone instructions had been urgent, he knew, but the calm voice had delivered the time and place of the meeting and even the way to walk there in exact tones. Hanley was to leave at the usual time, the voice had instructed. But how in hell did *they* know about the usual time, Hanley had thought, and then dismissed it. Of course they would have known those things.

It was not necessary to tell Hanley to be alone.

He had met the other man once before, during the Gdansk matter. This was much the same thing. Perhaps it was worse.

Hanley walked through the narrow lobby of the building to the door marked "Stairs," which led down a concrete well to the underground garage. There were two layers in the garage, according to the man who had telephoned him that morning at home. The man he would meet would be waiting on the lower of the two subbasement floors.

Hanley's steps echoed hollowly on the stairs as he descended slowly.

He had not brought a pistol, though he was authorized to carry one and had even been issued a standard .357 Colt Python revolver. He did not like pistols because he did not use them well. Besides, he could not believe there was any real danger; he was not a field agent; he was in Washington.

The message from Rome had started the business. He had received it thirty-two hours before.

Felker. He had disappeared before the final contact in Venice.

Worse, four hours later, the agent called Cacciato had been found garroted in the bottom of an empty Coca-Cola delivery boat floating free in the turgid waters of a back canal in the old city. It had been a picturesque murder, and photographs of the dead agent had been splashed across the front pages of the Italian newspapers. An anonymous communication sent to Reuters in Rome had correctly identified Cacciato as an intelligence agent of the United States and of R Section; but the part-time correspondent for Reuters who had checked with the American embassy had been informed that R Section did not operate in Italy. So the Reuters man guessed he was a CIA agent.

Hanley had received a facsimile of the front page of the Milan paper, *Corriere della Sera*. Cacciato, in his familiar bow tie, had appeared to be sleeping in the picture. There was scarcely a mark visible, the garroting wire had been so fine. A professional sort of job.

Before he had been killed, Cacciato had transmitted Felker's sample cipher to Hanley. The Section had agreed to pay off Felker, at least until he got to the United States. The book was important, but Mrs. Neumann thought Felker's message was of sufficient length to be cracked. It was a tedious task, and she and her "geniuses" in computer analysis were at the job now.

The Old Man had been distinctly unhappy over the development.

"Fucking Opposition," he had fumed.

"We assume so."

"What happened to Felker?"

"I don't know."

"Maybe he diced Cacciato."

"I don't think so; it really wouldn't make any sense. It's a possibility, but it wouldn't make any sense."

"The English were after Felker."

"They were miles away." Hanley had paused then. "At least, we assume they weren't that close on the trail. We haven't been able to get a flutter from Brit Intell."

And then, this morning, he had received the call to his unlisted home telephone, pulling him out of a foggy sleep. The call had amazed him nearly as much as the call he had received four years before after the problem at Gdansk and the subsequent foul-up. But that had been an entirely different situation.

The lower level of the parking garage was full of gleaming cars, sheathed in their stalls like so many hooded falcons. The instructions had been very clear about time and place, but vague about how long he would have to wait. They were probably observing him, Hanley thought, to be certain he was alone.

He did not feel afraid.

Washington was his cocoon, after all; he had lived in the city for thirty-one years. The bizarre world of spies and intelligence and covert operations that he directed as the second man of R Section seemed from this city nothing more than a mental exercise. At least, most of the time. Only now, when confronted with a physical presence and the promise of a threat implied in the death of a field agent, did the world of real espionage insert itself into the skin of his polite society.

Before he saw the car, he heard the motor.

It purred into life at the far end of the parking level.

Hanley stood still and saw the auto suddenly rush down the narrow aisle toward him.

He waited. The car did not have lights though the parking level was lit dimly.

The Cadillac stopped a few feet from him. He automatically took notice of the diplomatic plates and the license number; he had a remarkable memory for such things.

The door of the car opened and a young man got out of the driver's seat and walked around the front of the car and opened the right rear door. He then glanced at Hanley. With a shrug, Hanley bowed his head and stepped inside.

The automobile was very quiet, and a low musical sound seemed to come from hidden speakers buried in the black, plush depths of the interior. Hanley assumed they were musical bafflers, designed to shut out the probes of any directional microphones that might have been placed outside to spy on the conversations carried on inside the car.

The face of the Soviet agent was gray, as though he had been ill. His bulk was still massive, but there was a slackness in the body that indicated disease. He smelled sweet in the closed air of the car's interior, as though he had doused himself with cologne to cover up a smell of corruption. His eyes were gray but rimmed in red around the irises.

For a moment neither man spoke, and then the Soviet—he was, in fact, the third man in the intelligence section that worked out of the Soviet embassy—began without preamble. He spoke in a soft, whispery voice that was accented heavily.

"We had nothing to do with Cacciato."

"Why do you tell me?"

"Because he was your agent."

"No. We have no one there. He was Langley."

"No, Hanley." The bulk shifted next to him, but Hanley did not move. "We do not read Italian newspapers for information, as you do."

"I have nothing to say to you."

"But you came."

"I am always ready to listen." Hanley stared at the back of the leather cushion on the front seat. The Cadillac contained amenities, including a small bar that snapped open now from behind the front seat.

"You would have lunch now. I am sorry." The Russian seemed to speak with regret. "But we can give you a martini. I do not have food, but perhaps a glass of Russian vodka?"

"No thank you. I prefer the Polish vodka, since they invented it." It was childish and Hanley knew it, but he felt offended by the presumption of the other man.

The Russian rumbled into what was a brief flurry of laughter; it was punctuated by coughs. At the end, he wiped his lips with a well-used handkerchief. He studied the handkerchief for a moment and then pulled it away. Hanley noticed the gesture; when he returned to Section, he would make a memorandum about the health reports concerning the seldom-seen third man at the Soviet intelligence section of the embassy. Belushka was definitely ill.

"We would have provocation, Hanley. Felker murdered our man in England. You know this. And you were willing to make contact with him, to buy what he had."

"I don't know who you're talking about."

"I am talking about your dead agent. Cacciato. We do not eliminate him. Do you understand?"

"Why do you insist on telling me this?"

"Because we do not want a mistake. Like the matter in Gdansk. There was too much at stake there and too many wrong moves. On both sides."

Hanley said nothing.

"We do not want retribution, as there was after Gdansk. This was not our doing."

"I am supposed to believe you?"

"Yes." Softly. "You see, they have sent me. I never leave the embassy. In a little while, Hanley, I am going home. I have been relieved." The voice was hollow, turned in on itself. "I am ill. I know you see this, that you will make a report on it. It does not matter." He was silent. "I do not matter."

Hanley said nothing.

"It is important we do not misunderstand each other," the Soviet said again.

"Where is Felker?"

"I am not permitted to speak of anything but this matter. We did not kill Cacciato."

"But you brought up Felker."

"It was mistake," the Russian said heavily.

"And you have Felker now."

"You may believe what you wish."

"But Felker is part of the problem of the death of Cacciato." Said almost casually, slyly.

"I do not know this," Belushka said.

Hanley was puzzled; Belushka might be telling the truth, and that would be the most puzzling aspect of all.

"Will you tell them this? At R Section?" Belushka said with effort at breath.

"Perhaps," Hanley said. He realized with a start that it was Devereaux's usual response when pressed for a specific answer or commitment. Devereaux had never answered except in his own time and never explained. He had never accepted the role assigned to him.

"All right, Hanley," Belushka said with heaviness. "I give you this message and it is true; if you do not choose to respond, then it will be on your head. If you begin war with us over this, if you kill our agents, then we will kill yours."

"All right," Hanley said. He had agreed to nothing. He reached for the handle of the car and the door was opened by the young driver, who had stood outside and waited for the conversation to be concluded.

"Oh." Hanley turned in his seat back to Belushka. "One thing. Who follows me to lunch to see what I eat? Why would that be important?"

Belushka smiled. "Why do you think anyone follows you, Hanley?"

Hanley blinked and did not speak.

"Perhaps," Belushka said, "they are already there."

9
Paris

Jeanne Clermont was quite certain she had not been followed, especially by Manning, but the rules required certain procedures. She had entered the gray five-story apartment building at six o'clock and waited ten minutes until the door that led to the little garden in the back was opened. She had followed her conductor across the back to the red building on the opposite street, the rue Thénard. They had silently climbed the five flights to the garret rooms and shaken hands in that formal Parisian manner only at the door.

When she entered the low room, Le Coq was at the window, staring at the city.

She came to him and extended her hand, and he shook it; they might have been fellow workers meeting in the morning at the factory. Traces of the bourgeoisie always lingered, even in radicals.

"You're late."

"I was on time," Jeanne Clermont said, sitting down on a wooden chair. The large room with the low ceiling was badly lit by a single dim bulb hanging over the sink in the back of the room. It was covered with dust and old paintings; it had once been an artist's studio, but the artist had died, penniless and undiscovered. His paintings were quite bad in any case, and Le Coq saw no reason to get rid of them. Some in the cell occasionally took some of the pictures on Sundays to the quais along the Seine and sold them to tourists. Le Coq disapproved of this—it seemed so middle-class—but he did not intervene.

"In any case, how is it going with him?"

"It goes," she said.

"Has he made love to you?"

"That's not important. Not to you."

"Everything is important, Jeanne, you know that. I'm not asking you for any prurient reason, I assure you. I'm . . . attempting to gauge the degree of confidence he has in you."

She stared at Le Coq without speaking until he emerged from the shadows. In the half-light , he stood before her: tall, his face distorted by a vivid red scar that cut down his left cheek, drawing the skin in different ways, right through the socket of his left eye. For a long time, he had worn nothing in the socket, speaking of a glass eye as vanity. But the horror of his appearance—heightened by the eyeless socket, which seemed to stare with more accusation than his good right eye at those he confronted—finally drove his comrades to persuade him that a little vanity could be tolerated, for the sake of the cause.

His gaze was lopsided now as he held her fixed by his glittering right eye. He moved toward her, dragging the broken, healed remains of his right foot behind him.

Le Coq had red hair that stood in short, spiky clumps on his round head. "You look like a bantam rooster with your red coxcombs," Verdun had once joked of his appearance; and so "Le Coq," which was a not particularly appropriate nickname, had been given him. He was German, from Bremen, but he had no real home now except Paris. He had been in the city thirteen years and still spoke French with the peculiarly heavy German accent that seems to trample the delicate distinctions in the language. He was frequently misunderstood when he spoke, but Le Coq had become accustomed to patience. And to repeating himself until what he

63

wanted was very clear. Many people, even some who had known him longest, were afraid of him, though no one could remember any harm that Le Coq had done to them.

"The liaison has begun. That's all," she said. "William is not so foolish; I have to proceed cautiously in this—"

"Jeanne . . ."

She waited for him. She rested her elegant hands on the lap of her soft blue dress.

"Is there urgency to this?" she asked at last. Le Coq turned and looked at her.

"Why do you ask that?"

"Because you've summoned me twice in the past three weeks. Twice you've asked me the same question." She paused. "If this is more testing of me or my loyalty, then it has become tedious."

"I am not a waiter at Aux Deux Magots," Le Coq said. "Don't treat me as one."

"I'm sorry if my manner offends you; your questions offend me."

"It was the Company that gave you information about William Manning in the first place. . . ."

Now it was her turn to rise restlessly and go to the windows away from him and look out over the city. The view was cramped by a modern, white university building thrown up at the end of rue des Ecoles as one of the half-reforms the university promised the students after the riots of 1968. Its stark lines clashed hideously with the gentle, seedy, century-old buildings all around it.

"That he was an American intelligence agent," Le Coq said.

"Yes."

"It was not a test of you, Jeanne Clermont; we trusted you with information that you could have given to Manning, that would have allowed Manning to avoid our trap."

"Yes." Dully, not looking at Le Coq.

"And so we want reports, reports of progress."

"My life is my own," she said, turning, her blue eyes shining with dark contempt. It was as though Leq Coq's mundane utterances had offended her more than his first questions.

"Madame, your life is our life. La Compagnie Rouge. When you know of us, you accept us." It was meant as a threat, but she did not seem frightened. He took a step toward her, advancing slowly by dragging his broken foot behind him. "Madame, you gave your life to the revolution in 1968 and it was spared; have you grown so comfortable in living that you shrink from a total commitment now?"

"Why do you talk to me like this? As though I were a child at the Sorbonne you sought to recruit to ideals that you utter as meaninglessly as a priest muttering the blessings at mass? I'm not a child, Le Coq; I'm older than you."

"But Manning. You were his lover; perhaps you are again. It's what we wish, but perhaps you shrink from the commitment to what we intend."

"What do you intend?"

"In time."

"I won't kill him; I won't lead you to kill him."

"Kill him? Why do we want his life? He is useful only alive." Le Coq smiled, but it was a more horrible face than his frown.

She stared at him still with her eyes fixed on the horrible expression of his sunken face.

"The newspapers say the Red Brigade killed the American agent in Venice."

"Newspapers are tools, madame. You should understand that, you of all people. Who said it? *Le Matin? Le Monde?*"

"*L'Humanité,*" she replied, pronouncing the name of the newspaper of the Communist Party of France.

"What the Brigate Rosse does is not what we do. We are brothers in a cause, but brothers go their own ways at times."

"Where did you get information on William? Why did you give it to me?"

"No. The question is, why did William Manning seek you again? To seduce you again? Or to discover your liaison with our organization? Madame, why do you flatter yourself? To think that Manning came back to love you." Again, Le Coq smiled. "Are there no women in his life? Did he live like a monk for fifteen years after he betrayed you?"

"You tell me he betrayed me—"

"I can assure you he did. We know that."

"Why do you know? Why must I take what you tell me on your word?" She stepped toward him, and Le Coq retreated a step to the shadows along the outer wall of the room. "What will you do with Manning? I must know."

Silence.

And then Le Coq shrugged.

"We won't harm him. We have no reason to."

"That is not what I asked you."

"Madame, if it is a matter of kidnapping him, we'll do it." The voice was harsh. "We will do what we have to do to learn what mission he has come for. But there is no reason to kidnap him now."

"How can I believe that?"

"Madame, he is an intelligence agent. He has no propaganda value. When we kidnap an American general or a diplomat, at least it draws the attention of the masses to the American presence here. Who does not love to see an American brought low from his place of power? But an American spy? The agencies would disavow him and say he was not a spy, that he was a journalist or a tourist or some other occupation that does not interest the mass of people."

"So you would kidnap him. And question him. And then kill him."

"Certainly, madame. We would never let him go." The voice was soft, rushing like ice along a river in spring. She felt cold at his words but was determined not to show her fear.

"But if I can determine his mission . . ."

"Yes. Now you see, madame."

"Yes," she said.

Le Coq stepped into the light again. "You see, it is your responsibility."

And she realized, more profoundly than Le Coq, that Manning's life was in her hands.

10
Moscow

All the previous day, the probes by elements of the Czech and Polish army divisions had sliced deeply into the southern and central sections of Western Germany. The probes had been devastating—a large section of the restored center of Nuremberg had been destroyed by a Czech artillery battalion—but in the end, the Warsaw battalions had been stopped dead. During the night, when the generals of the East were congratulating themselves with wine and vodka in the buffet room at the central building, General Garishenko had ordered a new series of combination moves, including a daring penetration across the Czech supply lines by only a brigade from the 101st Airborne Division of the United States. In the morning, when the war resumed, it had been successful.

"Do you see? Do you see, Vasili Dmitrovich?"

General Garishenko could not contain his enthusiasm; all the months of study of the work of the Allied commanders, particularly over this same European ground in World War II, had paid off with the surprise drop by the United States airborne soldiers behind the Czech lines.

But Vasili, who was a captain seasoned by his work both within the Frunze War College and in the field in Afghanistan, could not be enthusiastic. He detested the idea of the war games played on computers; he detested the paper victories and the hollow flat result summaries flashed on the terminals. There was no real war, no blood, no smell of death and reeking flesh, no earth to win by inches, no clank of armor or bite of tank treads across the wet spring grounds; it was reduced to a game, and real war could not be reduced.

Still, Vasili said nothing; it was not wise to refuse promotions, even into sections of the army where no fighting was ever done.

"I cannot believe they didn't anticipate the orders," Vasili said at last.

"But they didn't, they never do, the strategy always remains conventional when the unconventional action is taken. They are the invaders, and from that act of daring they devise the most pedestrian strategy," Garishenko said.

"I still am waiting for the counterstroke," the younger man said with something like sullenness.

Garishenko smiled at him suddenly. "Poor Vasili. You have been picked to be on the wrong side. You cannot work up enthusiasm for our cause."

"Our cause?" The voice was sharp.

"In the game," Garishenko said, a smile still frozen on his small, round face. "We must do the best we can, you know, even if it is our lot to be the NATO forces. The validity of the games depends on it."

"Perhaps I am not suited to such games," the younger man said. He had a thick neck and a broad, Slavic face and dark hair; his appearance was almost brutish, but he was considered one of the best young commanders in the Red Army, and it was thought that some experience with computer planning, as well as working with

67

General Alexei Ilyich Garishenko, would round his continuing education.

They were seated in a bunker beneath the ground of Frunze War College in the southwest section of Moscow, not far from the Indian embassy. The bunker was without windows, without any season beyond the walls of the gray room. The walls were made of concrete blocks, sealed against the deep frostline of a Moscow winter and the sudden violent spring, when water seeped deep into the earth. The room was official, neither pleasant nor unpleasant. The desks were gray, the chairs gray, the carpet made of some nonspecific fiber from a nonspecific source, of a nonspecific color. Summer and winter, the air conditioning and heating exchangers hummed steadily and kept the buildings connected beneath the war college grounds at a constant temperature of seventy-two degrees with forty percent humidity. The care taken with the heating system was not for the comfort of the generals and students and technicians who devised the games and worked on the computers; it was for Naya herself, a lighthearted nickname given to the complex computer that was the heart of the war games.

Garishenko had added a single personal touch to the room: his own oiled walnut desk, imported from England at his own expense. The permanence of the desk in the underground room gave testimony to the permanence of General Garishenko in the games.

War games had been played on computer models for nearly sixteen years.

The games had originally been worked from a prototype developed by an American corporation in California, not far from Palo Alto. The California firm had devised it to plan competitive strategy for multinational corporations in the American and international marketplaces.

The Committee for State Security's special section—called the Committee for External Observation and Resolution—had simply stolen the program by bribing two young engineers working with the firm.

But then Bronsky had come into the plan. He was a brilliant mathematician and computer analyst who spent four years adapting the basic methodology for the new games and refining it to reflect a Marxist-Leninist view of history.

Garishenko, then a young army major, had been assigned to work with Bronsky as the games were devised. The games had liberated him, had given him promotions, had made him—since Bronsky's death—a leading exponent of the game theories in Moscow's government. But the games had also chained him to the life of a permanent outsider, even in the ranks of the army. He was the "against" man, he was the quibbler, he was the perpetual opponent in the games to those who devised new military strategies and tested them against Garishenko's skill and the impartiality of Naya.

Bronsky had devised the games from the bare roots of troop strengths, military hardware estimates, the logic of troop movements, and conventional strategy devised in such places as NATO headquarters at Brussels, at the National War College of the United States in Virginia, and at Heath House in London. But Bronsky had added a peculiar touch of genius that had entranced the government hierarchy from the first. Formally, the Bronsky touch was known as "The Index of Western Proletarian Discontent." Bronsky had delved into the raw statistical data of the West to find such mundane things as inflation rates, unemployment rates, frequency of urban riots, national opinion poll attitudes on matters such as race relations, religion, and a sampling on the basic optimism or pessimism that was the stuff of Sunday newspaper supplements.

The Bronsky index reflected a reality, but reality seen through the eyes of the Marxist philosopher.

The completed model, with all of the variations devised by Bronsky, had first been employed in a war-potential situation in the matter of Afghanistan. The game was coded "Kabul."

Garishenko had commanded the team that calculated the response of the Afghan peasantry to a Soviet invasion to prop up the ineffectual government of that country.

Garishenko's group had devised a guerrilla strategy of resistance. When Naya noted, impartially, that the rebels had no bullets and no guns, Garishenko replied with logic that they had the capacity to make such things. Garishenko also said the Central Intelligence Agency of the United States would help supply arms covertly.

Garishenko had won the game and lost the war. He had isolated the Russian divisions in the few cities of Afghanistan, but the results were not accepted at the highest levels.

There had been a party after the Kabul games. Even Garishenko, who was thought something of a leper by some members of the college staff because of his moodiness and his official position as "the man against," had been invited to the party. It was held in one of the large private dining rooms that Moscow's restaurants have for party functionaries who cannot be seen eating too much or drinking too freely in front of the proletariat.

At the party, Warnov—who was senior to Garishenko, but whom Garishenko considered a fool—had embraced him drunkenly and laughed and congratulated him on the fine job he had done in the games.

"But you see, my dear Alexei, the games are still games, still in the stage of being experiments."

"The games are the result of Bronsky's methodology," Garishenko had said coldly. He was not drunk, though he always drank too much; something in the room, in the patronizing smiles of the others, had made him cold.

"Yes, yes, and a brilliant man he was, but you see, the Marxist-Leninist models in the program were not sufficient. You underestimated from the first the spirit of the Afghans to accept peace and to continue to—"

"The Afghans have driven out invaders for twenty centuries, from the Chinese to the British. There is no reason to assume their response will be any different to us."

"But we do not come to conquer them," Warnov had said, still smiling drunkenly. "We come as comrades and fellow workers in a struggle for equality."

And Garishenko had known that night, from the drunken comments of Warnov and the others, that the results of the game had been rejected; more, that the game was a test for the invasion of Afghanistan, and though Garishenko had won, the game had lost.

They did not trust him. Not then; not now. If the computer called Naya was not sufficiently Marxist in its thinking, then perhaps Garishenko was not sufficiently Marxist as well.

The invasion of Afghanistan had followed the computer game, and after three years, the Red Army found itself isolated in that far, barren country, not winning the war and not losing it.

No one thought to suggest that Garishenko had been right and that the games had been an accurate projection of reality.

And now this new game, whimsically called "Paris." The proposal for the game had not come from the senior staff of the army or the staff of the Frunze War College. That in itself made the game unusual.

And three months before the game began, while Garishenko and his staff of nine were culling Western documents for information to place in the computer, Garishenko had been visited by a man named Lenovich.

The visit had come on Sunday morning, when he was alone in his apartment in the block two miles south of the War College.

Katharin, with whom he lived, had been visiting her relatives in Leningrad.

The visitor was one of those men who spoke softly and whose faces never showed emotion. It was not a trait of race but of training; men who did not admit they were part of the KGB.

The man named Lenovich had questioned Garishenko for a long time about the computer and about the Bronsky index.

The questions had been polite but thorough. Only after an hour did Garishenko finally begin to believe they related to the game that would be played, the game of the invasion of Western Europe called "Paris."

"And, Comrade General, how did you evaluate the election of François Mitterand in 1981? I mean, as a factor to the games."

"Everything to be related in the games was put into Naya," Garishenko said carefully.

"Of course, of course. But what was related?"

"In what sense?" Garishenko asked, pushing the question off as though it were an invader.

"In the sense that the victory of the Left, even of the Socialist Mitterand, shows the rising tide of sentiment for the policies of—"

"That is one interpretation, Comrade. It could also be noted that not much was changed in the election except that the Communist Party in France lost considerable power."

"It is only one election," the man named Lenovich had said.

"Exactly."

The KGB man had gone on to other questions, but the questioning always circled back to Paris, to the politics of the French, to the idea of what the French response would be to any invasion of Western Europe.

"Naya has not told us yet. We haven't entered all the raw data," Garishenko had said.

"Yes, yes. But you must remember that the philosophy of Marxism and Leninism must be adhered to in evaluating all such data."

"That is how Naya is programmed; that is what Bronsky invented."

"Yes, yes, but the results have not always been satisfactory, have they?"

Garishenko had become a little angry. "Do you mean in the computer game? Or in the field of battle?"

"Do you refer to Kabul?"

"Do you refer to anything else?"

"Comrade, the purpose of Naya is to improve the position of the Red Army, not to serve personal vanity or ambitions."

"Whose vanity or ambition? I do as I am told. I am designated as the Opponent. I will do the best I can, so that my army and my country are not misled by self-delusion into thinking they can win wars they cannot win."

"Naya is only a machine, after all," Lenovich had said.

"Yes. But you speak of it more as a god. Naya can only weigh the possibilities, explore the probable. It can only be as good as the program fed to it."

"Yes, Comrade General. It is well to remember that."

The last words had lingered in Garishenko's memory all during the weeks that followed. But he would not be bullied about the games; he would not do less than he was capable of doing.

The subordinate who was NATO field commander passed across a series of orders he had just fed into Naya. The games took several actual days because each possibility of troop movements was played again and again by the opposing sides.

In another windowless part of the labyrinthine bunker, a staff was assembled playing the game for the Warsaw Pact countries. In yet another hidden part was the Game Master, who judged verbal disputes that arose among the participants based on his own, neutral reading of Naya.

". . . Element 3 of the Z7 and Z8, U.S. Third Armored Division, engaged at Baden-Baden, will withdraw 0312 hours across Sector Z for rendezvous at Zebra 7 slash Arctic 5 with repositioned 8 element of Sector 12. Fallback positions 93 and 94 in Sector Scotland slash Tango will be occupied at—"

He read the numbers, movements, orders quickly; they were not numbers or games to him. He clearly saw men moving across the muddy face of the German midlands in late spring, falling back, cursing as they hacked their way up the long slope to Sector 93, where he saw a real village occupied by real people frightened by the approaching sounds of war. At night, deep in the self-induced stupor of vodka, he could see the faces of the American troops he moved so coldly in his orders of battle to Naya: He could see their weary faces beneath the helmets, see the blood seeping through the rough white bandages of the walking wounded, see the twisted bodies caught and frozen in the agony of sudden death. He could see the dull shimmer of a thousand rifles in the morning sun.

The first move of the war game called "Paris" had been given to the East fifty-one hours before.

The Ninth Panzer of the German Democratic Republic Army had leaped across the border into the West and smashed brilliantly and savagely in a fatal dawn raid at the Allied air force base at Frankfurt am Main while elements of the Seventeenth Wing of the Polish air force had bombed the American bases at Lakenheath and Mildenhall in East Anglia.

Yet, despite the surprise of the opening move, Garishenko had been most surprised by the Eastern decision to bypass French forces in Berlin and to be certain to notify the French "commander" (on Garishenko's team) that French territory would be respected. It was sophisticated of them, Garishenko had thought: They were finally using the Bronsky index, which took political dealings into consideration in these games.

"Don't they expect the French to support NATO?"

The question had been asked of no one in the war rooms in the bunker, and no one had answered Garishenko.

"Where is Tolinov?"

Tolinov was the French "commander."

He had been summoned from the bunker six hours before by the Game Master. He had not returned. The game was being delayed by his absence.

Garishenko fretted in his office as he waited for Tolinov to return.

He poured a glass of vodka from the bottle in his desk drawer and tasted it. The vodka was warm, but over the years he had come to drink the strong, unflavored liquor for its effect on him and not for the pleasure of the taste. The vodka isolated him but made him comfortable in his isolation.

Katharin had long ago soothed him. "Of course you are the enemy in their eyes, but you cannot be destroyed by this," she had said. "The army does not face the West, it faces you."

Katharin understood at least. She understood the pain of what he did, even if the others acted as though he were betraying the cause of the country.

"Theories in a game do not spill blood," he had said once to Katharin. "I can prevent war because I can contain the ambition of the foolish in Naya."

"But not in Afghanistan, not in the Kabul game," she had said bitterly.

"No. But they have learned; they must trust me, trust Naya, trust Bronsky's index."

The words had sounded hollow to him even as he said them.

Why must he be trusted? Paranoia was rampant in the upper eche-lons of the party and in the army; why would paranoia see the truth of what he was trying to do?

The headaches had come back to him two weeks before the games began again. Each night he had sat alone, in his chair by the window of the apartment, and drunk himself into a stupor while the pain traveled over the top of his skull and along the line of his rigid jaw, while the pain plucked at his eyes and made his pale skin wan and drawn. Katharin had known about the pain in him and had been powerless to prevent it. She only sat with him as he drank himself to sleep, listening to him when he spoke, covering him if he fell asleep in the chair by the open window.

"Have I forgotten anything?" He would ask the question again and again as he drove his staff to uncover statistic after statistic, to devise new elements for the program of the games, to make certain that the games would be so accurate that even the dinosaurs on the senior staff would accept the results this time. The invasion of West Europe. No, Garishenko had thought; there must be no equivoca-tion this time, no miscalculation on the part of men like Warnov.

The door of his private office opened now and Tolinov ap-peared. His young face was sullen, his blue eyes cold. Like the others—especially the young ones—he had resented assignment to Garishenko's side in the war game called "Paris."

"Where have you been? The game is delayed waiting for you."

"I was summoned by the Game Master."

"What did he want?"

Tolinov gazed directly at him. His eyes did not hide a certain contempt for the short, round-faced general who had mastered the computer games. "I cannot say."

"But I am the commander."

"I cannot say. It was forbidden."

"We have awaited your response," Garishenko said with sar-casm, holding his temper.

"I have made the response."

"Well, where is it?"

Silently Tolinov handed him a slip of paper on which a few characters were written. Garishenko stared at it.

"This is the French response?"

"Yes. There is no response. France will not act."

"You're wrong, Major Tolinov. France is the key to the games; of course France will respond."

"It will not respond," Tolinov said.

"Damn you, let me see your orders."

"I cannot, Comrade General. The orders are . . . my orders are not to respond."

Garishenko's eyes opened wide as he stared at the cold face and the blue eyes. The headache, which had flared and subsided over the days and nights of the game in the windowless room, now intensified. He felt the pain moving over his forehead, behind his eyes.

"Who gave you orders?"

"I cannot say."

"This is madness, this is no game at all. Of course France will respond. I will make France respond."

"It will not compute, General."

Garishenko roared then, a cry of pain and not of words. He rose up in his chair and staggered across the dull carpet to the computer console and sat down. His fingers danced over the keys quickly, putting in the access code for "France." He drew up a question, asking for present battle status of the French forces.

"STATUS: NORMAL ALL SECTORS."

Normal. Garishenko stared at the words and then typed in a single battle order, involving movement of the third battalion of the Sixth French Garrison at Berlin into East Germany Sector 973.

The computer flashed for a moment, digesting the order. There was a long wait. The screen faced them with a gray, blank face. And then words tumbled onto the screen.

"IT DOES NOT COMPUTE."

"This is wrong, this is wrong," Garishenko said, striking the access key again. "This is completely mad."

"General Garishenko," Tolinov said. "It's no use."

"Damn you, damn you, this can't be, we programmed the damned thing."

"General . . ."

Garishenko turned in his chair. "This has to compute, don't you understand? How can France not respond to the invasion of Western Europe?"

Tolinov said nothing.

Garishenko reached for the red telephone; it was the line to the Game Master. The phone clicked and whirred, and a voice came on the line.

"Naya is defective, it will not compute the French response."

The Game Master said nothing.

75

"Do you understand? It will not compute the French response."

"Perhaps that is the French response," the Game Master said at last in a dry, whispery voice.

"I programmed Naya, that is not the French answer to armed invasion."

"French territory has not been threatened."

"Dammit, this is wrong, this is completely wrong."

"You must play the game as Naya instructs."

"But there is a French response."

The Game Master spoke slowly then. "No, Comrade there is not."

PART TWO
REUNION

Things fall apart; the center cannot hold;
Mere anarchy is loosed upon the world,
The blood-dimmed tide is loosed, and everywhere
The ceremony of innocence is drowned. . . .
—W. B. YEATS

11

Herbert Quizon

It was just two when William Manning rang the buzzer at the door of Quizon's apartment.

When the old man opened the door slowly, he seemed startled for a moment to see Manning.

"You said two o'clock," Manning said, annoyed. He had not wanted to come here at all. Each visit with Quizon only dragged him back into the world·of shadows he had come from. They reinforced reality: His liaison with Jeanne Clermont was only part of a little job for the Section.

"Of course." The door opened wider. "As one grows older, one does not expect any virtues from the young." Quizon smiled at his own aphorism—as he did frequently—and stood beside to let Manning enter. The large oak door closed behind them with the clicking of at least two locks.

Manning waited in the foyer for Quizon to lead him across the hall. The flat was large, and Quizon had purchased it in a day when such an apartment on the boulevard Richard-Lenoir did not seem so expensive. The old man had lived alone in this place for nearly thirty years.

"Let's go into the little room," Quizon said. He led Manning down a dark corridor to a locked room. He removed the key from his flowered dressing gown—Quizon was clothed in shirt and tie and trousers and still wore a dressing gown until he went out at four in the afternoon for his first aperitif—and pushed the steel door open. Steel. It seemed such an odd precaution to Manning; and yet, everything done in the precise life of the old man seemed odd.

The room was bright with books and maps and yellowing copies of all the Paris papers. There were file boxes as well, stuffed with clippings accumulated from thirty years of being a watcher in Paris, first for the CIA and then, when he was cut as the CIA bureau moved into the city in numbers, as a retainer for R Section. Quizon had been a journalist all that time, free-lancing for one wire service or another, for one paper or another, and though he had achieved no fame as a reporter, he had a certain mystique in the ranks of intelligence. Quizon had seen all the changes and had predicted most of them correctly.

On a wooden table at the back of the windowless room were two large Panasonic radios. The first was tuned to the conventional shortwave frequencies; the second had been altered to pick up the conversations of official Paris, from the police and fire frequencies to the frequency used by President Mitterand's chauffeur. Mrs. Neumann, back at the Section, complained at times that Quizon's reports were larded with common gossip, and her complaint was largely correct; Quizon plucked his gossip from the airwaves. But Quizon knew that nothing endears a part-time agent so much as filing gossip with the home office. Quizon, in his years, had learned all the elements of survival of a correspondent far from home. Or a spy.

"Sit down, William, I think I have something that will interest you."

"I'm to see Jeanne at four."

"Yes. This won't take long." He paused and let a smile form on his thin, bloodless lips. "And it concerns her. And you, for that matter."

Manning sat down and waited. The old man had thin black hair without a trace of gray; Manning knew he dyed it. His eyes were brittle gray and his face, a jaundiced shade spotted with liver marks, was small and daintily formed. He had been in Paris in 1968, when Manning, freshly recruited, had infiltrated the left-wing cells at the university. Quizon had been his control officer then, as well. But he had been in awe of Quizon in those days. Now he was bored by the ridiculous old man with his fussy manners and his thin, high-pitched chatter. He might have been an aging queen but he was essentially sexless; he was, rather, a period piece, drawn out of a Proustian world of balls and days at the Longchamps race course and languid summer afternoons in the Bois de Boulogne.

Manning had not wanted to deal with Quizon as his control. Quizon was too much a part of the memory of 1968, of his first love for Jeanne Clermont; Quizon was the bad part of memory, the reminder of his betrayal.

"Information has come to me," Quizon began, placing the tips of his fingers against each other. "From a reliable person."

"In the government," Manning began.

"Yes. Of course. I have many sources—"

"*Le Matin, Le Monde, France-Soir,*" Manning replied.

"That is unkind but it is partially true. You prove again that courtesy is the preserve of age," Quizon said. It was as though each *bon mot* were plucked from a stream filled with them, held up briefly, and then thrown back into the waters of the mind.

"Quizon, without your usual preamble, what did you learn?"

"About Madame Clermont. Hanley had wanted to ascertain her worth. After all, on the face of it, it doesn't seem important to spend so much . . . er . . . effort on a person in the third ranking in the Ministry of Interior Reforms." Quizon smiled quite horribly, without mirth, and Manning felt himself becoming angry.

"The assignment came from Hanley; does he want to rescind it now?"

"He has had second thoughts. Something about the budget. I really don't understand it," Quizon said, dismissing matters of mere commerce with a wave of his hand. "But I think I have convinced him to give you a little more time with Madame Clermont. You see, my sources are impeccable."

"And what do your sources tell you?"

"Madame Clermont is worth our efforts," Quizon said. He stared across the room at a large map of Paris on the wall. The map was layered with colors, the blues dividing the arrondissements, the various lines of the Métro marked with distinctive colors, the whole map conveying a sense of the colors of the city visible to the naked eye.

"What do your sources tell you?" Manning asked again. He felt tired, tired of the old man and his mincing manner and tired of being reminded that he was only an agent in place, that what he felt now or had felt for Jeanne Clermont did not matter. Not to Quizon, not to Hanley, not to the computer clerk who had matched their names on a printout five months before in the Section. Mere emotions never entered into it.

"Madame Clermont was detached six months ago to a special project, as soon as she was appointed to the ministry. She had no known superior within the ministry, except for a functionary named Garouche who is not important to us."

"How does your source know this?"

"He knows," Quizon said. "He is utterly reliable; he has never been wrong before."

"And does he know the nature of Jeanne's project?"

"No. And absolutely no one does. She works routinely for days and then will disappear. Utterly disappear from the ministry. She makes no written reports, she keeps no notes."

Manning thought of her apartment, of the schoolbooks, of the photograph hidden in one dusty volume. He thought of the diary that told him nothing. No notes, no recordings, no secret places. It had not occurred to him at the time: It was as though her life were *too* mundane. It was as though she had created a portrait of herself without blemishes or lines of age.

"You haven't observed this, Manning? That she disappears for days?"

"No. We don't meet every day, that stage has not been reached. But if I say to meet on a Friday or Monday or whatever, she rarely begs off. I assumed she worked at the ministry every day."

"And I," Quizon said.

"Maybe she goes to the provinces. She mentioned she is doing ombudsman work in the field of primary education. Perhaps she's doing field observation."

"No. That's impossible. She is assigned to the sector concerned only with Paris."

"Then perhaps she just doesn't report to the office. I mean, there are a lot of explanations for this kind of thing."

"Don't you suppose I thought of that?" Quizon frowned, and the frown was just as unfriendly as his smile. "The least original thought is to suppose that one is vested with original thoughts."

Manning ignored the aphorism and the satisfied smirk on Quizon's face. He studied memory, and his eyes focused on nothing.

"What are you thinking now?"

"Do you think she's tagged me?" Manning said at last.

"It's possible. I don't know." Quizon rose and went to the radio and adjusted the dial. In a moment, the air of the small, windowless room was filled with the sounds of police calls. In formal, bored tones, the dispatcher at the Quai mentioned the possibility of a burglary in progress on the rue Cardinal Richelieu and a common street assault outside St. Eustache in the old Halles district on the right bank of the river.

Quizon tuned the dial finely. The squawks from the police dispatcher came clearly. Quizon stared at the black case of the radio for a long moment before he spoke. "Does she give any indication that she knows who you are?"

Manning slowly shook his head. "Once, a couple of weeks ago, she asked me . . . why I had come back. I thought . . ." What could he explain to this old man who showed neither emotion nor curiosity at the bizarre phenomenon of stalking the same woman again fifteen years later?

"Yes," Quizon said. "You thought she meant why did you come back to cause her pain again?" Softly. "You thought she was hurt because she had loved you once."

Manning could not speak. Quizon turned from the radio, and for the moment the hard angles of his thin, dandy's face had melted. Yes, Manning realized, Quizon had understood, perhaps had always understood, but a certain propriety that existed in his mind had kept him from ever speaking to Manning of such things.

"Perhaps that's all she meant. Perhaps she does know and doesn't care. There are so many complex strands when dealing with the emotions of a woman," Quizon said. "What do you want to do?"

"What does Hanley want me to do?"

"I can buy a little time, I think. This information is very good, very reliable. And I take it that Hanley is still puzzled by some aspects of this matter." Quizon resumed his old, hard face, a face that had no emotional involvement with the business at hand. "He won't share his secret with me, and I take it he did not share it with you. There is something larger here, Manning, something that even Hanley does not understand yet."

"Why can't your . . . informant . . . get closer?"

"I don't know. He has every resource. It's better not to . . . press him. He's a man of many secrets, perhaps he does not want to share this secret yet. I tell you, I didn't think this matter would become so complicated. Hanley won't tell me everything I need to know; he keeps secrets from you; and now, it appears, Jeanne Clermont has secrets as well."

"And it could all be nothing," Manning said. "We get involved in our secrets and sometimes miss the obvious. Your source, for instance—he might just be jobbing you, might just be looking for a little extra payment."

"He has never been wrong," Quizon said coldly. "I'm not in the habit of passing along information to the Section unless I'm certain of its authenticity."

Manning frowned. "Don't make speeches to me. What do you expect from me? If Jeanne Clermont has been tipped that I'm an agent, where does it put me?"

"Perhaps in danger; perhaps not," Quizon said. "I thought I should tell you."

"But you haven't told me anything."

Quizon blinked. The gesture was as owlish as Hanley's own blink when confronted with the outrageous.

"But I've forewarned you."

"You've given me the vague idea of a threat to me without telling me where it might come from. You've suggested Jeanne Clermont knows my mission or at least my identity and then agreed that it probably isn't true. You've paraded out an anonymous tipster in the government who may or may not have correct information—"

Quizon started to speak, but Manning held up a warning hand. His eyes had become darker, his face more pale; rare anger had boiled inside him, and Quizon had never seen the emotion in Manning before.

"I'm an agent and I do what I have to do, and when that little clerk in Washington told me to job Jeanne Clermont again because of a fucking computer link, I agreed to do it. You see, I do what I'm told. But I'm damned if I'm going to become a part of your little network, Quizon, your goddamn papier-mâché world of intrigues in intrigues inside of circles inside of secrets that don't even exist outside your own head. You're an old man, Quizon, I didn't want to deal with you on this; I told Hanley that—"

"I'm the agent in place," Quizon said.

"You're Herbert Quizon, you've outlived your time. And now

84

you want to muddy up a complicated business with an anonymous tip from an anonymous source about mysterious disappearances by a woman I have followed or spent time with for three months. I never saw her leave the city in that time. So what does that make your source? Dammit, I was there, Quizon, I wasn't spying on your fucking radios or tearing clips out of *Figaro* to fool Hanley into making out another voucher to you."

"I won't be insulted. Not by you, not by the Section. If that's what they think, they can go to hell. I can sell information to others."

But Manning would not be stayed. He wanted to wound the vanity of the old man; he wanted to lacerate him with words.

"You're a charity case, Quizon, you've been a charity case for ten years. You're past your time, you live in memories, and Hanley pities you."

"I don't want pity. You're lying to me, you forget."

"Yes. I forget. But you can't. You keep remembering your coups. But you won't retire, you won't leave the field. You're past it, Quizon; you have sources that were dry rivers years ago. You haven't had anything important since 1968, since—"

"Since the last time you were here," Quizon said. His voice was icy and brittle, like ice on a frozen pond on the warmest day of spring. His voice cracked, groaned, like ice breaking into chill waters. "Since the last time. You came here out of training, you were a puppy. You knew nothing, you didn't even know the dangers. You didn't even know the stakes. And at the end, you nearly blew the whole thing. You wanted to 'save' Jeanne Clermont. Do you remember when you told me that? You wanted to 'save' her from your 'betrayal.' Betrayal. Save. You were an agent in the field and you wanted to break the mission because you had fallen in love." He spoke each phrase with contempt, he made them sound like descriptions of a dull child. "A government was at stake and you had fallen in love with the first French whore you slept with."

Manning struck him, and the old man reeled across the small room and slammed against the wooden table. The two massive black radios jumped, and the squawks of the police dispatcher continued with calm through the crackling interference. Manning sat perfectly still; his hand stung.

A thin line of blood trickled out of Quizon's nose. It fell across the angled face. Quizon did not wipe at it, though it felt warm on his upper lip.

"You were going to blow the operation in 1968 and the Old

Man sent a hitter from Brussels. They were going to blow you away, Manning; you don't even know that, not even now. They were going to eliminate you because you had fallen in love. And I sent Hanley a long message and I said, I would take care of it for him. I said I would take care of the problem. I said, if necessary, I would kill you."

The words chilled him and sickened him. He thought of Quizon as he had been fifteen years before. Betrayal and betrayal; he thought he was the center of the storm and yet he was peripheral to it. Quizon could have killed him; they had wanted him dead. The operation was the only important thing.

"In the end, Hanley believed me. He knew I could handle things. He knew I had never failed the Section, never given them wrong information, never misled them. If I told Hanley that I would take care of you, then it would be done."

"You're making this up," Manning said dully.

"No. You know I'm not. You got out of Paris and mended your broken heart. You were in Laos, you were in Vietnam when November was sent home. You know I'm telling the truth. You've done your hits, you've grown up, Manning; you know what the world really is now." Quizon's twisted mouth was rimmed with congealing blood, but still the old man would not acknowledge the consequence of the blow. The blood dripped onto the flowers of the dressing gown and stained the roses a different red.

"Why do you suppose Hanley cares that you fell in love with Jeanne Clermont? Or anyone in the Section? Why do you think Hanley would care now? You don't wish me to disparage the honor of the 'lady.' I commend your gallantry, though I don't believe in it. You've been an agent too long to believe anything you've just told me."

Manning stared at the old man and realized he felt terribly tired. It was true, of course; Quizon saw things clearly, had always seen them clearly, and Manning had been playing a little game within the game.

Everything in Paris this spring had reminded him of the first spring, the one with Jeanne; everything had reminded him of the moments of his life before it had been colored by his first act of betrayal. Betrayals had followed in all the gray years since—death and secrets, lies and dirty little jobs that no one spoke of and that were never recorded, even at the Section—but this spring with her again had reminded him of the colors of his youth, before the world.

turned gray. He had been foolish and Quizon saw it and Quizon had thought to warn him now, even as he had saved him fifteen years before. Manning's life was of no importance to anyone but Manning. And in the years since that first spring in Paris, even Manning had come to value his life less dearly. Death seemed less awful as he grew closer to it. Until now, until he saw Jeanne Clermont again.

"I don't know what I should do," Manning said at last. The voice was hollow, barely audible above the hum of calls on the Paris police radio.

"There's nothing to be done," Quizon said. His voice had become gentle again. He had still not touched the smear of red blood on his upper lip. "There is nothing to do but what we have been told to do."

"If Hanley wants to end the assignment, it would be all right."

"No. It wouldn't. It wouldn't be right. Jeanne Clermont became important the moment the informant told me of her disappearances. You see that, don't you?"

Manning said nothing.

"There is nothing to do but to continue, at least for a time, until we find out the truth about Jeanne Clermont and find a way to use her."

"Again," Manning said dully. "Only this time to turn her, to work her for us."

"Yes." Quizon spoke with sudden gentleness, as though letting a child understand that there are truly demons in the world, more awful than those he has seen in dreams.

"I don't want to betray her again."

"But you will," Quizon said.

Manning only stared at him for a long time.

12

Jeanne Clermont

They made love for a long time. Twilight passed to evening and yet they were so intent on their lovemaking that neither noticed the changes of light or the passage of time. They might have been locked in a compartment on a sealed train through a foreign country, alone in the middle of an endless night, unable to experience any sight or sound beyond the locked windows. The journey might have had no ending.

Manning touched her for a long time as though retracing memory. He touched the pale skin of her gently rounded belly and then traced the form of her breasts as she lay on the bed next to him. Gentle night: beyond their windows, they could hear the explosions of glass that signaled the beginning of the commemorations. In May each year since those nights in 1968, the students of the Sorbonne had gone through the district and broken windows and raised again the cries of the revolution. Some were pranksters; some criminals; but most were quite serious, in the way that the young are serious about the world. Worlds are made to be made over; Quizon might have said it.

In the middle of the afternoon, Manning had staggered into the gray light of a sullen May day, and left Quizon's building on the boulevard Richard-Lenoir. He had walked across the city along the right bank before meeting Jeanne. In that long walk, he had seen everything clearly: Everything was constrained and preordained, in the way that all men know they must live for a time and then die.

He must betray Jeanne Clermont or use her. And if he did not, Jeanne Clermont would be of no use to anyone. She might, at the end, know that he had betrayed her again. Or she might not; it did not matter. Jeanne had her own role, ordained as surely as his, and she had accepted it a long time before.

When they met, he had few words for her. They had kissed and strolled arm in arm across the Ile St. Louis to the Ile de la Cité. As had become their custom, they dined at the Rose de France. When she spoke to him, he had responded sluggishly, like a sleeper who does not want to be awakened from his dreams.

He had watched her through dinner with sad, faraway eyes, as though seeing her from the perspective of a dead man given the chance to revisit the earth for a day.

And then, in the darkness of her rooms in the old apartment building on the rue Mazarine, he had hungered for her. He had touched her through her clothing, he had kissed her to breathlessness; he had made love to her for a long time and then, after scarcely a moment, made love to her again. He had consumed her on her own bed, tangled in sheets, wet with glistening sweat and the juices of their lovemaking commingled. No words. Only their sounds beneath the coverlet. His still-lean body had pressed itself against the gentle curves of her body. Once, she spoke his name, over and over, crooning as a mother croons to a sleepy child. Or a frightened child. Everything is all right; sleep will come.

At 2 A.M., while Paris slept uneasily, she sat at the window smoking a cigarette. She rarely smoked at all, but kept the cigarettes in a little case on a low table in her sitting room. She was naked but it was not cold; it had been a warm day, and the warmth had lasted all night.

He watched her smoking in the light of the moon.

He lay on the open bed, naked, one arm propping his body.

"I love you," he said at last.

She did not look at him but out the wide French windows. She saw the city before her. Her arms were folded across her breasts; her legs were crossed and she sat, Indian-fashion, in the leather chair that was next to the window. Her eyes shone brightly in the clear evening light; it was as though the moon had plucked at the soul behind the eyes and made it glisten with unseen tears.

"I love you," he said again, wishing the words had never been spoken before.

"When you left," she began slowly, like the beginning of a stream.

"When I left," he repeated, a child learning lessons.

"I was without consolation. I wept for three days. You told me you would leave, but after you had gone to Orly, I could only weep, I missed you so."

He stared at her, at the pale body in the moonlight, at the eyes seeing now only those things that had happened long before.

"You should not have left me, William."

"I never wanted to leave you."

She turned and looked at him. "I know," she said softly. And she turned again and stared out the window at the city. From far away, they both heard the sound of shattered glass.

"The events," she said, using the common French term to evoke the days of May of 1968. The inevitable riots would come again, the inevitable vandalism, the inevitable police cordons around the Pantheon and the riot police lined up indiscreetly along the boulevard St. Michel. The café owners in Cluny and along the boulevard would move their chairs from the windows so that patrons would not be splattered by broken glass if the worst happened.

The events. Manning thought it seemed every great thing mūst be trivialized with words: events, matters, incidents.

"The revolution that failed," she said. "Why don't they forget it?"

"Because it didn't fail," he said.

Another silence lay between them. She pushed out the cigarette in an ashtray next to her. She put the ashtray on the floor.

"Come to bed," he said.

"No. Not yet. I want to sit here."

"Jeanne," he said.

"I never knew I could cry until you left me," she said. Her words were soft but curiously without tone, as though they had come from some place in her so deep that all resonance had been lost.

"On the third day, William," she said.

He waited. Her words were like blows.

"Police, I thought. They were only police. They came about seven, they surrounded the apartment. You know who was there: Verdun, a couple of others. I must have told you. They had men at the back, in the courtyard below. I heard them on the front stairs as well. We had some papers, we . . . well, I flushed them down the toilet, but the toilet stopped. And then they came in the rooms. I remember one, he was quite large. In uniform, of course. He came into the bathroom and he pulled me by the hair and I screamed. Then he pushed my head into the toilet and flushed it. I felt the water go down my nose, my mouth, I thought I was drowning. When he pulled me up, by the hair, I was screaming. He laughed at that. He struck me once, but he did not hit me again. I've thought about it a long time; I think he was not so bad. I think perhaps he was as frightened as I was. I mean, he seemed frightened of what he was doing and yet he seemed to have to do it in any case."

He watched her eyes; he saw the soul shift, saw the eyes begin to glisten, not with tears but with the pain of memory.

"They put us in the patrol wagon and we waited for a long time. We could near noises outside but we didn't know what was going on. We stared at each other—Verdun and LeClaire and the others—we felt ashamed. It was as though we had been playing a game and our parents had caught us. Do you know the feeling I am describing?"

But he did not speak.

"After a long time, the patrol wagon was driven away. We

thought we were going to jail, to the magistrate's court. When I saw Verdun, it was much later—my God, it was more than a year— and he had been taken to a cell in the Palace of Justice and beaten. And they had let him go, just like that. He had wondered what had become of me, he had instituted inquiries, but everyone professed not to know. I was 'detained.' That is what they told him. Only Giscard—poor Giscard, rest his soul—would not be turned away. I think if Giscard had not kept at them, they would never have released me. Some of my friends . . ."

She paused, her mouth turned down in bitterness.

"Friends. They say I married Giscard out of pity. Why is pity so despicable an emotion? We praise love, but love can betray, love can anger. Love can drive one to murder. But pity is yielding, gentle, pity is God's kindness to us. Pity. I loved Giscard, perhaps differently from the way I love you, but I loved him. One man I loved and he left me; one man I loved and he died."

"Jeanne," he said at last. He sat up in the bed. "Come here."

But it was as though she had not heard him, as though he did not even occupy the same dark room.

"They kept me in a cell inside the palace for three days. They did not feed me. There was a hole in the floor of the cell to defecate into. There was a bucket of water, it smelled foul. It was like some sort of a medieval dream. I couldn't believe this had happened to me. I was Jeanne Clermont, I must be freed, I demand my rights. I even shouted these things, but there was only silence. On the third day, the matron came. She was a large woman. I'll never forget her name—Clothilde.

"Clothilde took me to a white room and she wouldn't talk to me. I kept asking her questions, I kept making demands. When we got to the white room, she told me to take my clothes off. I was wearing jeans then, I had a sweater. I refused. She hit me.

"I fought with her. She was so strong. I scratched her but she would not scratch me in return. She slapped me, and when I stopped fighting with her, she kept hitting me. There was blood in my mouth, I could taste it, and on my face. I took my clothes off as she had said. Do you know what she said? 'No wonder they called you a whore. You are built well, like a whore.' I will never forget that."

Jeanne Clermont had lit another cigarette. Her arms were still folded across her breasts, her legs still crossed in the chair.

"She took me into another room and I waited a long time.

91

There was only a bench. The room was cold. I thought I was being examined. She went away, but I knew that someone was watching me. After a time, they came into the room."

"Who?"

"Two men. One was Claude de Fouchet. The second was Michel-Jon Rosset."

He stared at her before she spoke. "How do you know their names?"

"They raped me. Perhaps that word is too strong; after all, I saw no reason to resist them. They wanted to use me; they wanted to humiliate me. Much later, I found out that it was not part of my conditioning, that the two men had been with the riot police the night they raided the apartment . . . after you left. Only three days after you left."

"Jeanne."

"It was rape, of course. It was against my will. But I did not resist them. I felt so broken; the large woman had hurt me badly. Do you know what they did?"

"Jeanne—"

"But I have to tell you everything." For the first time, she turned to Manning. Her eyes were fixed on the past, he saw; she really did not see him. He was a mirage to her. "Everything."

She turned away, back to the windows. "They raped me and then the first one, that was Claude de Fouchet, made me suck him. When he was done, the other wanted the same thing done to him. After a while, it didn't matter. After I sucked them, they left me. They left me like schoolboys, as though I had shamed them. I said I was hungry, and Claude came back later and brought me a loaf of bread. I was permitted to take it back to the cell. Even the large woman who had beaten me seemed ashamed. She gave me a blanket. I slept on the floor beneath a blanket on the third night."

"Why do you still remember their names?"

"They didn't tell me their names, if that's what you want to know." She looked at him. "It took a long time. Poor Giscard. He helped me, of course, he would have done anything for me. He never knew about the incidents in the room. With those men. It would have wounded him too much."

"My God," Manning said.

"Yes," Jeanne Clermont replied. "At times you must wonder, where is God in this? Why would He permit this to happen to me? Do you know I go to mass every Sunday at Notre-Dame? I stand there and try to feel all the centuries in that place. When I was young—when you first knew me, William—I never prayed. I knew there was no God. It was comforting. Now that I am afraid there is a God, I am never comforted. He exists and yet He torments me. He permitted my imprisonment, my humiliation, He permitted them to beat me and rape me—He permitted me to despair—and yet He did not give me any solace."

"I love you," he said.

"Yes, William. I know that. I knew that when you went away. The first time."

"It means—"

"What does it mean? Only that you love me. Nothing more."

"It means everything."

"Which is a way to say that it means nothing. We can only be certain of the specifics."

"Jeanne."

"William. They questioned me after that for days. First one, then the other. They kept at me. When I would not tell them what I knew, when I demanded my rights, when I accused those policemen of raping me, they took more drastic measures.

"I remember two. The rest, I'm afraid, are gone from my mind. Sometimes I dream about the other tortures, but when I wake I cannot remember them. I remember when they put the alligator clip onto my lips—my genitals, William. They shocked me. I cannot describe the pain of that. In the other, they wrapped wet towels around my head and tied me down and then poured water over the towels."

"My God," he said. Manning felt sickened, as though he had taken part in the tortures himself.

"Yes," she said. "I told them everything, I knew I would. I only hoped the others would be able to escape in time. I told them everything. I told them about the cell and about the structure of our organization and about the leaders. Much later, I realized they had managed to arrest the leaders because of my betrayal."

"Jeanne." But Manning realized he had nothing to say. Jeanne Clermont had recited all her horrors in the same flat voice, like a student required to tell a history of the First World War; it was as though what she described had happened so long ago that mere emotion was not permitted to cloud the recitation. He wanted to repeat her name again but he had nothing to say to her; he had no comfort to give her.

"I betrayed them." Her voice was dull and tired. "For a long time, I believed that my betrayal was mitigated by the torture. I was not a martyr, not a saint; I could not stand the pain. I betrayed them because I could not do anything but betray them. But those were rationalizations."

She turned and looked at him on the wrinkled bedsheet. "I could not be forgiven."

"Why didn't you tell me? Why didn't you reach me?"

"You were gone, William. You had said you would leave me. I had wept for you, but God had not permitted you to return and so I had stopped my tears."

"Those men."

"I could not forgive them. I prayed, you see, for a long time in the cells after the secret trial. I was charged with acts of treason, it was all absurd. There was nothing to do in the cells. I could stand the confinement but I couldn't stand the idleness. So I prayed; they would not permit any books but the Bible.

"I prayed for my captors and for my mother and father, who were dead; I prayed for the old and the starving and the crippled; I prayed for the two men who had raped me and humiliated me that third night. I prayed for you, William."

He did not speak to her.

"Did you hear my prayers? Did God intervene for you? In all the years you were away from me?" The voice was ironic, the tone was gentle; she might have been recalling a childhood fantasy that she regretted not believing anymore.

"When I was done with my prayers, God remained. I couldn't pray to Him anymore because He would not be reached by me, but He remained. He didn't need my prayers to exist. So I did what I had to do."

"How did you get out of prison?"

"Giscard. He had pitied me. I told you. And when I was freed, I found the names of those who had raped me. Poor Giscard. He thought I was deluded. I found them. One had retired from the police and bought a farm in Brittany."

He knew what she would reveal and he tried to stop her. He got up and went to her and held her. Her body was cold. She permitted him to hold her. She spoke softly, her voice to his ear.

"I reminded him. He begged my forgiveness. And then I killed him. But I couldn't kill the other. One killing was too much. I had been wrong, utterly wrong; they were made brutes that night they raped me, used me. I could not hate them all my life. I killed the one but I never sought the other."

"Don't tell me these things," he said at last.

"Why, William? Do you suppose I can pretend it did not happen to me? Or is it you who wants to pretend? Do you hold me? Or your memory of me? Fifteen years, William; I am not Jeanne Clermont whom you had loved."

"I love you," he said. "Jeanne Clermont. Now. This minute. Listening to the windows shattering in the Quarter. Now." He spoke with an urgent whisper and held her tight, but she did not respond to him. Naked, they stood in the balcony window, facing the city; his arms were wrapped fiercely around her.

"I love you now," he said again.

"Do you?"

"I love you."

And, at last, she let her arms come around his back, to feel the muscles and ribs, to touch the nape of his neck. She kissed him then and they pressed against each other.

He took her back to the bed and they lay down on the wrinkled sheets. He covered her again with his body. He made love to her. And they slept in their nakedness, arm in arm, breath against breath.

He woke and felt her next to him. He was very awake, as though he had slept all his life to this moment. He knew what he would do; the mission was finished, he would tell Quizon. He would not leave her again, he would not betray her again.

He got up and found his clothing and put it on.

The edge of dawn scratched at the dome of night over the city.

"William?"

Her voice was soft, full of dreams.

"No. Sleep, Jeanne. In a little while, I'm coming back."

"Don't leave me."

"No. Not now. I won't leave you again," he said, pulling up his trousers. He fitted the belt and pulled his zipper. He sat down on the leather chair and pulled on his socks.

"I have things to tell you. I want to do something first. I want to get . . . some things straightened out."

"At this hour?"

"Yes. Now. Nothing can wait until morning."

"What time is it?"

"Just after four."

She made a noise that was half sleep, half contentment. She pulled the sheets over her. She made the noise again.

"I love you," he said to her.

She smiled to him, half in sleep, half in the dim world of wakefulness.

He pulled on the light wool jacket. It was a matter of calling Hanley first; just before eleven at night in Washington. And then confronting Quizon.

Jeanne Clermont would not be used again.

The sleepy concierge, grumbling and full of resentment, watched him cross the courtyard out the front door of her building. Rue Mazarine was shuttered and sleeping, the cafés closed and the apartments shuttered against the light chill on the predawn breeze. Manning walked down the narrow street to the quai and the broad expanse of the sleeping dark river. When he had been young, he had walked in Paris before dawn; Paris had seemed less like a city than like a day that had to begin. He walked along the quai of the Left Bank, across from the Ile de la Cité. In the dim light that was half-night and half-day, the spires of Notre-Dame poked at the leaden sky.

I love you. It was the first time he had said it to her on this second, chance meeting with her. He knew it was not memory speaking; or lies of an agent. He loved her, and it was the first thing he had been certain of in fifteen years.

The black Renault car stopped abreast of him at the curb. The passenger door of the front seat opened and a policeman in uniform climbed out. Manning stopped and looked at him.

"Monsieur." The policeman spoke in the flat tones of official French. "May I ask you why you are abroad tonight? Do you speak French?"

"Yes. I'm an American. I'm going back to my room."

"And where were you, monsieur?"

"I'd rather not say."

"I see. Do you have a passport?"

Manning removed the blue passport from the inner pocket of his jacket. The Paris policeman pulled a penlight from a pocket of his uniform and threw the light on the page that revealed Manning's portrait. The policeman studied the photograph and then cast the penlight on Manning's features. Manning blinked. The policeman looked at his face for a moment and then looked again at the passport.

"Satisfactory?" Manning said, annoyed.

"There were many disturbances this evening. Because of the events. Were you on the rue Mazarine just now?"

"Yes."

"Shop windows were broken . . ."

"I'm hardly a student."

"What is your occupation?"

"Journalist."

"Ah."

"Yes. Ah. I'm an American. Can I have my passport?"

"One moment."

The policeman returned to the Renault and leaned in the rear window and spoke with someone in the backseat of the car. Manning could not see the figure except that he wore civilian clothing.

The policeman came back to Manning on the walk. His face was imperturbable.

"You will come with us for a while," the policeman said.

"I will not come with you. What's this about?"

"Please, monsieur."

"Can I have my passport?"

"If you come with us."

The policeman handed the passport back to Manning. Manning held it for a moment and then replaced it. He followed the policeman to the Renault. The car was without any official markings on it.

Manning opened the rear door and slid inside. His legs were cramped. Next to him was a large man with a large nose and comic eyes, like Fernandel. He appeared to be a caricature of a Frenchman.

"What's this about?"

"Monsieur," the civilian said. "You will be kind enough to come with us?"

"Why?"

"We have a few questions."

The car started up quickly and shot into the center of the street. Paris was empty; it was as though it had been only a stage play and all the actors were home. Only the garbage trucks moved slowly down the boulevard St. Michel, picking up the burdens left from the day before. The Renault made a left turn at the bridge and headed toward the cluster of gray, official buildings on the Ile de la Cité in the middle of the Seine.

"Are we going to the Palace of Justice?"

But the civilian did not answer. In the front seat, the two uniformed policemen stared straight ahead.

The car crossed the island and continued to the right bank of the river and made another left turn, this time heading toward the Louvre and the Tuileries gardens.

"Where are we going?" Manning said, and for the first time he felt uneasy. With a small movement, his arm pressed against the small pistol hidden in the sleeve of his jacket. He could not reach the pistol now in any case; but once he was free of the car, he would withdraw it.

The little car shot down a ramp near the Louvre and screeched to a stop on the empty quai. The black river surged beyond the ancient stones.

"Get out," the civilian said.

"What are you talking about? I'm not going to get out of this car!"

"Please," the civilian said, with courtesy and with a certain boredom of tone, as though he had said these same things a thousand times before.

Manning stared at the other man. But it was comic; he inspired laughter, not fear. Manning shook his head and moved out of the car awkwardly. He was not built for small cars.

Neither was the civilian. The civilian pushed his large legs out in front of him and heaved himself up. The two policeman were already out of the car. The car had no lights showing.

Gray Paris dawn broke reluctantly against the honeycomb of clouds.

"What's going on?" Manning said.

He saw the small weapons before they had lifted them. Part of his mind cataloged them as he stood frozen against the stone steps of the quai. Uzi. Manufactured by the Israelis and copied by the French. An automatic weapon capable of firing a forty-round burst in something under seven seconds. It was an extremely light weapon with a hollow handle that could be retracted beneath a jacket. Or a policeman's tunic.

I love you, Jeanne, he thought. You see, that was what I finally realized. I had betrayed you but that was not as important as the fact that I still loved you. I had never stopped loving you.

The weapons were without silencers.

They burst. He did not feel pain, only a certain sense of dread as he fell. This could not be reversed, he thought oddly; they could not be sorry for what they had done. They have killed me, he thought.

He fell across the stones. Blood seeped into the cracks of the stones.

The two policemen replaced the Uzis beneath their tunics.

The civilian grunted an order and pointed at the body of William Manning.

The two policemen picked him up and carried him—one at the shoulders, the other at the feet—nine steps to the edge of the quai. They threw the body into the river and it made a loud splash. The two policemen looked at the spot where they had thrown the body and then at each other. One led the other back to the Renault. Both climbed into the front seat. The civilian already sat in back.

Without lights, the car backed up the stone ramp to the level of the street.

In a moment, it had disappeared around the corner of the rue de Rivoli, leading west from the light of the new morning.

13

Devereaux

The Eastern Airlines 727 sat poised at the far end of the main north-south runway at National Airport on the Virginia side of the Potomac River. It had been waiting five minutes, not because the runway was occupied but because the destination—Kennedy Airport on Long Island in New York—was stacked up. Under the system devised since the air traffic controllers' strike nearly two years before, the planes were held up at the takeoff end of a run and not left to circle waiting to land.

At last the signal was given in laconic tones from the controller in the distant tower. The day was warm—it had been warm all week in Washington—and heat shimmered along the runway. The jet revved suddenly and strained at its own brakes and then began the galloping leap along the concrete. Roaring with a full-open throttle, the three-engine jet leaped off the pad 2,345 feet after starting the run and climbing slowly as the banks of the Potomac loomed ahead.

Suddenly, the plane veered sharply to the left and continued its tricky ascent, now paralleling the river in a northwesterly direction, rising above the squares and neat grid of streets of Washington on the right and Alexandria on the left. Washington was a quiet zone, mandated by Congress, and so each takeoff was forced to the left, away from the capital, until it cleared the metropolitan area. At three thousand feet, the no-smoking lights were turned off, but the strain of the climb was still trembling through the floor in the passenger cabin. Again the plane banked, and a broad portrait of the distant Blue Ridge Mountains appeared in the portholes.

Devereaux stared at the mountains. He thought he could see the lazy, sprawling curve of the Shenandoah River, but perhaps it was his imagination; in any case, the plane banked again and now was heading directly north by northeast for the short run to Kennedy.

"The situation has changed," Hanley said. He sat in the seat next to Devereaux and gripped its arms tightly with white fingers.

"Yes. You said," Devereaux replied. He turned away from the window and looked at Hanley. Meeting on the flight had been Hanley's idea; it was more than his usual paranoia about overheard conversations. Hanley had seemed genuinely frightened this time. "Security," Hanley had said. "We must take precautions."

"I thought you wouldn't come," Hanley said.

"I was curious."

"I didn't have anything to do with . . . the situation."

"No, Hanley. You were out of the line of fire, as always."

"Dammit. There were political considerations. The Old Man had his reasons to move on you. You have to admit that you've been . . . unorthodox in your approach at times."

"Did you call me to justify yourself?"

"I'm not explaining," Hanley said.

"No. And neither am I."

"What have you done since you quit?"

"Written a book," Devereaux said.

Hanley started and turned in his seat, but he was stopped by the trace of a smile on the winter-hard features. Hanley had felt uncomfortable from the first moment of meeting, when he saw Devereaux enter the plane by the cockpit door. He had chosen to meet Devereaux on this flight because it was a secure meeting—no bugs, no witnesses. And it was one of the new flights in the middle of the day from Washington to Kennedy Airport—most of the shuttle planes went to La Guardia.

"That's not a joke," Hanley said. "The Old Man is sensitive about that."

"About books?"

"You know what I mean."

"I wouldn't betray you," Devereaux said. "Any more than you would betray me."

"That isn't fair," Hanley said in the defensive voice of a bureaucrat.

"Nothing is."

"This is about Manning," Hanley said. "You knew him."

"He relieved me a long time ago. In Asia. You know that as well as I do." Devereaux's voice was cold and comfortless. He closed his gray, arctic eyes for a moment and saw Manning in his mind, coming off the plane at Saigon late in 1968. They had called Devereaux home and Manning had not understood the reason. Home. It was really an exile to the West, because Asia—even the Asia of Vietnam, scarred by war and corruption—had become the only place he had wanted to live. And after 1968, it was the only place denied to him.

Devereaux had refused to play the numbers game initiated by the CIA and accepted by the Pentagon and the Johnson administration. With devastating accuracy, Devereaux had prepared a report predicting the Tet offensive by the North Vietnamese troops early that year. The report had not been well received in Washington because it had contradicted everything from the CIA operatives. And when Tet *did* happen and toppled the Johnson administration, someone in some bureaucracy had remembered Devereaux's report and had pulled the proper strings to make certain that Devereaux would not go against the grain again. Not in Asia. His exile in the West had lasted until three months before, when the Old Man had forced him to move into the bureaucracy itself or resign.

"What about Manning?"

"He was a good man."

Devereaux understood the tense.

"Where did he get it?"

"Paris." Hanley's voice was soft. "We thought he had a little assignment there. A probe with someone in the Mitterand government. We weren't sure it would work into anything. You know he had been in Paris. I mean, before we sent him to Asia."

"Yes." Devereaux remembered Manning that night in a cheap bar down in the black heart of Saigon, telling him things he should never have confessed.

"I didn't tell him everything. Even when we started getting the links. In Tinkertoy, I mean. I told him to be careful."

"Sound advice," Devereaux said with sarcasm.

"I should have told him. After the business with Felker."

"Hanley, I don't work for you anymore."

Hanley stared at him as though not understanding him.

"I don't want to know your secrets."

"But you came to the plane . . ."

"I was curious. I told you that."

"Devereaux." Hanley paused. "We need an outside man. A contractor who can come in without any records, without anyone knowing."

"Even the Old Man?"

"Yes."

They were silent for a moment, feeling the plane shudder up through the layers of atmosphere.

"In the last six months, Tinkertoy has had problems. We have been getting a lot of information and it doesn't seem to fit at first, and then, when we double-check, it does fit. One of the things was a bunch of data that Tinkertoy put together that led us to tell the National Security Council there was solid evidence that the War-saw Pact maneuvers were a prelude to an invasion of Western Europe.

"NATO went to red alert and then called it off when nothing happened. And then this business in Venice. You see, the Brits were running a little network around our air force bases over there. They caught a Soviet fish named Reed, and Reed had some goodies, and their contract man—named Felker—decided to do Reed in and take the stuff and sell it free-lance."

"I thought this was about Manning."

"It isn't that simple. Dammit, I'm trying to make some sense out of it."

Devereaux did not speak.

"You see, this Felker contacted us in Venice, wanted to make a deal. The CIA was interested too. We moved as fast as we could and got one piece—just to check on Felker's bona fides—but then Felker was killed. So was Cacciato, our agent there. Do you know what Felker had stolen from Reed?

"The oddest stuff. It was in a pretty simple code. When we fed it to Tinkertoy, there were five items in all. Four of them checked out with Tinkertoy, but Tinkertoy threw out the fifth—it didn't work, it didn't background with all our other stuff in the computer. So Mrs. Neumann went in and checked out the four items that did make the grade, and all the support for them had come from *other* information that had been either fed in or altered in the last year in Tinkertoy. And it all had to do with stuff about a game at the Frunze War College in Moscow involving a mock invasion of Western Europe and . . . one bit had to do with Jeanne Clermont, some unconfirmed reports of her contacts with a terrorist group operating in Paris."

"What did that have to do with the invasion of Europe?"

"Nothing by itself."

"I don't understand you."

"This is the way Mrs. Neumann explained it. If point A of Felker's information was fed into Tinkertoy, it was accepted; it jibed with what we had known before. But if we went back to see what it jibed with, we found point AA connected to point BB and point CC, all coming through the same pipeline. And point BB, which had no direct connection with point A, was about Jeanne Clermont. Do you see?"

"Like second cousins who never met," Devereaux said.

"Except in Tinkertoy. No connection between Felker and Jeanne Clermont. Except through bits of information from a dozen sources that met inside the machine."

"If Tinkertoy isn't reliable, get rid of it."

"But that's it." Hanley stared hard at the seat back in front of him. "We don't know that Tinkertoy isn't reliable. If we guess about an invasion of the West, maybe the information is right and our guess is wrong. Maybe someone made a mistake, in either gathering it or feeding it into Tinkertoy. NATO was furious after they stepped down from the red alert. Said red alert stirs up the population and everyone in Europe is jittery now about this so-called peace movement. It gets the military upset."

Again, a ghost of a smile crossed the gray features of Devereaux's face. "Peace gets a bad reputation, doesn't it?"

"This is not a joke," Hanley said. "No matter how absurd, we still have two agents killed in the past three months. And now, this week, Frunze has started playing 'Paris.' "

"How do we know that?"

"We know that," Hanley said.

"And what's the outcome?"

"The game isn't over."

"Are we going to win the war?"

"This is not a joke. Not to them, not to us."

"Are we going to win?"

"No. I don't understand it."

"Maybe we don't have God on our side."

Hanley ignored him. "The Langley Firm is interested because they're afraid we are doing a little probe on their operations in Europe. Especially in the Mitterand government. It explains the message we intercepted in Rome. I had a meeting with the A.D. at Langley."

"You reassured him."

"No. I told him."

They could feel the thrusts of the engines as the plane now descended, pushing down against the waves of air that held it aloft, catching that balance between speed and attitude and altitude that made the whole thing work. Hanley gripped the seat again, forcing the blood from his knuckles.

"Manning was shot down and his body dumped into the Seine. Felker was killed in Venice, he was supposed to have Red Brigade friends there so that's where he hid out."

"How was he taken care of?"

"A water bus, actually. He was dumped in the Adriatic by someone and a water bus ran over him."

Devereaux smiled.

"Nothing in this is funny."

"Manning in the river, Reed in the broads, Felker in the Adriatic Sea. Perhaps the connection to all this is death by water."

"Sarcasm," Hanley said.

"What do you want from me?"

"We . . . need you."

"Because I'm outside," Devereaux said coldly. "Because you're afraid of what might be inside the Section."

"Yes. Something is wrong. Everything we do seems to be known. And yet we don't know what is really going on."

"Why did you send Manning back to her?"

Hanley appeared startled. "You knew then? About the first mission? Fifteen years ago?"

"Manning was a fool." Devereaux spoke with weariness clouding the words. "He fell in love with her."

"I didn't know that."

"Did you expect him to tell you?"

"Why did he tell you then?"

"Because I didn't matter to him." Devereaux paused, stared at the plastic interior of the plane. He saw beyond the plane and this place, perched ridiculously on waves of wind in the middle of an endless sky. "Manning came to Saigon. It was June. After Tet, after everything. It was all over for us but we dragged it out for another seven years. He hated Saigon, he hated the heat and the corruption of the place."

"But not you."

"No." Quietly. "Not me. But I wasn't staying; I was pulled back."

"I didn't have anything to do with that."

"I didn't matter to Manning. He wanted to tell me about this woman he had known in Paris. We got drunk one night; I think we got drunk. Maybe only Manning got drunk."

"It was against security for him to tell—"

"After a while, no one in Saigon believed in security." Devereaux's voice was flat and yet soft. "No one believed in anything. Saigon was all illusions, and so after a while no one had illusions anymore."

"I asked him if he thought it would work," Hanley said. "Going back to Paris, I mean. He said he would try."

"He wanted to see her again," Devereaux said. "He must not have gotten over her."

"That's romance," Hanley said. "I can't believe that."

Devereaux did not speak. His face was cold, pale, crosshatched with lines; his eyes were gray, reflecting the partial graying of his brown hair. "November" was his code designation in the closed files of R Section; the name suited his appearance and manner, the bleakness of his voice.

"If it goes bad," Devereaux began.

"You're on your own. You aren't on file. I have money from contingency funds. For . . . special payments. You don't have sanctions for or against; you're outside the rules."

The no-smoking sign flicked back on; they felt the flaps of the jet drag at the air rushing past the sleek metal fuselage; a fog-shrouded patch of ground loomed below. The landing gear whirred down and locked.

"There never were any rules," Devereaux said softly as the plane rushed down. "You never understood that." He paused. "Now start at the beginning, about Tinkertoy. And about Jeanne Clermont."

14

Garishenko

Garishenko woke as soon as Lieutenant Baliokov touched his shoulder in the darkened command room. His eyes adjusted a moment to the gloom and he wondered, like a child, where he was. His eyes glittered in the light of a single lamp on his desk.

"Sir."

"What time is it?"

"Morning 11, 0500 hours," the young officer replied.

Garishenko sat upright. He slept on a cot during the games. He was clad in underwear; his uniform was carefully hung in the closet. Next to the bed was a cup of cold tea. Cigarette butts littered a wide ashtray. He had read the orders of battle until he feel asleep. That had been three hours ago. He felt drained, cold, frightened; the game had turned against him in the last six game days—that is, the last forty hours—and the weight of impending defeat seemed to shackle his body. The headaches had returned, and so had a dull, aching feeling in his joints, as though the defeat of the NATO forces would be the defeat of his body as well.

"What change?" Garishenko said, blinking his eyes to regain a sense of consciousness.

"Naya says Amsterdam and Rotterdam have fallen and the eastern approaches to the North Sea are taken," Baliokov said.

"Then it's over. And still no response from France."

"No, sir. The premier—of the Soviet Union, sir—sent this message to the British this morning at 0430 hours."

He handed him a computer printout. Garishenko stood up and went to the desk and placed the piece of paper beneath the light of the single lamp. The words blurred for a moment, and he blinked his eyes again.

All military activity of the Warsaw forces has ceased from this moment and we are engaged in securing purely defensive and temporary positions in the Low Countries. I urge, for the sake of peace and for the countless numbers of our people who have

106

been made the victims of this folly, to begin the process of peace talks immediately while each side has its mutual advantages in the military sectors. . . .

Garishenko looked up. "The British won't accept this response."

"Sir, there were riots in Liverpool against the war two hours ago, as well as in Brixton and in London at Chipping Green and Nottingham."

"This is madness, what does Naya say?" But he had come to dread the response of the computer.

"Naya says the British commanders have ordered their forces to hold their positions."

"But time is crucial. If Warsaw is allowed to secure their gains in the Netherlands, the next move will be a pincer against France."

"The French have not responded, sir."

"Damn. Damn." Garishenko wiped one cold hand across his forehead. He was sweating, his face was drawn, the pain of the perpetual headache pushed at his skull. "This can't be. Even they can see that. They are dreaming, they are making their own wishes come true despite reality."

Baliokov stared at the general in his underwear. "Sir, do you remember the revelations last year? In America? The Central Intelligence Agency was revealed to have lied about enemy troop estimates before the Tet offensive, as well as to exaggerate the number of Viet Cong troops in the field? Simply to tell the politicians what they wished to know?"

"But this is a computer. We programmed the computer ourselves. It is the most secure in our country. Who tampered with it? Who would believe that anything could be done to our program? Unless we did it ourselves."

"You can call the Game Master, you can—"

"I have done that, Lieutenant. I have called him three times, and three times he has turned me down. He will not accept the perfidy of the computer as a reason to stop the game. Don't you see?" He looked up, his face drawn and pale. "They have a chance to fulfill their fantasy and they cannot accept the reality. General Garishenko is to be defeated; that is cause for celebration for them. I am haughty and arrogant. That's what they believe. They don't want an enemy, they want a shadow, one that will move as they want him to move. If they wish to devise a strategy believing that the French will not come in on the NATO side in an armed crisis, then they are delighted to have such a France given to them. If they wish to believe the English will sue for peace after all their military goals are achieved, then Naya gives them such an England. My protests are the protests of the losing commander. 'Something must be wrong, I didn't make that program.' "

"Perhaps their own information overrode your program. In the computer, I mean?"

"We had access to the same information, to the same profiles, to the same scenarios based upon past performances of everyone from the leaders of the West to the idiosyncrasies of field commanders. All to the best of our knowledge. And now Naya makes sport of everything we have taught her."

"What are you going to do, General Garishenko?"

Garishenko had known from the moment he had dropped off to a sleep filled with nightmares what he would do if this moment came.

"Damn," Garishenko said. "In that drawer in the cabinet."

Lieutenant Baliokov opened the drawer and took out the glass and the bottle of Polish vodka.

The aide poured a glass.

"And yourself."

"Please, sir, I do not—"

"You will now. This time. You will."

Lieutenant Baliokov poured a glass of the clear liquid for himself. The two men solemnly threw it down their throats. For a moment, the vodka stayed the pain that had been throbbing in Garishenko's head. For a moment, it steadied him. He had known what he would have to do.

He pulled out a piece of paper and carefully wrote down an order. Then he tore the paper from the pad and gave it to Lieutenant Baliokov.

"Feed this to Naya now."

Lieutenant Baliokov looked at the order and then at General Garishenko. "Is this possible?"

"Yes. It's the only alternative."

"Sir, would they do this thing?"

"Of course," Garishenko said.

"But this is monstrous."

"Defeat is monstrous."

Again, the young lieutenant looked at the order of battle for the eleventh morning of the game called "Paris."

"General, I beg you to think of the consequences."

Garishenko smiled slowly. "What do you think I have thought of for the past two days? What do you suppose I have tried to avoid each time I called the Game Master? Do you suppose the Americans would permit Western Europe to fall within the Soviet sphere of influence without a total struggle?"

"But, sir, there is England still, and France—"

"France is in the pincers of the Soviets now. France is lost. Tomorrow or the next day or the next game, France will be overrun without a shot being fired. Who will France deal with? No. The lesson of history is clear to me, as it is to the Americans. Europe cannot fall."

And the young lieutenant, who had never known war in his life, stared again at the order:

To the commander of USS Neptune from CC CINCANT (Commander in Chief, US Naval Operations, Atlantic): Code Red, instruction Z349; scramble back, double imperative. Target Soviet Sector 9Z.

Baliokov did not understand all of the order, only enough of it.

"*Neptune* is a nuclear missile submarine," Baliokov said.

"Yes," Garishenko replied wearily. "This is the first part of the order to fire."

"What is 9Z?"

"A target."

"But what is 9Z?"

Garishenko looked at him. "Gorki, Lieutenant Baliokov."

"But they wouldn't destroy a city. They wouldn't destroy a Russian city."

Garishenko shook his head. "They wouldn't lose Europe."

"But America would invite . . . would . . ."

"It is a risk."

"But, sir—"

"Please, Lieutenant. Please file this order now and wait. I will be in the operations room in a moment. That's all."

And Baliokov could think of no more objections to make.

Except that the horror of the order seemed more real than a game should have been.

15 __
Pim

Evensong had been quite magnificent, Pim thought with satisfaction as he crossed the broad green from King's Chapel to the commercial heart of the town.

Cambridge was at the most frenzied time of the year, when those about to graduate were racing up and down the narrow streets of the ancient city in caps and gowns, playing the last jokes of childhood, savoring the excitement of being upon a threshold of new life. Pim had come to Cambridge at this time in May for the four years he had been building his network around the American air force base; it refreshed him to think that the weary, cynical world he inhabited was only a small part of a larger, hopeful world all around.

Or perhaps all these young, still unmarked faces were the slivers of hope in the real world of gray. That thought, as well, had crossed his mind many times.

He went up a side street from the campus of the university to an even smaller street called Rose Crescent. It was his habit, before catching the train back to Lakenheath, to stop for two pints at the Rose tavern.

"Pepys drank there too," Pim once told Felker.

Felker. Poor Felker; poor Reed. It was all unnecessary in the end. Reed might have been turned and Felker would have been rewarded. Now Felker was dead and Reed was dead and the difficult job of building a new contact had begun. As yet, the Soviets had placed no one at the base.

At least, no one that Pim had discovered.

It had gone well with Auntie at least; Gaunt had done his bit in smoothing it through. Felker had been blamed on Mediterranean Section and there was a shake-up going on there now. Some in Auntie even hinted, somewhat romantically in Pim's view, that Med Section had done in Felker in Venice to get even with him.

"That would certainly set matters straight," Pim had joked to Gaunt, but Gaunt had not been amused. He had been nervous through the whole affair as he did his part in shepherding the little lie through Auntie. The lie that said Felker had killed Reed.

"Good evening," Pim said, entering the public bar.

The patrons of the Rose were mostly a mixture of local businessmen and shopkeepers and a stray don or two from the university itself. The pub had just opened for the Sunday evening trade.

The publican poured him a pint of bitter, and Pim tasted it with appreciation. It had been a satisfactory day; he had arranged to make some surreptitious rubbings from King's Chapel after permission had been denied him. They were wrapped in oilskin inside his long trench coat. The task of rebuilding the network at Lakenheath and Mildenhall, however tedious, was proceeding well. Gaunt seemed pleased enough, and that meant the superiors in Auntie were pleased enough; the incident with Felker had been smoothed over and, if not forgotten, at least the blame had accrued to the right place. It really had been Med Section's fault in the first place, Pim had assured Gaunt; and Gaunt had wanted to be assured. It was as though the two men had not killed Reed or dumped his body in the broad; Reed had been Felker's fault, and both of them half believed it.

After a second pint, he started along the winding high street toward the train depot, which was nearly a mile and a quarter from the town center. Pim did not mind the walk; the train was at seven-thirty, he had time for a last pint at the public house across from the station itself.

The sun was reluctant to set. May evenings were long and languid, like memories of younger days. Pim thought he felt sentimental for his younger self, the tough and assured young man out of the East End who, by dint of competitive examinations, had refined his accent and tastes and shaken off the odors of nine generations of poor families, poor cooking, and poor expectations of life. He had never gone back to the East End; he had never expected to, once he had gone up to London School of Economics and been recruited by the old MI-6. In the old-boy network then in place in British Intelligence, Pim's progress had been slow; they knew where he came from, they knew what his accents had really been. When did you decide to refrain from dropping your h's?, one had asked him once. He had not forgotten it; he had taken care of that slur, in his own way, at the end.

The train from London was exactly on time, and Pim stood in the aisle and watched the countryside roll by. He passed a planned

New Forest of straight poplars bearing the sign "British Trees for British Matches." He remembered the first time he had seen the sign, four years ago; he had not been pleased by the posting to Anglia, but with characteristic determination, he had set about making the network at the American bases work.

His posting would soon be up. He had applied for a transfer to the American desk. Perhaps they would send him to New York—or even the embassy intelligence staff in Washington. He had shown a peculiar genius for probing the American psyche, even while keeping an English perspective. That was what it said in one of the periodic Status of Agent reports filed on him; Pim had made a point of reading it.

He got off the main line train at Ely and walked across the platform to the shuttle for the little towns on the spur that included Lakenheath.

"This is Ely," said the elegant, nondescript British Rail announcer. She spoke the name of the city as though it conferred a special blessing on those who heard her voice. "This is Ely. The train at Platform 4 . . ."

He entered the shuttle and waited a moment. The conductor, in British Rail black-and-red, shuffled up and collected his ticket. Pim sat down heavily in the front seat. He liked to watch the track stretching endlessly ahead of him from the front window. He liked to think he ran the train.

Slowly, reluctantly, darkness began to tinge the growing green fields of the Suffolk countryside. The spring rains had been sufficient, the sun had been generous. Pim felt satisfied and a little tired; the outing in Cambridge had done him some good. He felt he would return to work tomorrow invigorated by the little holiday.

The train slid into the station at Lakenheath just at nightfall. Gates were thrown across the roadway to stop traffic, but none waited; the gatekeeper would be going home now; this was the last train of the day. Pim knew him well enough to wave as he walked down the three steps at the end of the wooden platform and waited for the train to pass.

The train chugged on, and Pim crossed the tracks as the gatekeeper swung back the wooden fences and opened up the road again.

"Good night," Pim said with a little wave.

"Good night to you, sir," the gatekeeper returned.

His automobile was parked a little way up the road, near the public house. He walked with his characteristic quick manner, as though he were late but not late enough to require an actual trot. Pim was always conscious of his own dignity, which sometimes made his gestures comic.

He crossed to the black Ford Escort in the car park near the public house door. For a moment he paused, considering the possibility of another pint before returning to his rooms, but he rejected the thought. He fished his key out of his pocket and stuck it in the door lock.

"Why don't you have a pint instead?"

He turned, bristling, his instincts suddenly revived. In the darkness, he did not see the other man until he stepped from the shadows near the door of the pub.

"Who are you?"

"Pim, I waited for you all afternoon. Where did you go?"

"Who are you? What do you want?"

"Let's have a pint and talk about it."

Pim considered for a moment; he looked around him. The public house was open, there would be locals inside. He could bolt now, but what would be the point? The other man knew him and had followed him, and Pim had been careless enough to let it happen.

"All right, mate," Pim said in a cheery little voice. It was the voice that had disarmed other enemies; it was the manner of the harmless cockney made up to be something he wasn't. A comic figure, not to be taken seriously. Not to be afraid of.

The other man remained in shadows until Pim opened the public house door. Framed against the light, Pim paused. Had he made a mistake? Was there danger?

But the other man pushed behind him, and the two entered the place.

The air was heavy with smoke. A darts game was in progress on the far side of the bar. On the wall was an appeal for the National Heart Fund. On another wall, a small fire added to the smoke of the room. The coals glowed brightly and gave their peculiar warm stench to the place.

Above the bar was a dirty mirror advertising the merits of Greene King ale. It was the favorite local beer in Anglia.

The two men went to the bar, and the publican, his face the face he always turned to strangers, came down to them. Some of the locals also studied the strangers.

"Pint of bitter," Pim said in his avuncular voice. He felt·the knife on the spring pressed against the flesh of his right arm. He was very good with a knife; he had learned the trade as a child within the sound of Bow bells.

"Vodka," the other man said. The voice was American.

"Vodka," the publican repeated, as though he had never heard the word before. "Ain't got no vodka, but we have gin. Gin good enough for you?"

"Good enough," the American said. His voice was low and flat, as though he had learned never to say more than he meant and never to raise his voice, to give any clue to his emotions.

The American put down two pound notes.

"He pays," Pim said, again pasting a cheerful mask on his piglike features. He turned to the American and held up his pint. "Cheers."

The American fished ice from a bucket and dropped the cubes into the gin. He did not respond to Pim. When he looked up, his eyes were gray, his face a winter landscape.

In the trade, Pim thought without panic. He was in the trade; there was no mistaking a man like him.

Pim tasted the bitter and put down the pint.

"I want to talk to you."

"Yes. I supposed so," Pim said, still smiling. The mechanism of the knife in the sleeve was simple: There was a safety catch and then the trigger button. Once the safety was off, the trigger could be set off by his merely banging the inside of his arm against his side. The knife would slide down into the palm of his hand. Stiletto, with six cutting edges of the best Wilkinson steel welded to the sides of the blade; from the point, the cutting edges formed a Cross of Lorraine of steel.

Pim touched his sleeve and pushed off the safety.

"About Felker."

"You wouldn't want to identify yourself first, would you? And tell me why you followed me?"

"Who do you think I am?"

"I haven't the faintest."

"You've run an espionage operation. Against our bases. Felker was part of it."

"You've got that wrong, friend."

"Pim, I don't have time for you. There is some urgency to this."

Urgency. He had used the word the night he had induced Gaunt to bloody his hands dumping Reed's body.

"What do you want?"

"I'm with Central Intelligence."

"Do you have some identity?"

Devereaux produced a card and flashed it discreetly at the bar. Pim stared: It was the same winter face in the photograph, the same seal of the United States covered in plastic, the same wording. He had seen the card before; yet the card didn't necessarily mean anything.

Not to someone in the trade.

"What's going on, then, mate?"

Devereaux stared at him for a moment. "I thought this could be handled reasonably," he said.

"I'm a reasonable man, everyone around these parts knows that," Pim said.

"Dammit," Devereaux said wearily. He stared at the glass of gin as though deciding something. He picked up the glass and drained it. "There isn't time to convince you. I need information."

"Just why do you come to me?"

"You're posturing," Devereaux said. "I told you that I didn't have time."

"Well, I don't know who you are then," Pim began.

Then he saw the gun.

Everyone in the public house saw the gun at the same time.

One of the dart players looked at it and then turned and finished throwing his last dart at the board. Oddly, because he was a good player, the dart missed the board completely. The player turned and stood still.

Everyone in the room stood still.

The landlord came down the bar. "Look here, what's this about? Is that a gun?"

"Come on, Pim," Devereaux said.

"You can't do this, you—"

Devereaux pulled back the hammer. They all heard the click, saw the hammer poised behind the firing pin.

It was extraordinary. Everyone stood still and did not speak.

Pim turned, looked at the country faces arrayed in the brightly lit bar. Then he started outside.

"These Wild West tactics won't succeed. You're in England and—"

"I know where we are. I want you to drive. Not your car, mine. Across the road."

The rental Toyota waited for them. The engine was powerful, and Pim bucked the car to life. Devereaux sat beside him but not within easy cutting range. The knife was in Pim's right sleeve, and he would have to reach across his own body to slash at the other.

Devereaux held the gun steadily.

"Are you going to kill me?" Pim asked. He was not even certain it was his own voice.

"No," Devereaux said. "I want information. I told you."

"About Felker. He bolted us. If you know who I am, you know that. Took the ferry out of Harwich last February was—"

"Who killed the Soviet agent?"

"Felker."

"No."

"Oh, you were there."

"No."

"Then you wanted information; I gave you information."

"I want the truth this time. This doesn't concern you anymore. It concerns us. I want information."

"What's your name?"

"That isn't important."

"Where are we going?"

"I want you to drive through the village and take the road you took to the place where Reed was found. You know the road."

"Yes."

"You took it there when you killed Reed."

"I . . . I killed Reed?"

"Of course. You or someone you hired. I don't care about that. I want to know what Reed knew; I want to know about Felker, what he thought he had."

Pim decided.

He had to get this man out of the car, into a position for a quick cut. Right across the face, push him back. Maybe right into the fen. The same place they had pushed the body of Reed.

"Reed was the Soviet agent."

"I know. But why did Felker bolt?"

"Found something. Information."

"And you went to Reed to find out what it was."

"Yes. How did you know Felker didn't kill him?"

"It made no sense. If he had what he had—if he had enough to try to sell it to us—then he had no reason to kill Reed and draw the trail to him. He had every reason to keep Reed alive. You were the network master; you had every reason to see him dead."

"You're a detective, a fucking detective is what you are," Pim said, his voice slipping into the rhythm of the East End of London.

"What did Reed know?"

"We never found out—"

"Nonsense. You wouldn't have killed him without finding it out. What did Reed know?"

"We turn here."

The Toyota followed the narrow road over the little hump of land and then down the same path to the channel cut along the farmer's land. It was the spot—or near it—where Gaunt and Pim had dumped Reed.

"Get out," Devereaux said.

Pim climbed out of the car. The lights were still on.

"Get over there."

Pim followed the way indicated by Devereaux's wave of the pistol. The black metal shone in the light of the headlamps.

Pim walked up the little rise to the embankment of the channel.

"Here?"

"Yes."

Devereaux suddenly put the car in gear and pushed into the grassy field. He stopped a moment before striking Pim. Pim felt he was on a precipice, with the fen behind him, the auto in front of him. Devereaux turned off the headlamps, but the engine purred on.

"Now tell me about Reed."

"This is ridiculous, Yank. We're on the same bloody side, ain't we?"

"The reason you were spying at Mildenhall and Laken-heath . . ."

"Countersecurity," Pim babbled. He felt the knife case, but it was hopeless. "We were trying to track down a Soviet agent."

"You were spying on the American base. The Soviet just fell into your net by mistake. And you killed him after you found out what you wanted to know."

"Look, can't we go back to the pub, just sit down and sort this out?"

"I told you, there's some urgency. If I hit you now, you'll go into the broad. I'm about ten feet from you. If I hit you hard enough, I can break your legs. There's a good chance you won't even live."

"Jesus, Yank."

"What did Reed know?"

"Nothing, not a damned thing—"

The engine roared.

"But wait! Wait! He had notes. He had kept bloody fucking messages!"

The engine subsided.

"What did the messages say?"

"I don't know."

The motor roared again.

"I don't know, Yank. I kept on him . . . after Felker bolted. It seemed pretty damned odd, some of it. I mean, why did he have all those bits of information written down? He was in an enemy country."

"Maybe he wanted you to have them. After you turned him."

"That doesn't make any sense."

Devereaux got out of the car and stood still, his pistol pointed at Pim but invisible in the rural darkness. The night sky was overcast, bereft of moon or stars; only the smell of the sea was in the air.

"If you had turned Felker, you would have had a bunch of goodies to bring back to London."

"I'm not denying it. That's what we're in business for. Same as you, same as me. Except Felker upset our plans."

"Maybe more than your plans," Devereaux said, seeing something beyond this moment. "Didn't you ask him about all those messages he had?"

"He had instructions. To save them." Even as Pim said it, both men knew it sounded incredible.

"I swear to God, Yank, that's what he told me."

"And you thought it was the truth."

"I knew it. Reed wasn't able to lie. Not after a while."

"Why did he save the messages?"

"He knew about Felker. Knew we wanted to turn him. He was playing a game with Felker. Felker had . . . had become his lover. Reed was a flaming fairy, bloody great queen."

"And he wanted something to bring across," Devereaux said.

"That's it," Pim said. "He saved messages and the code book."

"What was the code?"

"Dammit, Yank, I could slip and fall—"

"What was the book?"

"England Made Me." Pim managed a sneer. "Ever heard of it?"

"Greene," Devereaux said. "Published in the States as *The Shipwrecked.* I liked the English title better."

"So much for modern literature," Pim said. "Can I come down now?"

Pim felt the blade point against his arm. He was ready.

Devereaux was silent for a moment.

"What else was there?"

"It was all he told me. I didn't have much time, y'see."

"A matter of urgency for you as well," Devereaux said.

"What are you talking about?"

"Do you swim well?"

"What do you mean? I told you everything I know."

Devereaux got back inside the car.

"What are you gonna do? Yank? Yank?"

"Give you a moment to consider the alternatives. Do you want to jump into the broad? Or do you want to be pushed in by the car?"

"Dammit. This isn't fair."

"It's fairer than Reed got."

"Dammit, we're allies."

"Go ahead, Pim." The voice was cold, mild, even a little amused.

And then Pim thought of the brass rubbings. They'd be ruined, even in the oilcloth.

"One favor, Yank? One favor. Let me take out the rubbings."

"What?"

"Brass rubbings? Got them up in Cambridge today at the King's Chapel. Please. Let me take them out."

"Carefully."

Slowly, Pim unbuttoned his coat and opened it. He pulled out the oilskin and set it down gently on the ground beside him.

"Brass rubbings," Pim said with reverence. "I collect them."

Devereaux did not speak. He flicked on the headlamps again and Pim was framed in the piercing white light. Pim trembled with rage; he felt a fool. The Yank had made him feel a fool. There would be a time for avenging this. He was Alfred Pim, he wasn't from the East End anymore; no man told him his place, no man told him about dropping his bloody h's.

119

The motor roared.

Pim turned and jumped over the precipice into the murky waters of the broad, near the place where he had dumped Reed's body three months before. For a moment he held still as the icy waters closed over him, and then his feet touched bottom. It was barely six feet deep. He struggled up and broke the surface.

All was darkness.

He could hear the motor already roaring in the distance.

Damn. Damn him. Pim struggled to the reedy bank and lifted himself out of the water.

16

Jeanne Clermont

For a long time—she thought later that it had been at least two hours—the car was on the road outside the capital, fleeing down one of the empty predawn highways into the lush and rolling countryside. She could not tell the direction, but she felt the rise and fall of the Renault as it dipped and climbed, valley to valley; she guessed they were heading southwest, into the countryside north of Tours, not far from the Loire.

They had placed a blindfold over her eyes. They had been courteous but the requirement was firm. She had offered no resistance. She was still numb from the death of William, from the sense of anxiety that had turned to fear and then to the certainty confirmed on the third page of *Le Monde*.

The big Algerian named Bourgaine had come for her in the afternoon and taken her to Le Coq. The location of the apartment had been changed; everyone in the terror cell seemed on edge.

Le Coq had flown into her. "He was with you, in your apartment, madame, and then he was killed. Why did you kill him?"

"I didn't kill him," she said, her words offering no explanation and no defense.

"Because of your petty jealousies," Le Coq had screamed. "He betrayed you in 1968 and that was more important than the work of our organization. You would be avenged like a cheap Corsican whore, you wanted his life."

She had said nothing while Le Coq berated her, described fantastic scenarios, stomped around the room like a child.

"You killed him!" Le Coq had screamed at her.

"No" was all she permitted herself to say, sitting on a chair alone in the middle of the darkened room while the shadows of the others were around her. She thought of the torn body pulled from the murky Seine, the blood upon his beautiful face, the holes torn in the white flesh of his body. Was it a moment before that he had covered her with his body, alive, warm and hard, held her with his arms, let his warmth spread over her, engulf her?

William, she had thought as Le Coq berated her and then lashed out at the others. William. He had left her without a good-bye, silently fleeing the dark room in the morning calm of Paris. She dreamed she had heard the shots that tore his life from him.

And then, after what seemed a long time, the ravings were done and she still sat in the room and the others would not speak to her. Would they kill her? Would they banish her from La Compagnie Rouge?

But now it did not matter to her; all her life was drained from her in his wounds. What did revolutions or governments mean to her when William was dead?

Le Coq had made a telephone call finally and come back to her a chastened man. "Perhaps you had nothing to do with Manning's death after all," he had said with a gentle tone.

"It doesn't matter what you think," she had replied sadly. "I want to leave now."

"No, madame. Not now. The games are over," he said. "To-night you will begin your real work for La Compagnie Rouge."

And she had waited, in silence and alone, during the long night as strangers came and left the garret, as there were little muttered conferences in the corners of the room. After three in the morning, when most of the bistros and brasseries in the 5th arrondissement—the Latin Quarter—were closed and the streets were at last quiet, Bourgaine reentered the rooms and said everything was ready.

"She will have to be blindfolded," Le Coq had said, and every-one agreed.

""Why?" she had asked.

"For security."

She had stared at him sadly. "More games?"

"No, madame. No more games. From this night, the games are finished."

And so they had taken her in the car along the streets of the sleeping city, out past the Bois de Boulogne, through the suburbs, into the countryside. The games are over, she thought as the car hummed relentlessly down the road, and then she would think of William again and she knew there were tears pressed beneath her blindfold. It was better that they not see the tears, she thought; it would be better if she could not cry for him anymore.

Now he suddenly pulled her blindfold away, and Jeanne blinked at the morning light. The day was soft, the fields—there were fields of wheat in every direction—were damp with dew, and a little mist hung over the sprouting tops of the wheat.

They had pulled up at a small, stone farmhouse with a red tile roof. The house was at the end of a dirt road that wound around two low, brooding hills. The house commanded a fine view of the fields beyond; in the distance, nearly at the line of the horizon, the windows of a château glinted in the light. The day was calm, already full of promised warmth; a few fat clouds drifted against the clear sky. They might have been a thousand miles from Paris, but they had driven less than three hours, Jeanne knew.

The large man who had blindfolded her now helped her step from the small car. Her heels sank in the damp earth of the path that led to the wooden cottage door. Bourgaine pulled the car around the cottage and parked it behind a wooden fence at the back of the property. Without effort, the house was as isolated as one could be; it commanded a good, long view of the only road that ran near the property.

It was safe, Jeanne realized, and she felt again the excitement that had mingled with her grief at Manning's death. Everything that had happened in the last forty-eight hours had pulled her back and forth. If Manning had not been killed, they might not have trusted her enough to bring her here, to show her the secret heart of La Compagnie Rouge.

And what did Manning's death mean to her except an opportunity like this? She had been going to betray him in any case, just as he had intended to betray her.

Would Manning have grieved if she had died?

She stepped across the threshold and tried not to think of him, but he had haunted her in life and would haunt her again. She endured his memory as though enduring pain or an illness that must run its course; she endured her own grief as though it were something apart from her.

"Madame."

He was a short man with an enormous belly and a dirty beret perched atop his bald head. He might have been fifty. He had not shaved, and Jeanne could not guess from his appearance if he had been awake all night or had just gotten up. "Café au lait? Croissants?"

"Thank you." She stepped across the large room. It was a kitchen but it had not been well kept. Dirty saucepans littered the white ceramic stove. A loaf of bread was on the table, along with stale croissants and a scattering of crumbs and bits of jam from an opened jar. The big-bellied man took a pot of coffee from the stove and poured some into a cup along with milk and handed it to her.

"Not like Paris," he said with a chuckle. "We are simple people here in the countryside."

"It doesn't matter," she said. She felt enervated by the long ride, by the night of waiting in Le Coq's rooms, by the constant reminders in her memory of Manning's death.

She sat down on a wooden chair painted a hideous yellow.

Everything in the room spoke of neglect, as though the occupant of the little house was accustomed to living like a beast among the remains of civilization. She sat primly, her hands folded on her lap. She looked around again, and then she noticed the transmitter.

It was a newer model, she noted, quite compact.

The big-bellied man sat down across from her. He pushed a remnant of croissant toward her across the wooden table, but she did not touch it.

"Madame Clermont," he said.

She only stared at him. And then he laughed, a low and rumbling laugh like the sound of water rushing in a subterranean drain. His black eyes were without mirth, she saw.

"I am Calle," he said.

She waited.

He lit a cigarette wrapped in yellow paper and blew the harsh smoke across the table toward her. He smiled again, and the smile revealed yellow teeth with unusually large canines: the teeth of an old dog, still able to tear at the flesh of a rabbit.

She picked up the cup of coffee and milk and sipped it. Despite the milk, it tasted bitter, as though it had been sitting in the pot all night.

"Le Coq said you were ready."

"For what?"

The Algerian had entered the room and resumed his station at the door. The big man who had blindfolded her was not in the house.

"You see, there has been a matter of some urgency added to our usual caution," Calle said.

"I don't know what any of this is about."

"Who killed Manning?"

"I don't know."

"Is that the truth?"

She stared at him without a word. He studied her with small, black eyes, the eyes of a beast. Yes, she thought with a little shiver, he had the air of the beast about him, in his appearance, in his savage face and yellowed teeth, in his soulless eyes that studied her as a cat studies a trapped mouse.

"In any case, you are now at the heart of things," he said finally. "I asked Le Coq if we could trust you and he said we had no choice. He's right; there is no choice now. Matters have reached a point where we must proceed."

"Monsieur," she began slowly. "Two days ago, William Manning was killed. I don't know who killed him. I would not want him dead. Le Coq knew this; you should know this too."

"You were in love with him," Calle said.

"That is not for you to say or for you to speak of," she said in the same measured way. Her voice was soft but oddly tough, as though the softness of her words masked only steel beneath, naked and waiting.

"Madame, all matters are for me to study. Everything that affects La Compagnie Rouge affects me."

"Who are you?"

"Calle," he said again, smiling again, flashing the sharpened teeth. He picked up a dirty glass and held it a moment. Then he got up and went to the sink and took an opened bottle of wine from the drainboard. He poured the red wine into the glass and brought it back to the table and sat down. He sipped it and then stared at her again without speaking for a moment.

"You were useful to us in Paris. Le Coq convinced me of that. I approved using you, I approved Le Coq telling you that this Manning was an American agent."

"Who are you?"

"Be quiet, madame, for a moment." He drained the glass of wine and lit another cigarette. The room was acrid with the stale smell of burned tobacco from a long night of smoking Gauloises.

124

Butts littered the rough planking of the floor; the windows were clouded with the stains of tobacco smoke etched on the glass. Everything in the room was rank with the accumulated odors of strong cigarettes, garbage, leftovers, and dirty dishes.

"We wanted to see what would happen. With you and with your William Manning. What happened surprised us; yes, I can say it surprised us. We didn't expect his death anymore than you did. But perhaps it has added that sense of urgency to this matter that was needed. Perhaps it is our signal."

"To what?"

"What we all wish to achieve," Calle said. He smiled again.

"Have I been driven in darkness, blindfolded, to this place just to be confronted by another dreary philosopher of the revolution?" She spoke with a Parisian's instinct for the cutting remark carefully fashioned in the elegant sentence.

But the beast did not move or react. The beast stared at her without guile; the black eyes were fixed on her face as though she might have been a victim.

She waited.

"Madame, it is very close," he said finally. "These are not children's games anymore. When you were at the barricades in 1968, taunting the police, you thought it was for sport, that your idealism was a rite of spring, something that youth must do."

"No, monsieur. You misunderstand me if you think that." She leaned forward across the table. "My passion is not to be questioned. Not in this. I have earned your respect with every day I served in prison and with every letter I have written and every cause I have served and every time the Deuxième Bureau questioned me or blocked me or blacklisted me or defamed me."

"Madame, all that has been as nothing." Calle got up again and went back to the sink. This time he returned with the bottle of raw red wine and another glass. He pushed the second glass at her and poured a generous measure. She picked up the glass and tasted it; the wine burned her throat.

"Bourgaine," Calle said.

The Algerian nodded and opened the single door and went outside.

Jeanne Clermont waited. Her hand rested gracefully on the squat glass.

"You are in a position to know many things," Calle began at last.

She stared.

"The appearance of William Manning did not surprise us."

"What do you mean?"

"We had expected him from the beginning."

"How could you?"

Calle shook his head. "That cannot be explained. Not now. What I require of you is quite simple, but, unfortunately, it is not so easy for us to obtain. We could have obtained it in time, but now the time is short. Events move too quickly. It is May already."

"What do you want?"

"I have been afraid of you," he said. "Of using you."

"What do you know of me?"

"Everything."

"And why are you afraid?"

"Because there is nothing we can do to you."

"What do you mean?"

"Your husband is dead. And now your lover is dead. He might have been useful, but that cannot be helped. Your parents are dead, you have no family; you are quite alone."

She smiled then, with sadness, with a gentle memory revealed behind the eyes. "We are all alone at last, Calle; age assures us of that. Why are you afraid of a woman alone?"

"Because we must be certain of you."

"Why?"

Calle studied the remains of the cigarette smoldering in his large, hairy hand. He dropped it on the floor with the others and crushed it out. He lit another.

"What do you do with your reports?"

She seemed surprised. She sat up straight and looked at him and then answered. "They are filed with Monsieur de Forêt, you know that."

"Yes, yes. But that isn't what I asked you. What do you do with them? I mean, when everyone has seen them?"

"They're filed, of course."

"Of course. Where?"

"I don't understand what you mean."

"Madame, since 1974 the records of the ministries as well as the records of the Chamber of Deputies and the Senate have been filed by computer."

She stared at him.

"Is this correct?"

"Yes. I didn't understand what you—"

"Yes. What we want. Simple. What is the access code to the computer in the Ministry of Internal Reforms?"

"But I . . ."

"I what? It's a simple matter."

"But I don't use the computer, I don't know . . ."

"How difficult would it be to find out? How difficult? Will it take months, years?" He was sarcastic now, and Jeanne felt uncomfortable at the mean change in the tone of his voice. The voice still rumbled but it was the growl of the beast now, hidden in some depth of his soul.

"I don't know, I never thought of inquiring."

"There are two codes to the computer. One is general, for the entire ministry; the other is personal, for the individual who has access. It is important that the individual is of sufficient importance to have access to all other bins of the computer."

"I don't understand."

"Madame, the computer of your ministry is interlocked with other computers in the government. At each level, lesser numbers of persons have access to a wider range of computer storage areas. At the lowest level, a clerk—a file clerk—will have access to the computer of the ministry and only to the file in her small section. At the next level, her supervisor will have access to all the bins of all the clerks. At the next level, the departmental supervisor will have access to all the bins of those below her."

"And the highest level . . ."

"Will have access to other departments," Calle finished.

"But why do—"

"It is important that we have the access codes to the computers at the highest level. If it is necessary, we are willing to pay for the information." He said the last words with contempt, and Jeanne returned the tone in her reply:

"Who would you pay, Calle? Obviously, you have thought to bribe someone before you spoke to me. Do you want to pay me? Or is my loyalty to the cause sufficient?"

The man stared at her, wreathed in smoke from his burning cigarette. "That's the question, isn't it? I would prefer not to trust you."

"Why? What reason have I given you or anyone in the movement not to trust me?"

"None. That frightens me. Are you so dedicated after all these years? You flaunt your middle-class morality, you pray at mass every Sunday, and yet you sleep with your lover and you married your husband out of pity. I am frightened by that which I cannot understand, madame. You are a member of the petty bourgeoisie and yet you flirt with a revolution."

"My dedication is questioned," she replied, "because I prefer clean clothes to dirty ones, because I prefer to live as a human being in my apartment and not as an animal."

Again the rumbling, low sound, half of a man's laughter, half of the warning growl of the beast. "So Le Coq says we must trust you. You have fooled him at least; but you must do more to fool me."

"The code," she said. "This access code. I will get it."

"How?"

"Should I ask you why you want it? The computer is for storage of files; what files would our ministry provide you that I could not request myself?"

"How will you obtain the access codes?" Calle repeated, ignoring her.

"I don't know. I'll get them. From de Forêt."

"Will you sleep with him?"

"Why should that be necessary?"

"Is he in love with you?"

She waited for her voice to come back. "Who are you, Calle, to ask me such things?"

"It is too important not to tell you."

"Yes. You have said that. This is important and that is important. But I cannot be trusted."

"No one can be trusted," Calle said.

"Not even you."

"Not even me. No one."

"Why do you want this access code?"

"That's obvious."

"But what can you learn from a file?"

"Madame, who killed William Manning?"

"You asked me that at first, and I told you I don't know."

"But the question is more important than you answer. Madame, William Manning was an American intelligence agent who wanted to use you. Use you for what? He was killed. By whom? Do you see, you are at the center of this business whether or not you are involved. You were the conduit for Manning—but for what? And then Manning is killed. Why?"

"I don't know." But suddenly, a horror seized her and she

thought for a moment she would choke or faint or be overwhelmed by some force she never knew existed. For the first time since Manning's body had been found in the Seine, she saw his death clearly. All during the hours of agony, of studying his dead features in the daily papers, of sitting in gloomy silence in her rooms, of reliving again and again their last meeting until the pain of memory had opened every wound, until every moment they had spent together was remembered with sadness, Jeanne had not understood until now.

She had caused his death. If she had not existed, he would not have died.

"Madame?" The small man leaned forward. Her face had gone white with shock, her eyes had opened wide; he saw the horror reflected. "Madame Clermont?

Madame?"

She could not speak to him. In a moment, there would be tears. But now she could not speak because the inevitability of William's death was finally understood.

17

Simeon

Devereaux had arrived in Paris thirty-six hours too late. The police had already ransacked Manning's hotel room; his few, anonymous possessions had been removed to the evidence room in the basement of that part of the Palace of Justice devoted to the workings of the Criminal Investigations Division.

They would remain there, unclaimed.

No one would avow Manning's identity. After a time, his body—unclaimed by relatives or friends—would be buried in the potter's field in Neuilly, outside the capital. He had been single, his parents were dead. There was no reason for anyone to acknowledge that Manning had existed at all.

For two days, Devereaux had done nothing. The lack of action was not characteristic of him, but if the game had not changed—as he told Hanley—the rules had shifted, and he was not certain of his ground. Hanley suspected something was wrong within the Section and so he could not turn to the Section for aid. And so he could not interview Herbert Quizon as a member of the Section; nothing could be floated back to Section—by Quizon or anyone. Nothing could be confirmed by Section.

For two days, in the dull, old-fashioned rooms he had rented in the same hotel where Manning had stayed, he tried to feel his way beneath the skin of the murdered agent. If Lakenheath and Felker and the dead agent Cacciato were all linked back to Paris and Jeanne Clermont, what was the link? And why had Manning been killed when nothing in his reports to Hanley indicated that Manning had any clue to a link? Or to Jeanne Clermont's part in a supposed chain of circumstances that stretched across Western Europe? And why had Manning chosen this hotel to live in?

Devereaux had brooded as he sat, stripped to the waist, on the straight chair next to his bed. His room faced the busy length of rue des Écoles, a faintly shabby street that cut through the old heart of the Latin Quarter. Across the street, students lounged in the afternoon sun in a bar with a few tables on the narrow sidewalk. A mixed odor of strong tobacco and carbon monoxide from the belching and overstrained motors of the street traffic reached the window of Devereaux's room. He sat alone and stared at the street scene and did not see it; rather, he felt the presence of Manning entering into him. He had to understand him to begin to understand Jeanne Clermont.

On the table was a bottle of Polish vodka purchased at an exorbitant price in the store up the street. He poured a little into a straight tumbler and tasted it.

Manning.

He had been the man to replace Devereaux in Saigon in 1968. He had seemed shot then, as though he were going through the motions. Devereaux had said nothing because his replacement meant nothing to him; he had only observed Manning's condition out of curiosity.

And one night, in a bar in Saigon that was too loud and too small and that smelled of the peculiar sweet corruption that permeated that city as surely as the smell of cheap, burning diesel fuel, Manning had wanted to tell him. About Jeanne Clermont. About the mission.

Devereaux had not wanted to hear the story, but he had listened. Perhaps he had been burned out as much as Manning; perhaps the hopelessness of the Saigon mission had overwhelmed him;

130

perhaps he was merely tired of telling the truth when everyone preferred to hear lies.

Devereaux had waited for a long time for Manning to tell the end of the story. They had sat in silence, listening to the bar girls chatter and watching a desperately silly Marine captain make a fool of himself by singing college songs to a sour prostitute who did not understand the English used beyond the bedroom. Already, in 1968, the mood of the city had become desperate, as though all the horrors of twenty-five years war were now coming to a final horror that would be unspeakable.

"Why is he doing that?"

"What?"

"Why is that Marine captain singing those stupid fucking songs?" Manning had asked. "Doesn't he know he's making a fool of himself?"

Devereaux had not replied for a moment. "Yes. I think he knows what he's doing."

"You see, I keep thinking, it was my first assignment, maybe I was naïve. I'd been laid before, I mean; it wasn't that. No—it was that; it was everything about her."

Even now, in the cold quiet of the old hotel room five stories above the cluttered street, facing the French doors that opened to the Paris sky and the little ledge that was the room's balcony, Devereaux could see Manning as he had been that night in Saigon fifteen years ago.

"Who told you they hadn't harmed her?" Devereaux had finally asked.

"Hanley. He's a third man in the Section, in operations."

"You don't believe him."

Manning had paused. "No. That's it. I don't believe him."

"It's better not to," Devereaux had said.

"I can't forget her."

"Then don't forget her."

"But what do you do?"

"You do nothing," Devereaux had said, fixing his cold eyes on the drunken Marine captain at the bar. What had he been singing? A Yale song about the tables down at Morry's, a sentimental song that made the longings of youth seem important.

"You went into the game," Devereaux had said. "There aren't any rules but you chose to play by certain rules. They wanted you to set up this woman and you did it. So you chose their rules. You could have protected her, you could have saved her; hell, you could have quit the game. But you thought you could work it from every way."

"That's not fair."

"No. It's only true."

"But what did they do with her?"

Devereaux had put down his drink. "Do you want the truth or do you want Hanley to lie to you? Think the worst and then assume it to be true."

Devereaux picked up his tumbler of vodka and walked to the balcony and stared down at the hustling street full of raucous afternoon life. He had been to Paris before, for brief periods, but until now he had never seen the resemblance to Saigon in the noise of the street. But then, the French had made Saigon before the Americans made it over again.

And then he saw the man again.

Devereaux stared down at the few tables in front of the shabby bar-tabac across the wide street. Something had jogged his memory for an instant and now the memory was fixed, like a tape recording stopped by the pause mechanism.

It was the same man, he was certain, but in different clothes. Where had he seen him?

Yesterday afternoon. In the rue Mazarine, as he surveyed the street where Jeanne Clermont's apartment building was located.

He stared at the figure sitting at the small round table with a glass of red wine in front of him, reading that afternoon's copy of *Le Monde*. He had light brown hair and a pale face marked by large and dark eyebrows.

Devereaux stepped back inside the room and put the glass of vodka on the little table. He picked up the shirt hanging from the back of the chair and slipped it on. He went to the closet—it was actually a wooden wardrobe affixed to the far wall—and removed his jacket. On the closet shelf was the small bag that he had packed when Hanley called him that morning in Virginia nearly four days ago. It had clean changes of clothing and shaving gear and the pharmacopeia of the professional traveler, including pills for waking up and pills for going to sleep and pills for chasing away the dread that crept up suddenly on lonely nights in strange cities, when he was doing a dirty little job.

And the pistol as well. He removed the piece of black, hardened steel and hefted it and then slipped the Colt Python .357

Magnum into his belt. He closed the mahogany doors of the wardrobe and turned to survey the small room. The bed was made, the bottle of vodka sat next to the tumbler on the table, a damp towel clung to the back of a second straight chair in the room. Scarcely a trace that the room was occupied at all; Devereaux had lived in hotel rooms for most of his adult life. He had learned the trick of coming and going without leaving marks of himself, like an animal that cannot be tracked through a dense forest.

He reached into his inside pocket and felt the passport and the bills that Hanley had given him. If he was killed now, there was nothing in the room that would trace him back to Section, no way to trace him even to a specific address in the United States. It was the macabre caution that all the agents learned.

He opened the door of his room and closed it.

He took the stairs. They wound down to the lobby at a dizzying scale.

He crossed the lobby. The clerk looked up in the suspicious and bored way of French hotel clerks and then looked down at the *France-Soir* spread on his desk.

Devereaux stepped into the street and started west, into the eye of the dying afternoon sun. In the reflection of a shop window that displayed English books he saw the man at the table across the street rise and fold his *Le Monde* and begin to follow him across the way.

The street was crowded with traffic; long lines of Citroëns and Renaults and Peugeots jostled for position at the lights as though the intersections were starting gates. He passed a pâtisserie with its array of fresh breads and stale quiches in the window and a bored, fat woman sitting behind the counter. He stared at the display for a moment as though he intended to buy something; in the reflection of the window he saw the man across the street pause as well and then go on.

Devereaux turned the corner and started north toward the river. In the next block was the entrance to the Métro. He decided to give it the test and started down the steps quickly; he noticed the name of the Métro station on the large, illuminated map inside and then shuffled into the line for purchasing tickets. He pushed over a ten-franc note and took his change and the ticket.

Out of the corner of his eye he saw the man descending the stairs.

Devereaux pushed through the turnstile and down another

flight of stairs to the platform. He walked the length of the platform, to the far end, and turned again. The stranger was on the platform as well. He raised the copy of *Le Monde* to cover his face.

Not a very good job, Devereaux thought. He knew how difficult it was to follow someone, but the other man had been clumsy. As though he did not expect Devereaux to be on his guard.

The underground train whooshed quietly into the station, and after a moment the doors slid open. The cars were full of afternoon faces, tired and dour, each hiding private thoughts and mundane disillusions. Devereaux stepped aboard and then looked out. The other man had already gotten aboard.

A terrible job of surveillance, in fact, Devereaux thought. The other man should have waited until the train was about to go and then gotten aboard.

The doors slammed shut and the train slowly picked up speed. Devereaux glanced out the windows. The next station was Odéon; the train was heading west across the left bank of the Seine for Porte d'Auteuil, near the southeast edge of the Bois de Boulogne, the giant wooded park on the western edge of the city.

As the subway roared along between the walls of the narrow tunnels, Devereaux thought of the man who had followed him. Since he had made no contacts in Paris yet, they had to know he was coming. But from where? What was the connection with Jeanne Clermont?

And was it worthwhile to make contact or play out the game?

Hanley had spoken of time; there was some vague urgency to everything that Devereaux had to do. He was instinctively against forcing a decision, but the stranger who followed him had made changes. Something would have to be done.

The train pulled into the farthest station west on the Number 10 line twenty-two minutes later, and Devereaux got out of the last car with a few others and headed for the exit. He did not look around; he knew the stranger was following him.

In the fading sunlight, traffic crawled painfully through the place de la Porte d'Auteuil, accompanied by horns and the roar of tiny engines and the strident whistles of the uniformed traffic policemen in their pillbox hats and white gloves. Nothing seemed to move; it was simply part of the twice-daily ritual of the Paris rush hour.

Devereaux crossed the place near the south end of the Auteuil racetrack and found his way into the woods. He walked quickly, as though he were going to a rendezvous; he wanted to be deeper into the woods of the park before he turned on the man who followed him.

He climbed a steep path toward the Butte Montmartre and then turned into the woods itself. Beneath the green canopy of the mature elms and poplars and chestnuts and maples, the sunlight was cut down. The woods were darker, and they muffled the sounds of traffic beyond the preserve.

He could not hear anyone behind him.

He crossed carefully into a roadway; there were no cars and no strollers. He went to the other side of the road and back into the woods. Then he turned and waited behind a massive oak.

A minute passed, and then another.

No one crossed the roadway.

In the third minute, a bicycle came speeding up the path, the driver intent only on the pleasure of the empty road and his body pushing against the machine. The head of the bicyclist was low over the handlebars, and his muscle-knotted legs were blurred as they pushed the gears.

Devereaux nearly smiled. Perhaps he was so inept that he had gotten lost.

The roadway was empty again. Devereaux waited and felt the weight of the black pistol at his belt.

"Monsieur?"

He turned suddenly and a man with large, sad eyes and a mournful face was in a small clearing fifty feet on the other side of him. Devereaux waited and did not speak.

"Do you speak French?"

"Who are you?"

"It is more important that I ask you."

Devereaux waited. His brown corduroy jacket was unbuttoned; the pistol could be brought to firing position in a quick move of his practiced left hand.

The man who had followed him had not shown. And in his place appeared this large Frenchman in trilby hat and tan raincoat, the English clothes utterly failing to disguise the Gallic features. His nose was long and broad, the eyes were wide-set in a wide face; the ears were long, with large lobes. The eyes seemed amused and sad by turns, as though what they saw never failed to cause one emotion or the other.

"I didn't understand what you said," the Frenchman said.

"I said nothing," Devereaux replied.

"Why are you here?"

"Taking a walk."

"Are you American? Your accent is American."

"I didn't know I had an accent."

The Frenchman grinned. "Precisely."

"Who are you?"

"My name is Simeon, Inspector Simeon with the Criminal Investigations Department."

"Has something criminal taken place?"

"Perhaps it might."

Again, the two men did not move but played on the silence between them.

Devereaux could not see the road now behind him. Maybe the two men—the stranger he had spotted and this Frenchman—had worked together and the other man was now circling him. But how had Simeon gotten behind him?

"Let me be clear. I've followed you since you came to Paris. Your name is Clay and you are an American exporter. That is what your entry visa says and that is what you told customs. But you came from Britain. I am curious about you."

"The French police must have a lot of time to indulge their curiosity."

Simeon grinned broadly. "This is not a matter for humor," he said, but the grin remained. "Why do you come to the Bois?"

"Why do you follow me?"

"Because I am curious. About you and about why you have taken a room in the hotel that was the hotel of William Manning." The grin remained as a ghost of a moment before, but the voice was quick, harsh, even brutal. Beneath the comic exterior, something existed that was a lie to everything Simeon appeared to be.

"Who is William Manning?" Devereaux said calmly.

Simeon removed a small pistol from the pocket of his coat. It glistened in the thin light of the dying afternoon. Above their heads, the trees rustled in a slight wind; the sounds of traffic were distant. From a café hidden by the trees, they could now hear the clink of glasses and low voices.

"You are an American agent," Simeon said. "You have an interest in William Manning and you have an interest now in Jeanne Clermont. I am a simple policeman; I have to know the truth of the matter."

"Do you suppose I killed Manning?"

"Someone did."

"What did you find? On his body?"

"The usual things. And a photograph. It was a photograph taken a long time ago—the type of film is obsolete—at the Louvre. It is a picture of a young man and his woman."

What a fool, Devereaux thought suddenly. Manning had not forgotten her in all the years between; he had been in love with her. And then he had been killed, and now his stupid romanticism had complicated matters with this policeman.

"All right," Devereaux said slowly. "I want to give you some identification."

"Yes. Slowly," Simeon said.

Devereaux removed the black case and opened it and held it up.

Simeon walked across the grass to a place ten feet in front of Devereaux.

He glanced at the card and then at Devereaux. "You have a pistol. Remove it and drop it on the ground."

Devereaux removed his piece and dropped it. The pistol made no sound.

"Central Intelligence Agency. You have no authority here."

"One of our men was killed," Devereaux said.

"But this is France; you have no authority. Why didn't you establish contact with the Deuxième Bureau?"

"This was a private matter," Devereaux said. He held his hands apart from his body; he watched the policeman. The pistol was steady; the policeman stood too far away from him. There was nothing to do.

"How many others came in with you?"

"Just me. We want information."

"We had watched the hotel. You inquired about Manning. The girl at the concierge desk notified me, of course. It was routine."

"Someone followed me just now. Was that you?"

Simeon appeared puzzled for a moment. "I don't know about that. I have followed you. What did you expect to learn here?"

"Who killed Manning."

"No." Simeon grinned. "That is not very important to you, I think. I think you want to know why they killed him."

"You speak like an intelligence agent yourself."

"No, only a policeman. I don't like any of this. I don't like Americans playing gangsters in my city."

"Americans? Did it involve other Americans?"

"It involves you. It involved Manning."

137

"And Jeanne Clermont."

"Yes. That's what I want to know. How is Madame Clermont involved in this?"

"You must know."

"No. I know nothing. I have a photograph, I search the files. We have a file on Madame Clermont. She is in the government, in the Ministry of Internal Reforms. She was a radical. You know that? In her youth? She was arrested and she went to prison."

Devereaux said nothing.

"But you, Monsieur Clay. What is the interest of the Central Intelligence Agency in Madame Clermont now?"

"I don't know."

Simeon was a large man but he moved with surprising grace. The pistol hand flicked out with scarcely a warning; Devereaux managed to turn away from the blow so that it caught him, not in the face as Simeon intended, but behind the ear. The blow stunned him; he fell. He felt nauseated and the earth did not seem firm beneath the touch of his fingers. He was on his hands and knees when the second blow came. Devereaux had expected it but he could not move, and it caught him in the ribs. He fell forward, and the third blow—another kick—cracked into the side of his chest. The policeman had not spoken as he worked. Now he stepped back a pace and the voice was heavy with labored breath.

Devereaux retched and the fluids of his empty stomach stained the ground. He pulled himself up to his knees and tried to rise further, but he couldn't. He waited.

"Do you think your reply to my questions could be improved now?"

Devereaux said nothing.

"You're a tough guy right?" Simeon took a step forward and raised his pistol hand again.

This time Devereaux drove the fingers of his left hand into the big belly before him, and at the same time pushed his shoulders against the other's legs. Simeon swung down with the gun hand, but he was was off-balance; in a moment, he was stumbling back, even as Devereaux rose and grabbed the pistol hand.

A single shot broke the silence. The trees rustled accusingly, like scolding aunts.

Simeon did not cry out as Devereaux wrenched the pistol out of his hand, nor when Devereaux's second blow landed heavily on his nose. Blood stained his face. The third blow sent him reeling onto the grass.

Devereaux regained both guns and stood, propped against an elm. He watched Simeon on the ground. Simeon half rose, wiped his nose, and pulled out a handkerchief.

"Throw your identification over here," Devereaux said.

"You can't get out of the city, let alone France."

"Here."

The Frenchman pulled out a wallet and threw it across.

Devereaux squatted and flipped open the card case.

Simeon.

His photograph stared back at him.

But he was not with the CID.

Devereaux looked up. "Deuxième Bureau."

"This is nonsense," Simeon said. "Why don't we be reasonable men?"

"There's nothing to reason about. You followed me or had me followed. You've made your connections. Now I want to know what you're doing about them."

"A foreign agent was killed in Paris. Why? Why was he here? You have no right in this matter."

"But I have the pistol." Devereaux's voice was low, plain, without traces of sentiment or pity.

"You can't get out of Paris without me."

"I don't intend to leave right now. What did you find when you found Manning? Why did you know he was an agent?"

Now Simeon smiled and removed the bloodstained handkerchief. Again, the grin was unnaturally broad, as though he were enjoying a good joke. "We picked him up the moment he entered France four months ago. He went through customs using his own name, his own passport. It was the work of an amateur."

"He had no reason to disguise it," Devereaux said. The hard gray eyes stared into the comic face, as though they could penetrate the mask that Simeon offered.

"We had his name."

"Why?"

"From . . . from before."

Simeon frowned, annoyed by the slight hesitancy.

"That's not possible," Devereaux said. It was only a guess.

"But we knew. From 1968."

"You never had the name of our agent. You never dealt with him directly. The information was passed back to CIA and traded to you."

"By the R Section."

"They were couriers."

For the first time, something like doubt crossed Simeon's features. He began to struggle up.

"No," Devereaux said. "Stay where you are."

"This is absurd."

"Manning was our agent, at Langley," Devereaux said. "He was pulled in and then we used R Section to make the camouflage trade with you."

"That's a lie," Simeon said.

"It was 1968. We had done badly on Tet, there were internal memos that said we had lied in our gross estimates on Tet, on enemy strength, on where the enemy would strike. We needed R Section as a screen to trade information with you, so that we wouldn't become involved either publicly or in private."

"Why should I believe you?"

"Because the information was good," Devereaux said. "He gave you Jeanne Clermont, he gave you a nest of radicals in the Sorbonne, he gave you their plans. After all, we were all on the same side."

"Then," Simeon said. "And now?"

"I don't know. Who was the thin man who followed me?"

"I don't know."

"Is that the truth?"

"In this case, yes. He was a complication to me."

"And what about Jeanne Clermont?"

"There is no suspicion of her. She is in the government; her records are all cleared. But why did Manning have her photograph in his pocket?"

Devereaux stared at the other man for a moment. "Perhaps he remembered her," he said at last.

Simeon laughed then and got up despite Devereaux's warning. He brushed bits of grass from his coat. He grinned again at Devereaux. "Well, Mr. Clay or whatever your name is, we know where we stand. What will you do now?"

"I don't know."

"I think you should be on the evening flight to London. That's what I think. I think you should return my pistol and you should let me escort you to Orly and wait until you get aboard the plane. That is what I think."

Devereaux stared at Simeon for another long moment, trying to decide.

Simeon was the wrong complication; he didn't know if the

French agent believed him or not, but he couldn't even return to his hotel room. He had money, he had identities. But time had run out, if Simeon pressed him.

And why should he trust the other man?

"Turn around," Devereaux said.

"Are you going to shoot me?"

"Turn around," Devereaux said. But the large man with the large brown eyes would not move.

"I have three choices," Devereaux said. "I could do as you say. I reject that. I could kill you. I could simply give myself time to get away from you. I would rather not kill you. I want to tie your hands and then get away."

"But I can help you get away," Simeon said, flashing the smile again. "I promise you I will take you to Orly."

"No. I don't think I want your promise. And I don't think I want to take any more time."

Simeon shrugged then and turned and placed his large hands behind his back.

Devereaux reached for the piece of copper coil at his wrist. It was the sort of device worn by those who believed it cured arthritis; in fact the coil resolved itself into a long, thin strand of garroting wire.

Devereaux took a step and quickly wrapped the wire around the large man's wrists.

"It's very tight."

Devereaux pushed him and tripped him. Simeon hit the ground heavily on his stomach.

He groaned and struggled for breath.

Devereaux removed Simeon's shoes and pulled the laces out and tied his ankles together. He picked up the shoes and threw them, in different directions, into the woods. He reached without a word into the pocket of Simeon's coat and removed the bloodstained handkerchief. He turned Simeon over and shoved the handkerchief into his mouth and wrapped his own handkerchief around the Frenchman's face to hold it.

"If you don't choke to death, someone will find you eventually," Devereaux said.

Simeon stared at him with his large eyes. But now they were hate-filled; the comic veneer had dropped away.

Devereaux got up and quickly crossed the woods back to the path where he had waited for the stranger who followed him.

He went down a little knoll into the woods on the other side.

The sounds of the distant, unseen restaurant were more clear.

He didn't know what he wanted to do, but he had to find a safehouse, he had to operate now outside both the Section and the law of France.

It was growing lighter in the woods; the streaming sunset was now so low that the long shadows of the trees were silhouetted in the golden haze. The scene reminded him of a painting by one of the French Impressionists he had seen once as a child at the Art Institute in Chicago.

He stumbled across the body just before turning south toward the park entrance.

It was the face of the stranger. A copy of *Le Monde* lay open on the grass. The face was bloodless, the eyes staring.

Devereaux caught his breath, felt the adrenaline surging through him. He knelt down and reached into the pocket of the dead man's coat.

A British passport registered in the name of John Alexander Gaunt.

Gaunt. Devereaux stared at the features of the dead man for a moment as though memorizing them. The face was like the face of a skull drawn with flesh that had been pale in life and was now ashen in death.

Devereaux turned the head slowly and saw that Gaunt's neck was broken. A sharp blow, perhaps the blow of a man's hand.

A large, powerful man like Simeon, who had not seen anyone follow Devereaux. Who had disavowed this stranger.

Who had probably killed him.

Devereaux's knees cracked as he rose. There were too many complications now, and yet he felt he was close to the heart of the matter. Jeanne Clermont. It all came down to her.

18
Hanley

"There are complications," Devereaux said. His voice was laconic; the mood was conveyed clearly despite coming across the transatlantic telephone cable.

Hanley waited. He was alone in his bare office, but he cupped the receiver with his hand with characteristic caution. He was a man of little cautions, picked up one by one after thirty-four years in the trade of espionage.

That morning he had brought two men from the plumbers' unit to sweep the lines in his office, looking for taps or other signs of electronic surveillance. The plumbers had been called the black-bag boys before Watergate offered them new nomenclature to play with. They had not detected any taps on the lines and were amused by Hanley's fussbudget way of overseeing their work. Hanley had even changed the code on the double-scrambler box connected to the phone. The box tore the sounds of conversation apart into meaningless bits of noise for those who might tap the lines.

Every caution was observed.

Devereaux did not exist in the Section anymore, and Hanley knew he was playing a dangerous political game. So this conversation could not be taking place.

"Complications here as well," Hanley said.

"A French policeman. At least, he had that identification. Jules Simeon. And a British agent named John Gaunt."

"What do they have to do with this?"

"Gaunt is dead. I think Simeon killed him."

"You were only supposed to go after—"

"Goddammit, Hanley, I didn't want these complications any more than you do."

"Gaunt was the British control. On that business at Lakenheath."

"Everything links back to Lakenheath and Felker. And Jeanne Clermont."

"Could you get Manning's things?"

"No. The room had been sealed by the Paris police. This Simeon had the identity of a cop but I think he was something else."

"Deuxième Bureau."

"Yes," Devereaux said. "He knew about Manning. Not the way a policeman would know about him."

"This has to do with Lakenheath," Hanley said.

Now Devereaux waited at the other end of the line with patience. In all the years as agent and control officer, neither man had been forthright in these conversations. Agents always held back; it was almost a rule of the trade. And the controls, from their desk far away, tried to keep agents fragmented from others, to seem to be the repositories of all knowledge so that no one agent would finally break the control.

But the rules did not apply. Even Hanley had said it. Devereaux had resigned and Hanley had brought him back, through a door that should not have existed.

"Mrs. Neumann thinks that Felker's information—actually, what he stole from Reed—was a plant."

"Great minds," Devereaux said. "So do I."

"But she doesn't understand it."

"Because whatever is gumming up Tinkertoy is supposed to gum up whatever the British use for a computer."

Hanley was silent for a moment. "Do you know that?"

"No. It only appears to make sense. Reed was too easy. He was supposed to have been turned by the British. He was supposed to have turned over his information."

"Then the Soviets are feeding us. And feeding the British and God knows who else."

"We always did it," Devereaux said. "They've just gotten more sophisticated. The computer is blind until someone says it can see and takes the blinders off."

"But what's the point?" Hanley's voice was nearly petulant. "Why warn us about a Warsaw Pact strike against the West? I mean, if it's going to happen, why warn us? And if it's not, why get us ready to repel it?"

"I don't know."

"And why take the trouble to put Reed at Lakenheath, and how could they have known that these English agents would try to turn him?"

"I met one of the Englishmen, and the other one is dead." Devereaux's voice was dry. "They're a long way from James Bond. Lakenheath was a low-level operation for the British. They had low-level people there. It would be a perfect way to worm into Auntie."

"Mrs. Neumann says she can't even begin to figure out where the bad information started and where it stops."

"Everything in Tinkertoy is infected?"

"Yes. Until we isolate it."

Devereaux spoke after a moment of silence. "Then the KGB took care of Felker."

"Why?"

"He upset their plans. He wasn't supposed to steal from Reed."

"But I received . . . an assurance . . . from a source that the Soviets were not involved."

"And you still believe everything you read in the papers," Devereaux said.

"They went out of their way . . ."

"Dammit, don't tell me what the fucking Russians told you!" Devereaux's voice had changed to that of a snarling, suddenly awakened animal. It was the animal of the streets that always slept inside the cold, calm exterior cage of the body. "I don't give a fuck what the Russians have to say about anything!"

Hanley flushed. Every dealing with Devereaux was tense because of these rare moments when the beast was confronted; when the cooled anger inside the frame of his control suddenly flared to flames again and Hanley could see the edge of the restless soul.

It was as though all the contradictions inside Devereaux existed along a fault line that shifted from time to time, suddenly erupting into the pattern of the savage street kid who had once killed for survival on the streets of Chicago and who, by the odd results of intellect and opportunity, had put a polish of civilization over the veneer of the jungle. The Old Man had wanted to get rid of Devereaux. He had simply been afraid of him. "Devereaux is a dangerous man," Galloway had said, and it was perfectly true.

"The contact was extraordinary," Hanley said with stubbornness.

"Tinkertoy makes the links," Devereaux said. "It's your goddamn machine. Felker was killed and Cacciato was killed."

"The Russians didn't want retribution."

"But maybe they'll get it anyway."

"You're not sanctioned."

"Yes, that's right, Hanley. Don't forget it. I'm not sanctioned for anything, but I'm here, even if my name is not on the roster at Section."

Hanley did not speak for a moment, and then he veered away from the dangerous ground. "What about this Clermont woman?"

"I don't know. It's a matter of the approach. I didn't expect the complication with this Simeon."

"Did you . . . take him out?"

"No. There was no point to it."

"What do you want to do?"

"I need a little time. A distraction."

"What kind?"

"Quizon."

"What about him?"

"He doesn't know about me, but the Deuxième Bureau has to know about him. He's been in Paris too long."

"What about him then?"

"Make a diversion for Simeon," Devereaux said.

"What do you want done?"

Devereaux told him. Hanley listened and did not register any emotion on his colorless face, but when Devereaux had finished, his voice was soft, as though recovering from an illness.

"But what would be the point?"

"The point is simple. Someone knew about Manning from the beginning. From the moment he came to Paris, perhaps before. Maybe Jeanne Clermont was a plot by the Deuxième Bureau itself, for some reason we don't understand. In any case, Manning was blown the minute he came to the city."

"You're guessing."

"Yes," Devereaux said. "I'm not as certain about things as Tinkertoy. I can only guess, but Manning is definitely dead and that's not a guess, and an agent of the Deuxième Bureau knows all about me and that's not a guess."

"No one knew about you," Hanley began to protest.

"No. Not me. But about someone else coming in after Manning was killed. The possibilities are not endless. There was Manning himself. Maybe he gave it away to Jeanne Clermont; maybe she set him up. Maybe the Russians have penetrated the Section and they were set for me here. Maybe someone in Paris had to know about Manning."

"Quizon. But Quizon wouldn't betray us."

"It doesn't matter. Not if he's as tapped as I think he is. Someone had to talk too much. It has to be Quizon."

"But Quizon isn't that important."

"He's a link. Just one more link. But when Tinkertoy started making its connections, it never connected Quizon, even though Quizon was the control officer for Manning."

"You mean that someone has manipulated Tinkertoy?"

"What does Mrs. Neumann think?"

"Everything you suggest," Hanley began vaguely. He paused. How could he convey this sense of being lost as though the underpinnings of the Section he had built and nurtured for twenty years were coming undone?

"Everything you suggest can't be true," Hanley said with weakness in his voice.

"If it's not, then Manning isn't dead and Felker isn't and Cacciato isn't. You don't trust Tinkertoy now, and neither does Mrs. Neumann." Devereaux spoke softly but his voice was plain, flat, and the very plainness made the words fall one by one, like a bell tolling. "The computer is fouling and you've had six months to find out why and you can't. So you've put me back in the field to do the job backward."

"And to find out why Manning was killed."

"Yes." For a moment, there was only the crackle of the line. "And why he had to be killed now."

Hanley was suddenly startled; his senses were alert; adrenaline rushed through him. Something in the tone of Devereaux's voice had changed.

"Now? You mean time has to be a factor too?"

"Yes," Devereaux said. "It's the only part of the whole thing that would make any sense."

"But how much time is there?"

"I don't know," Devereaux said. "But it can't be very much. Until whatever is supposed to happen happens. Or they wouldn't have taken Manning out."

19
Simeon

Simeon moved slowly along the brown canvas wall division set up in the large room. The Pompidou Center Museum was not crowded; the exhibit had not excited much interest. On the walls were photographs taken nearly forty years before, showing the landings of the Allied crafts at Normandy and the subsequent celebrations in the little villages along the coast liberated after five years under the Nazi heel. June 6, 1944; Simeon had remembered the day, had remembered the news coming over the wireless from the BBC. He had thought it was a trick until the adults had begun to celebrate around him in that apartment in Paris, when his father brought out a hidden cache of Cognac and even offered him a drink. They had been so absurdly happy; his father had said, again and again, "Vive les américains."

Vive les américains.

Simeon smiled, his grotesque clown's face an odd counterpoint to the grim black-and-white photograph mounted on the gray mat before him. It was a photograph of the part of the Normandy coastline called Omaha Beach. The bodies of young men, twisted in death, had been captured by the photographer.

Simeon grunted, his hands behind his back, and turned into the next room.

It was empty. In the entire room was only a single photograph, blown up to gigantic proportions. The photograph was of an American soldier bending over at the waist, burdened by his tools of war, his combat uniform caked with mud, his face made old by what he had seen and done, offering a candy bar to a child in neat but ragged clothes who carried a small American flag in her hand.

What genius of public relations or propaganda had decided on that? Simeon smiled again. The exhibit amused him with its crude idealism, with the sense of the romantic adventure conveyed in the stirring sentences that captioned each pathetic photograph. Idealism and the fervor of war; everything fades at last, and what is left but these souvenirs?

Simeon thought then of his son, David, who lived in Rouen. David once argued with him about the horror of nuclear war in Europe. David did not remember his father's war. David could afford idealism because his memory was uncrowded by remembrances of war.

Simeon had come to the museum in the remains of the old Beaubourg quarter because of the agreed signal that morning. When he had left his apartment building, there had been a letter in his mailbox. Inside the envelope was a postal card picturing the hideous bright bulk of the modern museum that squatted in the ruins near the old Halles district.

The time of the meeting was always the same, but not the place. The museum was immense, stretching up several floors to a rooftop restaurant. It was for Simeon to search the building, bottom to top, while they decided if he was alone and that contact could be made.

Now, in this empty room near the back of the third-floor exhibit, he saw the other man.

The other man wore an old-fashioned black coat and a large black hat, like an English butler. He crossed the room slowly and came beside Simeon and stared at the same photograph. The other man smelled of onions and liquor; his breath was foul, even as his face was bloated beneath the black hat.

"What did your signal mean?" His French was flawed, and Simeon had difficulty understanding him at times.

"Just what it means," Simeon said. "We had eighteen CIA agents marked in place. And now there is this one from R Section. I don't know who he is or why he has come. Except it must be about Manning and Madame Clermont."

"This is a complication. Does it involve us?"

Simeon smiled. "Is that for you to tell me or for me to tell you?"

"There is no levity in this."

"There is no levity in the Russian soul," Simeon said. For that moment, his innate contempt for the people he dealt with was betrayed. He had never been to the Soviet Union but he felt that he could draw an accurate picture of Russian life just from talking to these secretive, paranoid, moody people who had streamed through Paris over the years on behalf of their country.

"Does this man present a threat to us?"

"I don't know. I report to you and you pay me for my reports. You and I both know the complexity of the next . . . operation. Perhaps this American agent will help us, or perhaps not."

"What do you want to do with him?"

"Find out more about him. Watch him for a time. Let him be afraid of me. Let me see if he conspires with Madame Clermont."

"Are you worried by her?"

"Not as long as I can control her," Simeon said. "The problem is in understanding what game she actually plays."

"These are not games," the Russian said severely, like a reproving parent.

"No. Not for you. You must struggle in deadly earnest to even survive," Simeon said with a smile. His eyes were mocking because the words had come too fast for the Russian to translate. "You don't understand, do you?"

"Does it satisfy you to mock me?" the Russian said. "Then be satisfied for a time. But remember that the events of June 6 cannot be delayed. And if this American is in a position to hurt our plans . . ."

"Then he will be taken care of. Yes, your pedantic warning is noted," Simeon said. "Isn't it ironic to have this exhibit now? No one attends. Everyone has forgotten the war. Everyone wants to remember how long peace has lasted."

"We do not forget the war," the Soviet said. "Not in Russia."

Simeon smiled still, his face mocking the other man. "No. You do not forget it; the Soviets have long memories but learn nothing."

149

"I do not understand."

"Nothing," said Simeon, still smiling. "I said nothing."

"Do you mock the cause?"

"Of course," Simeon said. "There is no cause, or I am my own cause. As long as your pay is generous, your cause is just to me."

"You are too cynical not to believe . . ."

"In what? In a Communist god or a Christian one? In France, in la patrie? Vive la France, is that what you wish me to say, to wrap myself in the tricolor, to march on the Champs on Bastille Day? No, life is too short for causes, little one." And in that moment, he thought of his father opening the Cognac hidden for five years against the Boches in the grimy little apartment on the outskirts of Paris. What did he come to celebrate finally but his own death in the same miserable conditions he had lived under during the war?

And he thought of David, an absurd and touching pacifist. Simeon was the only generation of realism between the patriotism of his father and the pacifism contained in his son.

"No causes," Simeon repeated, not to the Soviet but to himself. To the memory of his father.

To his son.

20
Garishenko

The war game had ended three hours before and the machines had been shut down and everyone had left the bunker for bed or for a postmortem in the officers' and faculty lounge of the Frunze War College located in the basement of the main building.

Only Alexei Garishenko remained, slumped at his desk, staring at the bottle of vodka that had been drained an hour before. He had no energy, he had an overwhelming sense of dread. The room was dark; there was a single light still illuminating the remains of the operations room beyond his private quarters. He did not even hear Warnov enter the room.

Warnov sat down in the British officer's chair across from his desk and crossed his legs. Warnov lit a cigarette, pulling the smoke slowly through his thin lips and letting it escape just as slowly through his nostrils. His eyes were shaped like almonds and were as flat as a cat's eyes. His fingers were narrow, stained yellow by tobacco. He stared at the slumped figure of Garishenko without speaking for a long time.

"Why don't you come over to the college with me? We can have a drink and something to eat."

"I've drunk enough," Garishenko said. "Nothing works on me anymore. This damned headache; I can't get rid of it."

"It was a game. You were well prepared, but it was a game," Warnov said.

"It was more than that," Garishenko replied slowly. His voice was the voice of a sleeper. The darkness of the room without windows seemed to shroud it. "You know that."

"I know what I am told to know," Warnov said. "Do you deny that the victory was logical?"

"Yes. I deny it. Nothing in the West indicates what Naya supposed. France did not enter the war until it was too late; the British suddenly sued for peace after the Americans bombed Gorki from the Lakenheath base. That's absurd; worse, it is fatally wrong."

"The computer is the mirror of the reality we give it," Warnov said. "If you do not trust its judgment, then you question your own judgment."

"Naya was wrong," Garishenko said. "You know it, the Game Master knows it. It was wrong, it was not logical."

"What did the Americans say when they sold us Naya? 'Garbage in and garbage out.' It is true, Alexei."

"Dammit. There was something wrong. But you chose to believe it because you wanted to believe it. And now? What now? Will you act?"

"I cannot say."

"You know this is a prelude. Every war game involving Western Europe was a prelude for action."

"Was there war? Was there ever a shot fired against the West in all the years since 1945?"

Garishenko knocked the bottle off his desk onto the soft carpet of the floor. The room was soundless except for the hum of a generator that penetrated the air-conditioning ducts. Garishenko had not been outside these rooms for thirteen days; had spring come to Moscow?

"A last spring," he said slowly, like a man awaking from a nightmare.

"What are you talking about?"

"This dreadful game." He glanced up. "Do they believe it, Warnov? Are they celebrating their victory now in the lounge? Are they speaking of how easy it was to invade Europe and make it a Soviet sphere? Do they believe that the English surrendered or that the French were so easily bluffed or that the West Germans were so defenseless?"

"They celebrate their little victories," Warnov said slowly. "You have done well, Alexei. They think that to defeat you is to defeat reality; they think that you are the world of the West, contained in your person, contained in all you have placed inside Naya. Naya is the West standing against us, threatening us; Naya has been defeated and you have been defeated, and because of your ego you cannot believe this has happened."

"It will not be so easy for you."

"What?"

"When you send the tanks across Germany. When it is flesh against flesh and machine against machine. It will not be so easy."

"No struggle is easy, but the prize of our ideal . . ."

"No. Not ideals. In twenty years, we will have bound the rest of Europe to us as surely as the East is bound. In twenty years, they will be ours; they will burn our gas and our oil and they will be grateful for it. The American day passes in Europe. But we must be so impatient, we must have war."

"Perhaps not. Perhaps it is only preparation," Warnov said.

"No. The Kabul game was not preparation; the Paris game is not preparation. The war has already begun, and you know it and so do I."

"General Garishenko," Warnov said, again with softness. But the voice of the other man was broken with pain, a sense of grief and bitterness.

But Garishenko could not be consoled. He was a soldier and could not cry; he was a man of reason, of intellect; what he saw clearly he could not deny.

It was too late.

The generals had chosen to believe the computer and to see the game as reality.

The war had begun but the shots were silent for a little time, while the thought of inevitable victory settled into their minds. Tomorrow or in June or the next month, it would begin. And then, Garishenko thought, in the noise of death, no one would be able to admit they had been wrong.

21

Mrs. Neumann

Mrs. Neumann had guarded the thought all day, telling no one in computer analysis, not even Marge, who had become her best friend there in the past two years. The secret thrilled her because it was so unexpected.

Hanley had been dour as always, and they had gone over the same dreary ground at the morning conference on The Problem. It was now referred to in capital letters.

"Why do I keep feeding Tinkertoy this garbage? Garbage in and garbage out, you've been told that enough times."

She had been given two new names and new links.

"Yes, Mrs. Neumann, you and everyone in comp an have told me the same things," Hanley said testily.

"Who are these people? More information from Quizon culled from the French newspapers?"

"No. Quizon is not the source."

"Then who is?"

"I can't say."

"Oh, damn and double damn," she said, realizing her own nerves were on edge. The months since Tinkertoy began fouling had cost her tranquility; she had fretted over the machine as she might worry about a child slow to learn to read.

"Mrs. Neumann." Hanley had leaned forward over his desk gravely, folding his colorless fingers together in vague imitation of sincerity and frankness. All of his gestures seemed acquired, as though he had studied them for a long time and picked them up step by step and used them frequently, but without confidence and without certainty that their purpose was served.

"There are no coincidences," he had begun. "We always assume that. Why has Tinkertoy made these links over the last six months? Why do your geniuses—I beg your pardon, your people—

make these rash conclusions from Tinkertoy's ideas? Are the Warsaw Pact countries about to erupt again? Will there be a new Poland? Or will there be war in the West? All the scenarios are provided from what Tinkertoy tells us. 'Garbage in and garbage out.' Yes. But what was the garbage? Or is it garbage at all? Are you right in your assumptions? Can we go to the National Security Council with your conclusions, based on calculations made by Tinkertoy? Obviously, we have told them some things but we cannot tell them all."

"They're on alert; what more can we do?"

"Find the truth," Hanley had said.

"But what is the source of this new data? I need sources."

"Why, Mrs. Neumann?"

"Because we always have a source code for the data."

Hanley had stared at her. "I don't understand that."

"There are access codes to Tinkertoy and source codes. Access shows point of origin of computer information—from me, from Marge, from National Computer Center in Roanoke, wherever. And access leads to source—access and source meet and . . ."

And then she had stopped speaking and she had stared at Hanley with her mouth open. She had gone into a reverie in which she was no longer in the small, cold room deep in the bowels of the Agriculture building explaining elements of Tinkertoy to a man who did not understand. She was in Tinkertoy in that moment; she thought finally she understood everything that had gone wrong.

If anything had gone wrong.

"Mrs. Neumann? Are you all right?"

"It couldn't be that simple," she had said at last, still entranced by her vision.

"What couldn't be?"

"Of course, we never went back over the data for source after it was established. Marge punched the garbage in. It was from Quizon, part of it. . . ."

"What are you talking about?"

"Don't you see?"

"Mrs. Neumann . . ."

"It doesn't matter, Hanley," she had said, snapping into the present again. She got up from the single straight chair in front of the metal desk and pulled the loose sweater around her. So damned cold in here, she thought again; he's crazy.

"Everything matters. What's this about access and source?"

She had smiled then. It was so rare an event that Hanley was startled by it and leaned back in his chair as though she had struck him. "I'm going to put Tinkertoy through a few paces this evening," she had said. "After the others are gone. I want to be absolutely certain about this."

"This is about The Problem then?"

"Of course," she had said. "What the hell do you think we're talking about?"

"I hadn't the faintest idea for the last five minutes."

"You see, we checked the sources and we double-checked. Everything. Marge even ran an access check once. But what about source and access together? You see, I'll have to get the logs together." She had rubbed her hands in anticipation of the task; she was not a person to enjoy idleness or frustration in her work. This would be satisfying. "It's just dreary work, Hanley, and there's no point in explaining it to you. But it will work. It will."

"But what are you going to find out?"

"If there's garbage in Tinkertoy."

"And if there isn't?"

"Then you're a damned fool not to go ahead and give the Security Council everything. I mean everything. If everything computes and we're sure of the information and the sources and the access and everything checks with the log, then . . ."

"What?"

"Then it means Tinkertoy is right."

"But your computer analysis may be wrong. In projecting scenarios."

She had smiled at him like a mother. "Hanley, everything we offer is fraught with human risk. Perhaps we are wrong and maybe the general sitting in his war room is wrong, but we're the best we've got. If we can absolutely vouch for the information. And Tinkertoy."

She had spent the rest of the day gathering up the logs necessary for the task. There were time in/out logs from computer analysis, from the control sections, from operations—which counted the field men, including agents, stationmasters, watchers, and freelancers—and logs for her own clerical staff. She would start from the beginning.

She had been so happy that Marge had caught her whistling to herself as she worked at her desk around four-thirty.

"Lydia?" She never called Mrs. Neumann by her first name

during the working day, but that had ended a moment before.

Marge looked in the doorway of Mrs. Neumann's friendly little cubicle. The office was in keeping with Mrs. Neumann's pioneer-woman way of dressing. On the walls were bits of needlepoint and a sampler that said: "Garbage In, Garbage Out." It had been done for her by a whimsical aunt long before, when she first began to work in computers and was full of the jargon of the trade.

"Hello, Marge. I haven't seen you all day."

"I was in Five Section, we're overloaded with that Middle East stuff again."

Mrs. Neumann smiled. "Have some coffee?"

"No. I'm just leaving, it's four-thirty. Bill is going to meet me at the Mayfair, we're with friends tonight. The ones from St. Louis, I told you?"

"Four-thirty already?"

"Working late?"

"Just a few things."

"I thought we had been all caught up at this end," Marge said. She put on a worried frown that did not suit her bland features. She was conventionally pretty in a fussy way, like a doll dressed in elaborate clothes that no woman could actually wear through a day. Somehow, Marge Andrews managed it, just as her hair managed never to seem unkempt, just as she never seemed to have a cold or to appear in an awkward moment. Some of the men in comp an flirted with her, and she responded in a sweet, unbeguiling way. She might have been out of a Doris Day movie; her taste in clothes matched her taste in music and literature. Lydia Neumann was not well read in other fields but she had a native shrewdness that instinctively knew that there was a little bit of the practiced phony about Marge.

And yet, over the past two years, Marge had filled the older woman's need for companionship and a patient soulmate to share her own anxieties with. Girl talk, Leo Neumann fumed at times when Lydia would delay coming home for a private heart-to-heart with Marge at the cocktail lounge across the way from Ag building. But Mr. Neumann was a patient man as well and understood that his wife could not share some things with him. Marge was good for Lydia, Leo had once said, and that was what everyone thought. Including Mrs. Neumann.

"Well, this is just a little something I want to try on Tinkertoy," Mrs. Neumann said vaguely, with the same smile on her face

156

that she had worn all day. She was on the hunt; she was sure she would find the flaw in the computer.

"Anything I can help you with?"

"No, no. Just run along."

"Is it about—about the problem we've been having?" Marge kept the worried look pasted on her face. Her pretty blue eyes— there was no other way to describe them—were opened as wide as a china doll's.

"No," Mrs. Neumann said quickly. Both of them realized it was a lie, but Marge Andrews's features did not change. She only blinked her eyes and made them wider.

"Just something I've been working on to . . . improve some of the programming capabilities, especially in the area of . . . of recasting the anagram code."

"Oh," Marge Andrews said.

"You run along."

"Oh," she said again.

Mrs. Neumann smiled maternally. "Been showing them Washington?"

"Who?"

"Your St. Louis friends."

"Yes. They want to go to the top of the Washington Monument, can you imagine anything as corny as that?"

"Why don't you take them on a tour of the Capitol? As long as Congress is still in session, I mean. I can get one of the boys from Senator's Cox's office to take them around."

"Oh, I'm so tired of that. It's so dreary. All that garbage . . ." She stopped. "Well, I mean, I suppose I wouldn't have to go around with them."

"They'd like it."

"Yes. I suppose they would. Yes, I'll suggest that to them. They've never been east. Bill knew him from college and we've traded Christmas cards. Bill wanted them to stay with us, but they didn't want to impose. They're sweet. People from the Midwest are sweet."

Mrs. Neumann said, "I'm from Omaha."

"Yes. I know. I meant it as a compliment."

"I know, Marge. There. You run along, and I'll call Connie over in Senator Cox's office tomorrow and she'll get one of the boys to take them around. Whenever they like."

"All right. Good night, Lydia."

"Good night, Marge. Have fun."

She turned then, slowly and almost with reluctance, and started down the corridor. Her ruffled white blouse was unsoiled by the day's work, her light brown hair was perfectly groomed, her makeup was discreetly doing its job.

Mrs. Neumann closed the door.

Within a half hour, the section of computer analysis that housed Tinkertoy's monitors was closed.

At midnight, the cleanup crew would come in and search the place for scraps of paper that had been shredded during the day and dumped in wastebaskets. The floors would be swept and mopped and the desk tops cleaned off. And if anyone left anything on a desk top, it would be reported the next morning to the supervisor of security and there would be a great hullabaloo.

Mrs. Neumann would be undisturbed for nearly six hours. It might be enough time. She knew the questions she wanted to ask Tinkertoy now, finally, after six months of dead ends and blind leads and frustrations. She had the logs, the sacred books still kept in the old-fashioned way, each log item entered laboriously by hand and signed by the person entering it. Log and computer, old and new. She thought with satisfaction: Now we're going to find out what's gone wrong with poor old Tinkertoy.

She closed the door of her office and locked it and started down the darkened corridor for the security door, which led to the main security desk and the elevators. She had been in the building for nearly sixteen hours but she did not feel tired. Her step was light on the polished floor. She passed the supervisor of maintenance, and he nodded to her, and she gave him a smile that he would remember much later, when he was asked about it.

"I'll drive down to get you," Leo had said, but Lydia Neumann had demurred.

"I can get a taxi around the corner."

"But it's nearly midnight."

"I'm all right. They've got a guard on duty right on the steps. I'm all right. I've worked in Washington for thirty years and I've never had an incident."

"So tonight could be the first time. I want to come down to meet you."

"You need your rest."

"Listen, I can rest better when I know you're in the house."

158

"Leo, I'll call for a taxi before I leave the building, all right? Then there'll be one waiting for me when I get out. All right?"

"I can still come down and get you. How come that slave driver Hanley's got you working so late?"

"Oh, Leo. If I could only tell you. I can't, but I can tell you it's all right now. I think I really understand everything now."

"About what?"

"I can't tell you."

"You're teasing me." Leo Neumann laughed.

"Of course. You and Hanley. I can tell him tomorrow. It was so simple, but really, I was amazed. It was beautiful. I don't understand all of it and why it was done, but it was a beautiful job."

She had called the taxi company and they had promised a driver to meet her on the Fourteenth Street side of the Agriculture building at the right hour.

She passed through security and then the main desk security and was let out of the locked door into the darkened street. Official Washington: glum, low buildings hidden in stately ranks along tree-lined streets. All doors were locked against the anarchy of the night city streets. In the distance was the sound of an ambulance or the wail of a fire truck. Washington burned and died and killed and raped and stole at night in the shadows of the great government buildings; Washington was angry, tense, hateful at night, a jungle of a million beasts, each turned against the other beneath the orange glow of the anticrime lights along the streets. It had still been a sleepy Southern sort of city when she had first come here. She remembered feeling thrilled by the cherry blossoms at night along the Potomac in spring and by the sweet, magnolia smell that seemed to float over the concrete hub of the city, even when there were no magnolia trees to be seen. That sense of the city had changed for her and for her husband, who had lived in it for a long time, and they had long since fled to one of the outer suburbs. By day, the city was an ersatz Paris, devoid of street life and the bizarre juxtapositions of shabby businesses alongside great monuments in that French city, but still with some elements of nervous grace in the little shops and restaurants and tiny parks alongside sweeping thoroughfares. But at night, it was a merciless place, full of silences and screams and terrors kept outside locked doors.

The taxi was waiting at the curb, and she crossed the walk to it.

"Is this for me?"

159

"Mrs. Neumann?"

"Yes."

She climbed inside awkwardly. She was awkward in many things because her gestures were too large for her frame and for the compact nature of the society she moved in now.

"Where do you want? That address in Alexandria?"

"Yes, please."

The meter had been running, she noted, but nothing would sour her tonight. This was a triumph, albeit a quiet one; she could tell no one but Hanley. Not even Marge. Not yet.

The car fled quietly down Fourteenth Street toward the bridge over the Potomac. It was the sort of cab sealed against violence from passengers: The driver rode in a cocoon of bulletproof glass and plastic that cut off conversation between the front seat and the back. The doors could not be opened without a release from the driver. Everything had been done to protect him against crimes of violence from the public at large.

Mrs. Neumann felt pleasantly tired. The air conditioning in the cab brushed against her face. She smiled. Once, when she had been a young woman, she had smelled the magnolias blowing in from the parks along the river.

She reached for the lever to open the window. Perhaps she would smell the magnolias again. She felt young tonight, as though she had begun all over again.

The lever was stuck; the window remained closed. She forced it with her strong hand, but it would not budge. She pulled, and the lever came off in her hand.

"Damn," she said, and pushed it back into the socket. She leaned over to the other window and forced the lever there.

It did not work.

The cab crossed the Fourteenth Street bridge. Below, in the placid waters of the Potomac, an airliner had gone down the previous year. The cab continued into Virginia, past the gentle embankments on that side of the river. Home in a little while, she thought peacefully. She rapped at the bulletproof glass to get the driver's attention.

He did not turn in his seat.

The car continued down the desolate streets, heading south.

She struck the glass again. He didn't understand, she thought with impatience. She struck it again, much harder.

The car glided past the street where it should have turned.

She looked for the license number; she would report him to his superiors. Mrs. Neumann was not a woman to suffer nonsense or fools.

There was no license card and no number in the cab.

For the first time, her anger was replaced by a sense of dread. What was happening here?

She hit the glass very hard, as though she intended to break it. She kicked very hard at the back of the front seat.

The driver turned and looked at her for a moment and then turned back to the windshield.

They were rapidly passing through darkened hills of darkened homes.

She looked around her but there were no cars. There were no people on the streets.

Jungle, she thought.

She swung with her might at the side window. It shivered with the force of the blow of her doubled fist but it did not break.

And she knew what was happening. She felt the giddiness rise in her, the sense of losing control that she had once felt on a Ferris wheel that had malfunctioned and sent her whirling too quickly around and around until the hand safety brake had been set. She had been quite dizzy and afraid.

Leo, she thought.

Her arms; she couldn't feel her arms. They were floating away from her body.

She tried to swing her fist again against the window, but the fist would not respond.

Her knees. Her knees were on the floor of the cab.

My God, she thought, I have to fight this, I should never . . .

She slumped forward and pushed her feet against the door. She pushed and could not feel her legs. And then she felt the pleasant giddiness pass and felt another wave of emotion come to her. She was sleeping again and she must wake up; she was dreaming that she was awake and it seemed very real but she also knew she was only dreaming. If she could just awaken, then it would be all right.

She tried to rise.

Yes, she thought with wonder. She was rising. She was floating upward. Her head pumped briefly against the roof of the cab and then she was through it, rising above the cab and above the street, rising above the city.

The Washington Monument. She was at the same level as the

red warning lights set into the top of the obelisk like the red eyes of a monumental Klansman. She stared at the red eyes.

And slowly, they winked at her.

22 _____
Quizon

The funicular advanced slowly up the steep ascent of tracks and pulleys toward the square at the top of the hill. On the square was the strange white bulk of the church of Sacré-Coeur with its minaret towers gleaming in the soft morning light. Below the church, stretching out on a broad plain on either side of the meandering Seine, was Paris, wrapped in a light haze of ozone.

Herbert Quizon watched the city fall away below him as the car ascended. It never failed to startle him by its beauty, perceived from the heights of Montmartre.

Quizon brushed an imaginary speck from the lapel of his lightweight sports coat and repositioned the flower in the buttonhole of his lapel.

He was an old-fashioned bachelor with old-fashioned mannerisms that seemed parodies of a dandy's gestures in a turn-of-the-century melodrama. His hands were elegant and his fingers were long and carefully trimmed at the nails; he always carried a walking stick that would not have supported his weight if he had been required to use it as a cane. He seemed suited to Paris, but a Paris of another time.

With a grinding lurch, the funicular cars reached the top end of the short run and locked. The doors slid open and Quizon stepped off through the turnstile and ascended the few steps to the square that surrounded the white church.

He knew where to go from the instructions; they had met here before.

He strolled around the edge of the square to the fenced-in park that clung to the side of the hill rising to the church. The steep park was laced with paths, cleverly concealed in the rocks and among the bushes and trees that stretched down the side of the hill.

For a moment, Quizon leaned against the fence and looked

down at the city he loved, and again marveled at all the changes that had been wrought in it in the forty-two years he had lived here. In the hazy distance, great office tower blocks marched along the rim of the old city, spoiling the sweep of the low buildings of the city center. The strange, hideous bulk of the ultramodern Pompidou Center Museum with its exposed piping and escalator tubes on the outside of the building in the old Beaubourg district offended Quizon's eye. He turned his lips down in a practiced pout and then lowered his gaze to the park in front of him.

He opened a gate and started along the path that wound down the hillside.

The man he had come to see was sitting on a bench behind some shrubs, regarding the same view that had entranced Quizon a moment before.

Quizon sat down next to him without a word.

They waited in silence for a moment as though this was a ritual they had to observe; in fact, it was elementary caution. Perhaps no contact should be made; perhaps someone had followed Quizon.

"A fine day," Quizon said at last, his French lisping easily into the rhythms of the capital dialect.

Simeon said nothing.

Quizon touched the flower in his lapel again and rearranged it minutely.

"Who is the man?" Simeon said at last. His voice was rough, low and hard and without humor, though the comic arrangement of features of his face could not be altered.

"I received a message from Hanley," Quizon began. "This morning. After you asked for the meeting. Hanley said that Mme Clermont would make contact with me in six days and that she was working for us."

Simeon stared at the small, birdlike man in his straw hat and bow tie.

"What kind of nonsense is this?"

"I'm telling you what Hanley signaled me. This morning at seven."

"This is impossible."

"Why? It would explain other things."

"What things? Manning was sent here to spy on her. Do you mean now that Manning was sent here to turn her? And that she was flipped after he was killed?"

"I don't know, Inspector. I'm just reporting."

"I wanted to know about this man. The one in the Bois de Boulogne."

"It can only be Devereaux," Quizon said. "But it can't be him either. He was separated from the Section six months ago. Resigned, they said."

"Are you sure?"

"I have my own sources. . . ."

"Your sources are *Le Matin*," Simeon said. "You know nothing that I don't tell you."

"I know about the Section."

"Then why has he been sent here?"

"I don't know. Especially in light of this business about Jeanne Clermont. Why would she contact me?"

"You're the station man here for the Section," Simeon growled.

"But Manning gave me no indication . . ."

"Manning was going to quit the assignment," Simeon said. "That was the indication he gave you. You told me that afternoon."

Quizon was silent. He stared at the city and smelled the trees in the park around him. So peaceful, he thought, and yet we talk about murder. Of course Simeon had killed Manning; it was the inevitable act after Manning indicated he would not compromise Mme Clermont.

The thought of Manning's death did not horrify him; he was accustomed to death, because he was growing old and too many of his friends of youth had died.

"Why would Hanley tell you this? So suddenly?" Simeon spoke out loud but he was not asking Quizon a question, and Quizon kept his silence.

"Because," Simeon answered his own question. "Because it is not true."

"What?"

"Because it is not true," Simeon said, staring again with his large, comic eyes at the little man. He stretched out a paw and placed it on Quizon's frail shoulder. He felt the bones beneath his hand. "Do you see, Herbert?"

"No."

"Devereaux. Devereaux is working for Hanley, Devereaux has not contacted you—"

"I'm just a station man, sometimes they don't contact—"

"No, no, Quizon, you don't understand at all." Simeon smiled then, a vicious cunning smile like the smile of a cat with a mouse in

164

its mouth. "They don't trust you anymore. They are passing along disinformation. To whoever they suspect you work for. They are giving you the wrong information to give Devereaux time. But for what? To get to Mme Clermont and try to trace back through her to whoever killed Manning. It's not such a bad idea, but I'm afraid they didn't understand you would tell me. If I had taken it from a tap, I might have believed it. They didn't understand that you work for me."

"Inspector." Again the little man wriggled beneath the heavy hold of the other's hand. Simeon was powerful, both physically and in a sense of presence. Simeon had concluded an arrangement with Quizon eight years before. The choice for Quizon had not been difficult. Simeon would have deprived the old man of the only thing he had loved in his life: the city of Paris. "You see, my friend, we are on the same side in any case, but I want you to be more on our side than on the American side." So Simeon had argued that day in Quizon's rooms eight years ago. "If you can accommodate us, then we can help you. First, you will remain in Paris. Second, we will supplement your income. There will be no danger for you."

"But I would be a traitor," Quizon had argued.

"Are you such a patriot?" Simeon had laughed then. "You have lived in Paris since you were eighteen. You were here during the occupation of the Germans. You have not been to America for thirty years. Where is your loyalty then? To Paris? Or to some faraway Washington and some bureaucrats you never see."

"I was in Washington just two years ago."

"For four days. Four days in thirty years. There is no choice, my friend. You will accept my offer or you will be exiled from Paris within twenty-four hours. I promise you there will be no hearing, no plea, no appeal. You will never set foot in France again."

Quizon had argued but it had been fruitless. Simeon had presented the choices brutally and honestly; he had lived up to his word. And Quizon, for the sake of the only thing he loved, had agreed, little by little, day by day, to compromise himself and the workings of the Section.

It was all routine and nothing had been done with his information, so far as Quizon could see. Paris had not been an important center for espionage since the NATO headquarters was moved to Brussels; Quizon lived in a sort of information backwater, and his dealings with the agent from the Deuxiéme Bureau were not frequent.

Until last November, when Simeon began to make a series of

165

demands on him and requests for odd bits of information on the workings of the Section.

"So they don't trust you, little friend, and they are afraid of me. And so they are giving you this lie to pass along to me. Well, let us use the lie." Simeon smiled. "Maybe we can turn it back on them. Yes. I think that would be possible."

"What are you going to do?"

"The question is what this man Devereaux is going to do. And I think he will see Mme Clermont as soon as possible."

"I don't understand any of this," Quizon said.

"No. And it's better for you not to. Manning could have been useful to us—until he decided he could not bear to betray Madame Clermont a second time. A weak fool. Well, we will make do; we will make Monsieur Devereaux useful to our purposes."

PART THREE
SOUVENIRS

They will supply us with the materials and technology which we lack and will restore our military industry, which we need for our future victorious attacks upon our suppliers. In other words, they will work hard in order to prepare their own suicide.

—V. I. LENIN, 1920

23
Moscow

General Garishenko entered the dimly lit room and looked around quickly. There were nine others in the room, and each face was lit by a single lamp set on the long conference table. Ten lamps, nine faces. General Garishenko took the empty leather chair near the head of the table and turned on the lamp.

Beneath the circles of lights were ten copies of the report, each covered by a plastic sleeve. No one had moved to open the report; no one had spoken since entering the room. This meeting was so extraordinary that Garishenko had had no inkling of it. In a state that worshipped secrecy, the existence of this group and this meeting had not been hinted at except in the highest reaches of the bureaucracy.

The room was without windows because it was the end room of a basement corridor that had been built fifteen years ago at the rear entrance of Lubyanka Prison, which itself was part of the complex of buildings on the square controlled by the Committee for State Security, which included the GRU, the military branch of the KGB, and the Committee for External Observation and Resolution, the covert operations arm of the civilian branch of the KGB.

Garishenko looked around again in the silence of the dark room and recognized only a few faces. One was General Warnov. Another was Supreme General Karoshenkovich. He did not recognize the man at the head of the table who would chair the meeting.

"Some of you are known to each other. Some are not. There will be four such meetings, with four different groups within the Presidium. I am permitted to speak with the authority of the first secretary. I am Gogol."

Gogol. The director of the Committee for External Observation and Resolution. Not his name, of course, but one of the names used for the anonymous mandarins who actually directed operations within the KGB. Gogol was the keeper of the dead souls, of the secrets within secrets buried deep in the collective mind of the Soviet state. Gogol was never referred to except in whispers among friends, and it was a tribute to the man who was Gogol that he always knew what was said of him.

"General Garishenko."

Garishenko looked steadily at the wizened face of Gogol. In the dim light, he was difficult to see clearly; he might have been an illusion except for the clear sound of the dry voice. His face had vaguely Oriental features; he might have come from Soviet Asia.

"You found the responses of Naya to be difficult during the war games concluded," Gogol said quietly. His voice was like the sound of dry papers rustling in a dry, desert wind. His voice was hollow, almost ghostlike; when he spoke, his lips drew back slowly from his dry mouth, revealing small, sharp, extremely white teeth.

"I did not find Naya to be difficult," Garishenko said slowly, his voice carrying a stubborn edge. "I found Naya to be wrong. I programmed the computer and the responses were not credible."

"And so the game was lost. Some would say it was your ego that made those charges after the game."

"I beg your pardon, Comrade. I made these accusations during the games, but the Game Master would not entertain them."

"And who was the Game Master?"

"I don't know. That is never known."

"I. I was the Game Master, General Garishenko."

"Then why would you not accept my protests?" Garishenko said. His voice carried conviction; some would have said he had been in the West too long, that he had programmed the responses of the West for too long and that he had learned to speak out of place.

"Because there was a game within the game," Gogol said, smiling again. His eyes seemed liquid in the small circle of light that exaggerated and distorted the features of his faintly yellowish face.

"I don't understand."

"'Hurricane.' That is the force that NATO has planned for ten years to repel the Soviet invasion of Western Europe. Hurricane was the plan completed within five years of General de Gaulle's decision to commit France to a separate force and a separate policy, apart from the North Atlantic Treaty Organization."

Garishenko listened with partial attention as Gogol recited the history of Hurricane; he knew all about Hurricane, but there was a sense that others in the room did not.

"In 1980, when it was necessary to redirect the political and economic forces of Poland after the temporary anarchy of the Solidarity experience, new calculations were made by the research bureau of the committee based on the Western response to those reforms."

Gogol paused and looked around the room. "The first page summarizes the Western response. It was uneven at best. The United States, predictably, was belligerent in tone, but without substance because the Western alliance was fragmented."

Garishenko looked at the page of summaries hidden beneath the plastic sleeve. Old history, he thought; Gogol is preparing a case like a lawyer. But what was the case?

"Two factors were calculated by the research bureau to further fragment the Western alliance. The first is the existence of the natural gas pipeline which our country will construct from the Siberian fields to Western Europe. It is to be financed by the West, and the states of the West have already agreed to this; it is to be constructed in time to tip the balance of energy power away from the Middle East to the Soviet Socialist Republics by 1995.

"And the second factor. What do you suppose it was, General Garishenko?"

Across the table, Warnov stared at Alexei. They all stared at him from their circles of light, like disembodied heads at a meeting of ghouls.

"The election of François Mitterand as president of France," Garishenko said, realizing for the first time where the meeting was leading, realizing why Naya had not worked, realizing how close events had been forced to a conclusion. He had been a mere cog, a toy of the gods who had known the outcome of the war game called "Paris" long before it was played.

"Correct, Comrade. Exactly." The whispery dry voice continued:

"The United States is at the point of losing Europe for the West. Not that it will fall into our orbit immediately, but the influence of the United States has reached a critical point. One more step, and it will fall from the ledge. Force Hurricane will be shattered without a shot being fired."

Garishenko, without permission, turned the page and read quickly.

Gogol noticed and smiled. "Do you see now, Alexei?"

"Coup d'état," Garishenko said in his precise French. "The assassination of Mitterand and his ministers by agents provocateurs of the United States."

"Of the Central Intelligence Agency, to be exact."

Gogol smiled. There was an audible gasp in the closed room. "In three days, on the sixth of June, President Mitterand will go to Normandy to again walk along the paths where the Allied forces invaded Europe in 1944. He has done this often and it is officially planned.

"At the same time, American agents will attempt an unsuccessful assassination of Georges Marchais, the chairman of the French Communist Party. And they will strike, with more success, at Mitterand. NATO forces have already been on alert in Europe since our successful tampering with the American intelligence agency's computer apparatus, the so-called Tinkertoy machine."

"And Tinkertoy is the sister of Naya," Garishenko said suddenly.

"Yes, Comrade General. The same companies made components of both machines, the same companies set out programs for both machines. Before Afghanistan brought the American embargo on certain software and hardware in the electronics field, the American business sector was very willing to sell us their secrets." Gogol smiled. "And to finance the sales for us."

"And you tampered with Naya . . ."

"Because the Americans tap Naya and already have the results of our games."

"And you have found a way to enter Tinkertoy."

Gogol nodded. "That was the secret. Until now, General Garishenko, it was necessary to keep this secret. We have had some successes in tapping into Tinkertoy, but the codes are changed so often and are so infinite that it was hardly worth all the efforts. But now we can enter Tinkertoy and pass through the system without leaving any muddy tracks." Gogol laughed. "Yes. We can program Tinkertoy from within, you see. We no longer want to know what Tinkertoy knows; we have the ability to give Tinkertoy our information."

"But what will put the blame on the Americans?" It was Warnov and his voice was complaining. He didn't have any real understanding of Tinkertoy or Naya, and he was annoyed that Gogol seemed to be talking directly to General Garishenko. He was annoyed that Garishenko had been right after all; that the war game called "Paris" had been fixed by the KGB to be won by the Soviets, all to carry on a deception half a world away in Washington.

"The Central Intelligence Agency has fourteen agents in France, and nine are specifically assigned to infiltrate the national government in Paris. The number of agents was increased by six after the election of Mitterand. One agent will accompany the press party with Mitterand to Normandy on the sixth of June. Another will attend with Georges Marchais and the other officials of the Communist Party a memorial to the war dead at the Arc de Triomphe in Paris. Mitterand will be killed at three; at the same time, an attempt will be made upon the life of Marchais."

"But the CIA won't do these things."

"Our terrorist cells within France will carry out the overt actions. But the blame has already been placed with the CIA. American forces are on alert in Europe. Since March, they have predicted a Soviet invasion of the European continent by Warsaw Pact forces. That is the work of Tinkertoy. We had even planned rather carefully to feed the same information into NATO from the British intelligence operation, but the plan . . . failed." For the first time, Gogol's dry and confident voice seemed to falter.

"What happened, Comrade?" asked Warnov, eager to stamp his presence on the meeting by asking a question that at least could be answered in plain Russian and not laden with computer gobble-degook.

"The human factor," Gogol said, smiling again. "We had an agent planted at Lakenheath air force base in England and he had information that he would turn over to the British when the British managed to make him a double. Unfortunately, an opportunist named . . . well, that's not important . . . took the information from our dupe. We didn't want the information to fall to the Americans, it might have given them a clue about Tinkertoy. It was too bad, but we decided it wasn't necessary for the success of the mission."

"The Shattered Eye," Garishenko said.

"Yes," Gogol responded, noting that Garishenko had turned to the third page of the report. "The operation is the Shattered Eye. A poetic fancy. The Eye of Force Hurricane is France; it can be shattered in one blow, in one day. The time is exactly right. The peace movement is at a furious pitch of activity. Mitterand has universal respect as a man in France, although some dislike his politics."

"And there is France itself," Garishenko said. "Idiosyncratic at best. Force the Americans to make a premature move against us at the same time they are assassinating the left-wing leaders of France. It is too mad not to be exactly real." Garishenko spoke softly, with awe coloring his slow words.

"Yes. On Sunday, the sixth of June, a red alert will be sounded at the American air base in England. The American alert will trip alerts at all NATO bases from Turkey to Norway. The Americans will have initiated the alert; they will have initiated the act of war against the leaders of France. Within three hours, the American agents in France will be exposed and the coup d'état will be crushed. Georges Marchais will become the president of France without ever understanding why."

"And if the populace does not react as Naya predicts?"

"Then whoever will take over the French government after Mitterand will have the support of the rest of Europe in severing all ties—economic and military—with the United States. In any event, the warmongering posture of the present administration in the United States will be discredited and the forces of peace will be encouraged."

"Our forces of peace," Warnov said.

"Yes. Precisely. We will make no act in response to the American feint against us on the sixth of June. We will not comment until the French themselves have discovered the duplicity of the American agents in their midst."

"And communications . . ."

"Yes. The last detail, resolved just this week. We have our agents in place. Six months ago, the Americans were lured into making contact with one of our number, a French woman. She has access to the new codings of the French government computer system. With her entrée, the computer will be fouled—by the

Americans. And she, in turn, will denounce the American agents who have used her. It is an authentic plan from every angle."

Garishenko sat for a long moment in the silence of the room staring at the final page of the report on the Shattered Eye.

All the complex plottings had been broken down simply into thirty-one lines of type on the last page of the report. So simple but so complex that he realized only a couple of people in the room understood it as well as he. And now he understood why Gogol had spoken to him; with an odd quirk of vanity, Gogol wanted one man to understand the strategic brilliance of Gogol's plan.

Garishenko let a slow smile cross his pale face. For the first time in two weeks, he did not have a headache. He felt nothing. There would be no war, only a victory; and he had been duped by the machine along with the others as a final test to prove that the Shattered Eye would succeed.

"And who conceived the plan?"

Gogol turned his eyes to Garishenko, who sat at his right side.

"Many committees," Gogol said vaguely.

"The Committee for Terror," Garishenko said.

"Among them. Yes. Many committees."

"And what did Naya say?"

Gogol turned and smiled. "Do you suppose we ran a game to see if it would work?"

"Of course."

"There were many variables."

"And Naya said the plan would work."

"Yes. Even the computer the Americans sold to us said it would work."

"And France will be neutralized."

"That is almost certain."

"The military situation—for the West—would be intolerable then. Would they go to war?"

"No."

"Naya says they won't go to war."

"With ninety percent probability."

Garishenko frowned. "Such a risk. Even a small risk."

"Comrade General, every proposition has its risks attached."

"Even those proposed to a computer," Garishenko replied.

24

Fairfax, Virginia

The music was ethereal, nondirectional, coming from everywhere and nowhere, vaguely reminiscent.

Mrs. Neumann listened for a long time with her eyes closed. The air was damp, close, hot; where was the music?

She opened her eyes and saw nothing. Her right arm felt heavy, as though a hand held her wrist down. Then she realized it was not a hand, but metal, strapped tightly around her wrist.

She could not see in the darkness. Somewhere, beyond the music, there was a noise like a furnace or an air-conditioner compressor thumping on.

Yes. Exactly.

She felt sick, her stomach grumbled to her. She was alive and yet she was suspended in a sort of limbo of darkness and the vague, dreadful music, like the music piped into an elevator.

Yes. Exactly.

She realized she did not feel afraid, only curious. She tried to sit up, and managed it with difficulty. With her free left hand, she felt along the edge of the platform she sat on. It was a cot, an ordinary wooden folding cot. She felt the canvas beneath her.

Her shoes were gone, and her stockings.

She pushed behind her and touched fabric. Fabric on the right side as well. Like a tent, the fabric was slippery to the touch, and damp.

She blinked at the darkness all around her and imagined she was beginning to see a shape to it. In front of her was a pole, a tent pole.

Beneath her feet was bare concrete. It felt cold, but the air was warm and stale and sticky.

"Hello," she said. Her voice was cracked and dry.

"Hello," she said again. "Who's there? Where am I?"

There was no answer, only the continuing sounds of the music.

She felt overwhelmed by tiredness suddenly and lay back down on the cot. It creaked beneath her weight. She kept her eyes open in the darkness, as though it was less dreadful if she could stare at it.

She slept; or did she only dream that she slept?

Her eyes were open and the darkness pressed around her. And silence. The ethereal music was stopped. And then she heard them.

The sound of a zipper, and the front of the tent was thrown open.

It *was* a tent, she thought, disoriented by the sudden light and the figures at the entrance.

"Are you all right?"

The same voice she had heard for years, only now tinged with a hardness at the edge of the words.

"Marge! What's going on?"

"Oh, come on. Little Miss Busybody, you can figure out what's going on. You've just ruined everything. Nearly."

She stared at the young woman in the embroidered blue sweater and the schoolgirl skirt who was leaning in at the entrance talking to her. Marge, little Marge in computer analysis.

Lydia Neumann understood in that moment, and the puzzle vanished from her thoughts. Of course: Marge would have had to be the final link, the final clue.

"What are you doing?" Mrs. Neumann said.

"What do you think we're doing? We're playing with Tinker-toy." She smiled, hideously innocent, her soft features framed in Mrs. Neumann's eyes by the thought of what she was doing.

"This is monstrous," Mrs. Neumann said.

"We want something, Lydia, something very important, and since you're the one who screwed everything up with your source books and logs and your government overtime, you're going to have to help us."

"Who are you? Where do you have me?"

"Don't you know me, Lydia? Is your brain rotted?"

"What have you done to me?"

"Kidnapped you."

"How long have I been here?"

"Two days. You were sleeping a very long time. We weren't sure if we'd end up needing you, but I told Bill we would and so they kept you here. Do you like it? Bill used to use it for camping when we were first married. I hate camping but Bill likes to get out. He goes out to Maryland on the weekends sometimes, alone. You know? Out west of Hancock in the Cumberlands."

The young woman chattered inanely, as though she were stop-

177

ping by the door of Mrs. Neumann's office before going home at four-thirty.

The mundane situation dizzied Mrs. Neumann. She suddenly felt faint, and nearly fell off the cot.

"Don't do that." Marge's voice was sharp, as though she were admonishing a two-year-old. "Sit right up."

"Where am I?"

"You're not supposed to know that," Marge said. "Now, Lydia, I want to talk to you. Everyone in the Section is in an uproar with your disappearance. They brought in a team this morning from National Security Agency to check through Tinkertoy and see what you were working on. So why don't you tell me and we can erase the evidence and everything will be hunky-dory."

Lydia Neumann stared at the all-American-girl face, at the soft brown hair carefully feathered at the edges of the face, at the soft brown eyes.

"Who are you?" she said again in a cracked voice. She felt dry, she felt tired, she felt confused by the sudden stab of light behind Marge's figure in the entry of the tent.

"You know me."

"You. Terrorists? KGB? Who are you?"

"Why do you want to know?"

"Because I want to know," she said, childishly. Everything in the conversation was surreal.

"We work for a cause," she said.

"A cause? What cause?"

"Peace."

"Goddamn you," Mrs. Neumann said.

"Now, don't get upset. Would you like some water and food? Better yet, how about a cup of coffee? We only have instant, Bill doesn't drink coffee that much—"

"We're in your home? Your home?"

Marge bit her lip and looked annoyed. "That was stupid of me, wasn't it? I'm just not very good at these one-on-one things, but Bill said I should try you first, in case it would work out. Before we had to . . . well, let's not talk about that. I want to talk to you about what you found out. I mean, why were you working so late that night? And when you called your husband—"

"You tapped my phone," she said. Her voice had grown stronger but now it was weak again, as though she had met too many defeats in too short a time. "How long did you tap my phone?"

"From the beginning," Marge said.

"You had clearances, the highest security approvals."

"Well, that just goes to show you," Marge said.

"How long have you been working for them?"

"For who? You mean for peace? All my life, Lydia. You have to understand that, that I'm really committed. This isn't just a crush, you know. Can I make that coffee for you? You like cream, right? We have that nondairy, but it's just as good. If you don't mind instant. Or would you like tea? I've got some ginseng tea and some Lipton. Bill drinks the Lipton, he doesn't like coffee that much."

"I want to get out of here. I want to go to the bathroom," Mrs. Neumann said.

"No, dear. That Porta-Potty is going to have to serve for a while, I'm afraid."

"This is humiliating. How could you do this to me?"

"Really, Lydia, it's not as though anyone has hurt you. We put you in a tent by yourself and give you a toilet, and I even put some Mantovani on the stereo for you, I thought it would be relaxing." Her voice took on a tone of annoyance. "We really don't have that much time, Lydia, I'm sure you can understand—"

"Go to hell."

"What?"

"Go to hell, all of you." Quietly.

"Lydia, I really hate that kind of language."

"Go to hell."

Suddenly, a male voice came from somewhere beyond the walls of the tent.

"Honey? Is she talking to you?"

"I just started, dear."

"Well, we don't have that much time, you know."

"I know it, Bill."

Mrs. Neumann listened as they ragged at each other, and again felt a dizzying sense of complete disorientation, as though she had stumbled into a movie comedy and was now on the screen, vying with two-dimensional figures in a plot she did not understand.

"Let me talk to her," Bill said, and he came around the tent opening. For a moment, both of them were in the opening, half leaning over to speak to her. She felt ridiculous, chained to the cot, talking to two suburbanites who had made the matter of terror mundane.

"Look, Mrs. Neumann." He was blond and pleasant, as featureless as Marge in a male way. They might have been dolls. "I don't want to go into all the consequences, but it's pretty important that you give us some idea of what you've found out of that computer and what the traces led back to. Now. Marge and I are personally opposed to violence of any kind."

"That's right," Marge said.

"But we're part of a larger group and we have to consider the group good."

"You're mad, both of you, completely mad," Mrs. Neumann said suddenly, the horror clutching at her throat. "Get me out of here. Now."

"No. Not now. Look, Mrs. N.," Bill said slowly. "You know we've tapped your telephone, you know we know where you live. We've been keeping an eye on Leo for the past couple of days, too. Naturally, he's frantic with worry, but there really isn't anything to worry about. Really. And we would like you to think about what could happen to him. I mean, some others in the group are just not as reasonable about this."

"Don't you threaten me, don't you dare threaten my husband, you—"

"Now take it easy," Bill said, smiling vaguely. "Nobody threatens anyone, but we really have to have your cooperation, or else we're going to have to tell the group that you didn't go along with us. And, as I said, some of them are really pretty tough about this. I mean, I'm for peace, and I've always been for peace. And so is Marge. But look at it our way." He blinked earnestly. "After all, you're the one who brought this problem on in the first place, right? If you had just let things go for a couple of more days."

"But there's nothing I can do," Mrs. Neumann said, weakening for the first time. She thought of Leo and she yearned for him in that moment; and then she thought of Marge and Bill staring at her through the opening of the tent. They would kill her in any case, she realized with a sort of intense clarity. They would kill her at the end, but maybe there would be time to save Leo. After they killed her.

She thought of her own death for a moment, staring at them from the cot. She had thought she was dying in the back of the sealed cab; when she had first opened her eyes in the blackness of the tent, listening to the vague music, she had thought she was dead.

She smiled then.

"What's funny?" Marge asked with that pricklish tone of annoyance again.

"You. Both of you. You're ludicrous. And you're mad, both of you."

"Is that what you have to tell us? Are you forgetting your husband?"

"No. I'm not forgetting him, no. But there's nothing I can do. Every time you made an entry into the computer, Marge, you didn't make the handwritten entry into the logbook. Especially when you were entering bogus materials from abroad. Quizon, for example. He had an access code number that also had to match a source code, and then it had to agree with the time of entry and the time of transmission logged in the book."

"No one would have thought to go back through all that," Marge said.

"I did. It took me a long time but I did. When they go through Tinkertoy, they're going to single out the bogus items, and then they're going to do what I did. Go into the logs. And they're going to get you."

"You knew it was me."

"No. I knew it had to be someone in computer analysis. There are twenty-five of us. I would have found you eventually."

"So they're going to change the coding . . ."

"Of course," Mrs. Neumann said.

"Damn," Bill said.

"Bill, I really don't like that language, it's not the least bit attractive."

"Sorry, honey. Well, Mrs. Neumann, what should we do?"

"Let me go. Now. Get away as soon as you can."

"No. I'm afraid we can't do that."

"I know," Marge said, like a bright student. "If I had your access number, Lydia, I could go into Tinkertoy myself and erase the 'boges' before the NSA people connect them."

Mrs. Neumann stared at her. "But maybe you're too late," she said.

"No, I don't think so. You know how long it's going to take to even get the setup to purge the computer. Everyone's in on it—we had people from DIA in today for the first time."

"I won't—"

"Please, Mrs. Neumann, don't be that way."

"I can't."

"Please, Lydia, it would be so much easier," Marge said. "Think about it for a little while. I'll come back later and I'll bring you some coffee. With cream. And then while we're gone, think about Mr. Neumann. I mean, you've got to get your priorities straight."

"Monsters," Mrs. Neumann said, but the tent flap closed and she heard the zipper and she was in darkness again. She sat waiting in the darkness and thought she heard them move away from her. In a moment, the air-conditioner compressor hummed again.

And a moment after that, the music began again.

Mantovani, she thought, her eyes open, trying to stare beyond the darkness all around her. Monsters.

25 ___
Paris

The president of France rubbed his hands slowly back and forth as he sat in the large leather chair next to the fireplace in his private audience room in the palace.

De Gaulle had used the room for his secret briefings during his war on the OAS in France. Pompidou had used the room to plan his strategy against the terrorists and anarchists who had nearly overthrown the Fifth Republic in 1968. Giscard, who had more secrets than his predecessors, felt he had no need for a secret room and had scarcely used it at all.

The staff at the Elysée Palace informally called it the hidden room, though everyone knew the location of it. During the regimes of de Gaulle, it had been soundproofed and fitted with electronic screens to ward off wiretaps; it had also been fitted with several hidden entrances that provided access and egress without anyone else in the palace knowing the identity of the people who came and went. Thus, in a government ridden with gossip, in which routine secrets were made public, the president of the Republic was able here to conduct affairs of state in absolute secrecy.

The room was decorated in the style of Louis XVI; that is, with highly polished woods and elegant chairs and little desks and banquettes that suggested both intimacy and opulence.

The president rubbed his hands because he had developed a skin disorder in recent years that manifested itself in times of stress. It resembled psoriasis, and his hands would become inflamed and itch. Sometimes, if not treated right away, the skin of his hands dried to blisters that broke and bled.

Across the white rug from where he sat, a woman spoke in low, sure tones. Her report had continued, with only a couple of interruptions for questions, for fifteen minutes. She did not speak from notes. The notes and reports would be written later.

It was nearly as bad as he had feared, but he did not show any emotion. His large eyes were calm, his manner characteristic of a politician who had known great loss over the years, and great pains, and who now, in power, considered the vanity of believing that power could achieve all his goals.

François Mitterand had become the first left-wing president in twenty-three years, and the bureaucracy, an establishment of the Right, conspired against him. And so did the shattered remains of the French Communist Party, which he had taken into his government but which was being strangled in the hug of his moderate embrace.

The woman now finished speaking and waited for him to respond. Her hands rested on her lap. She held herself erect, her light eyes changing color in the glowing half-light of the room, sparkling in the reflection of the fireplace. Though it was June, the room was always too cold for Mitterand, and the perpetual fire was one of the luxuries of office the simple man demanded.

"Madame Clermont," he began, "it would seem that the Deuxième Bureau has been less than efficient in this matter." The sarcasm was intended.

Jeanne Clermont did not gesture as she responded. "This is more than a laxity. I am convinced of it. For two years, there have been bombings of synagogues, killings of American military officers, as well as that matter with the American chargé d'affaires."

"And now your American agent. Mr. Manning."

Jeanne Clermont stared at him but did not show any emotion. "It was not the terrorists," she said at last. "I am convinced it was from within the government. From the Deuxième Bureau, the CID, from some security source."

"When the army sought to overthrow the government in de Gaulle's time, after the Algerian settlement, there were pockets of resistance to democracy, one might say," Mitterand replied.

"What more can be done, Mr. President? La Compagnie wishes the communications code access and source route, and they have indicated to me that the matter has some urgency." She spoke quickly, with the conscious understatement of the Parisian, who used the language to play words against each other for a subtle shading of effect.

"And so you think it involves me, when I travel to Normandy this Sunday."

"Yes."

For a moment, Mitterand studied the painting of Charles de Gaulle that dominated the far end of the elegant room. De Gaulle was pictured in gray uniform, standing in his stiff and yet oddly graceful way, one hand resting on the same table that Mitterand now sat next to.

"How far we have come," the president said. "When de Gaulle—of all people—sought to settle the war in Algeria, the rebels in the army sought to assassinate him. And from that moment, we have progressed to the point where the faction that wishes to destroy the Right works to sabotage the Left first. Right against Right, Left against Left, all in the name of reason and logic."

"I must give them the code," Jeanne Clermont began.

"No, madame, that is what you must not do. There is nothing more to be gained by your dangerous liaison with La Compagnie Rouge or by risking anyone's safety. In forty-eight hours we shall begin the arrests and break the back of the conspiracy."

"They are terrorists. I have only uncovered a part of the group."

"Madame," the president said, inclining his head in a little bow. "You have been courageous, as courageous as the women in the Maquis during the war. More than that; your duty was not as clear to you as it was to them."

Jeanne Clermont smiled sadly at that, at the irony of her betrayal of the cause. No one would call it betrayal, of course, except her.

"You have served France," Mitterand said. "Perhaps you have served peace."

She did not speak to him further. The president touched a button at the side of the elegant table, and in a moment two men appeared, dressed in the stiff collars and soft suits of the civil service. One was the minister for Internal Reform, the other the secretary of the Deuxième Bureau, the supreme intelligence agency of the French government. Both men had been summoned to the Elysée Palace and made to wait twenty minutes outside the hidden room for the private interview to be concluded.

The minister appeared startled to see Jeanne Clermont. She barely glanced at him.

"Gentlemen, this is Madame Jeanne Clermont, who has worked for me, secretly, for nearly a year. She has much to tell you, and then, I assure you, you will have much work to do. Everything will be said only here, in this room. Even as the operation is carried out, the secrecy must be maintained even when dealing with your trusted subordinates. And, Mr. Secretary, Jeanne Clermont is to be protected from this evening. Taken from Paris to one of our safe-houses in the South. Until the matter is concluded."

The puzzled secretary of the Deuxième Bureau could only nod in agreement.

"There are other matters," the president said vaguely. He turned, and the interview was concluded. But he turned back again and went to Jeanne Clermont, who rose from the armchair where she had delivered the names of La Compagnie Rouge into the hands of their enemies.

"Madame, you have served our cause all your life without rewards, and there will be none this time, only thanks, offered in secret." The large head, the large eyes so clear and shrewd beneath the dark eyebrows, stared directly into the eyes of the woman before him. "Do you feel you betray the Left when you work for me in this matter?"

She did not speak, but the president waited a moment.

"Terror, madame. Two hundred years ago, it nearly destroyed the Revolution and gave us dictators and wars. We cannot let our revolution go the same course."

He shook her hand in the formal way of Parisians and turned again, this time leaving by one of the doors that led back into the passages of the palace.

"Madame?" The minister spoke softly, awed by the moment and his presence in the hidden room.

Jeanne Clermont stared at him for a moment and then began to speak of the things she had learned over a year with La Compagnie Rouge and with the terror cells she had penetrated.

Two hours later, the secretary for the Deuxième Bureau made a discreet telephone call to the superintendent of liaisons, the officer in charge of "arrangements."

"We have a holding matter," the secretary said. "Who do you have?"

"Who is it?"

"A woman named Jeanne Clermont. She lives in the sixth arrondissement, on rue Mazarine. Can you have someone—discreetly—remove her at eight tonight?"

"Yes. Does it matter which house she is to be taken to?"

"No. Out of Paris. She is in extreme danger and it is a delicate matter. From the palace itself."

The superintendent paused. "I can give it to Simeon. One of the old-timers."

"Good. At eight."

"It will be done."

The connection was broken and the secretary began other calls. The matter was put out of his mind.

26
Washington

Bill had been right all along. He had taken the Polaroid snaps of Leo Neumann and presented them to Lydia. The threat against Leo was implicit in the fact of the snapshots; she had given in and told them everything. There was still time; the NSA computer analysts hadn't even gone through all the background sheets yet.

The room was dark; it was nearly seven o'clock at night. Marge preferred to work in the dark, but she couldn't during the day because the others objected. Marge liked to sit before the green glow of the computer display terminal and punch in letters and numbers and watch the computer respond with its flat declarations and sharp questions. It was like watching a program on television in a darkened room; all the senses became tuned to the display as the real world around faded in the blackness. At these moments Marge felt she had fallen into Tinkertoy, like Alice through the Looking Glass.

She couldn't explain the sensation even to Bill, who understood most of what she told him. But Bill wasn't a romantic; perhaps that was why Marge kept these things secret.

"What are we going to do after I expunge the material?"

"Don't worry about it, honey."

The conversation had taken place that morning in the kitchen as the two of them prepared to go to work. Bill was an assistant systems evaluator in the Department of Defense. He shared an office with two other junior men on the third floor in the south ring of the Pentagon. Marge and Bill had met at Ohio State University at Columbus and dated from their sophomore year. They were married at twenty-two, when they were both getting into government work. They were thirty-one now, they had no children, by choice; they had a pleasant three-bedroom home on a broad, pleasant avenue in Fairfax, Virginia. Every summer, in August, they traveled. One year they went to Hawaii. One year to England and Scotland. Another year to Scandinavia. What their passports never revealed was the trips to the Soviet Union. In fact, a number of things about Marge and Bill Andrews were never revealed.

Her fingers clattered over the nearly silent keys.

Lydia Neumann had been clever, of course, or she wouldn't have caught on to the game.

It had been a matter of exaggeration. When the routine reports came in from the field, Marge routinely typed them into Tinker-toy—but with little differences at key junctures. The first report she had altered nearly eighteen months before concerned the strength of the Ninth Polish Armored Division on maneuvers with the First Czech Armored Brigade in the fields thirty miles southeast of Krakow. The observer had passed along the information on troop strength, on tank and artillery numbers and kinds, and the rest of it. Marge had received her instructions through the man called "Courier" that day as well.

"For the next two months," Courier had explained, "you must double the size of the troop counts along the East-West European border."

And so seventy-five tanks observed became one hundred fifty observed, and the nineteen new Soviet-made rocket launcher vehicles became thirty-eight. Marge did not understand the need for the obfuscation, then or now. It was merely important, and she had a little thrill each time she fooled Tinkertoy.

Gradually, the disinformation had grown to a patterned structure that still did not make sense to her but was part of a larger scheme, she knew.

And now it was necessary to shift the disinformation around, to bury it inside Tinkertoy by creating new access and source codes that would temporarily blind the investigators. Time, Bill had said:

"We need four days at least, and then we can get rid of all the garbage."

No one would have understood them, Marge thought as her fingers selected the keys in rapid-fire sequence.

They certainly weren't Communists. They had been to Russia enough and they had tolerated the pathetic attempts of the Soviet officials to show them the glories of the Communist system.

"My God," Bill had said at one point, "they still have tubes in their radios."

"And the food," she had replied. She had hated the food most of all, the heavy rich creams and the sweet-smelling cabbage, and the permanent odor of onions that was everywhere. And the bread. Everyone had said the glory of Moscow was the bread, but she had hated it. It was dark and coarse and it had too many flavors.

No, they weren't Communists. They weren't dupes or fools. But peace required all sorts of alliances that were not pleasant at times. "After all," Bill had told her once, "no one thinks that Roosevelt wasn't justified in his alliance with Stalin during World War Two. It's a matter of priorities. Are the Russians going to attack us? Are they going to invade New Jersey? No. But there's always the chance of accidental war, and that's what we have to overcome."

They were dedicated to peace.

And, in time, they found the extra money delivered by Courier to be useful as well. It wasn't a matter of working for the money—they would have done it for nothing—but the money was not unwelcome.

There was the sense of danger, too, and that attracted them. It was as though they were invisible. They walked through the paces of the humdrum days, they did their work, they made their office friendships, they had friends in at night to share their latest video-tape rental movie, they had ordinary vacations at ordinary places, they went back home to Ohio at least once a year to see the friends and relatives left behind—but in it all, they knew what they really were, and the sense of constantly living a double life put a fine edge on the dull side of their existence.

"It's like being a spy," Marge had said once.

"But you are," Bill had laughed at her. She loved the way he made her feel so girlish at times. He would call her "little girl" at tender moments and she would feel as she had when she was nineteen and had just met him and first loved him.

"No. I don't mean working for R Section. I mean . . . what

we're doing. It's like we're moving through a foreign country or something. On a secret mission."

"It *is* a foreign country. Not the country we thought it was when we were kids, honey."

And they would talk again about her brother, Bobby, who had been made a quadriplegic in Vietnam, and they would talk about the kids shot down by the Guard at Kent State when they were just kids, and about how they had been radicalized and then recruited to the movement, and finally, how they had accepted a lifetime dedication to work for peace.

The thoughts washed over her memory as part of her brain concentrated on the dull work at hand.

"And now the next step," she said aloud and looked down at the piece of paper in her hand. It was the new access code she had gotten from Mrs. Neumann, the code that would scramble the identity of the source of the disinformation. Everything in Tinkertoy was double-guarded so that no one could casually penetrate the memory bank from without; but Tinkertoy, like all computers, could be penetrated easily from within.

This was Mrs. Neumann's own code, the one with the highest priority to access of the computer at all levels.

She typed: " T E 9678/11/LL2918/C ROMEX 4."

The last digit flashed on the screen and then the screen went blank.

She waited for a moment.

She touched the "Answer" key.

She waited.

The screen remained blank. Even the cursor that marked the part of the screen that was alive was gone from the screen.

In the language of computers, Tinkertoy was down.

Marge got up from the console and went to the light switch and turned the lights on and walked back to the display terminal and stared at it.

She walked around the machine and looked at the wires streaming from the back of it. Then she walked into the next room.

The terminal in the next room was "on." Tinkertoy wasn't down after all; the system was still functioning. But something had put down the terminal Marge Andrews worked on.

For the first time, she felt a shiver of fear.

She took the note pad and carried it to the live terminal and sat down quickly and began to tap the same code into the machine:

"T E 9678/11/LL2918/C ROMEX 4."

The computer swallowed the information when she pressed "Enter." And then, just as suddenly, it shut down. The cursor disappeared from the screen.

She got up quickly and went to the telephone and dialed the number in Fairfax. There was no time for caution. The phone rang and rang, and finally she heard Bill's voice.

"She gave us the wrong code. Tinkertoy shut down."

"Can you get out?"

"I don't know. I'm scared, Bill."

"Just leave. Now. Quickly. Just get out."

She slammed down the receiver and grabbed her purse and started down the hall to the central corridor of the part of the building that housed the R Section.

Her heels clattered on the floor. She had worn a summer dress, a white silky thing that had wilted in the heat of the day. Her hair was not so carefully arranged as it had been that morning.

She opened the doors of the central corridor and saw two security men with weapons drawn and the chief of security.

She walked toward them.

"Hello, John." She knew the security chief from working late with Mrs. Neumann.

"Mrs. Andrews. The computer put out the emergency signal."

"I didn't hear . . ."

"Mrs. Andrews, no one can leave the building until we determine if the signal is a malfunction." The security chief was in his early thirties; his face was the blank face of a cop suddenly transformed by duty into a machine. He had joked with Marge in the past, even flirted with her; once, at a Christmas party, he had made a slight pass at her; but now it was as though she did not exist.

"Of course," Marge said. "I'll go with you."

They walked back down the side corridor that led to computer analysis. The flooring was standard gray-green government tile, designed to look like no color at all. It was shiny because the cleaners had just been at it; the buffing machine had created whirls of wax rings, endlessly interwined, all the way to the end of the corridor.

"How are you, John?" she said nervously as they walked along. The two security men brought up the rear.

"Were you working on the machines?"

His voice was abrupt, without friendliness, the voice of a traffic cop cataloging details of an accident.

"Why, yes, I was in fact, I—"

"We were signaled two terminals were down. They were fed the emergency shutdown code. Only six people have that code."

"I don't understand."

"You're not one of them, Mrs. Andrews."

"John—"

But they had already turned off the corridor into the nest of offices that huddled along the south wall of the building and were used by the computer analysis section.

They entered the second office and the blank computer face, now a dead gray, faced them.

"Were you working in here, Mrs. Andrews?"

"I . . . no, I wasn't . . ."

"But no one else is here," he said blandly. She turned. The two uniformed security guards were staring at her. She turned back, and John stared at her. They stood in an awkward tableau for a moment. "Look," she began, "the machine must have malfunctioned."

John said, "Yes. That must be it."

"Is this going to take long?"

"We notified Mr. Hanley. He wanted to be notified if anything . . . happened."

"But what's happened?"

"The machine, Mrs. Andrews. It shut down."

"But we've had shutdowns before."

"Yes, ma'am." The voice was becoming more distant, cold.

"But am I going to have to wait for Hanley? I have to meet my husband . . ."

"Yes, ma'am, I'm afraid you're going to have to wait. You see, I'm just in charge of security, I don't have anything to do with the machine."

"But what did you do before? I mean, when the machine shuts down."

"We notify Mrs. Neumann." He stared at her. "But she isn't here now, Mrs. Andrews."

27 ____
Paris

Evening lingered in the glow of the afternoon sun, which still brightened the clear sky but cast the buildings of the rue Mazarine into colors of purple and gray. Lights were on in the cafés, and the evening menus were posted on chalkboards in the windows of the narrow streets in the 6th arrondissement. Cars crawled slowly through the narrow ways; dogs—hundreds of different kinds of dogs—loped along the sidewalks, sat outside the cafés and brasseries with begging looks; the streets were beginning to fill for the evening with mingled throngs of students and tourists and the residents of the villages and ordinary Parisians taking part in the carnival life of the evening city.

Jeanne Clermont saw all these things and saw none of them. Her thoughts were turned back, to the reports she had given three men in the Elysée Palace. She hurried along the rue Mazarine, neatly sidestepping clots of tourists who blocked the way by crowding around the menus posted in windows or in stands on the street, and arguing in loud English or American voices how many francs equaled how many pounds or dollars.

She pushed through the massive door at Number 12 and crossed to the large room at the back of the building. The concierge looked out from her little cubicle at her.

"Bon soir, madame," she said automatically. But the concierge did not return her greeting. The old woman was cross and civil by turns, each mood lasting about a day, a woman who lamented life and celebrated it by the seasons of her emotions.

Jeanne Clermont climbed the winding stairs to her apartment. Not for the first time in the past month, she thought of that last evening with William Manning, how he had trailed her as they climbed the stairs and then the touch of him at the door, next to her, his breath—sweet with wine—against her cheek. There were matters that could not be put in reports or spoken of to anyone; there were private griefs that no one could know. Giscard—sensitive soul—had told her once as they walked along the Quai des Grands Augustins on a perfect autumn afternoon:

"See them, Jeanne? How many private sorrows do ordinary people hide when they walk on this street on this magnificent afternoon?"

"What do you mean?"

"I think," Giscard had said, "that as one grows older, one begins to associate all pleasant moments in life with a remembrance of some private sorrow, so that even a beautiful afternoon becomes tinged with melancholy. Will you think of this afternoon someday and be sad because it will remind you of other afternoons when you thought you had been happy?"

Both of them knew that Giscard was dying.

"Yes," she said now, to herself, to her locked door as she inserted the key in the lock. I will think of William on these stairs, I will think of him next to me as we lay on the couch, watching the thunderstorm come over the city. I will think of Giscard on a perfect afternoon in autumn when he was dying.

She opened the door and went inside and set her purse on the little elegant table in the entry hall and flicked on the foyer light. In two hours the police would arrive to take her to a safehouse in the country before the operation began.

She closed the door behind her and then looked at the apartment. Everything had been made a shambles.

Books. Papers. Clothing. They were scattered on the rugs in the front room.

She felt suddenly sickened and afraid.

To cover her fear, she walked quickly into the front room, where she and William Manning had stayed and slept and loved while the storm shook around them.

A man was sitting on a chair of green cloth near the tall windows that opened to the balcony. The windows were shut, as she had left them in the morning. Nothing else in the room was the same; even the paintings on her walls had been removed, and some had been pried from the frames. It was not vandalism, she saw; the paintings rested on the floor, leaning against the walls. There were only the remains of a methodical search of everything she owned.

She stared at the unmoving, silent man.

He was in middle age; his hair was gray streaked with dark brown strands. His eyes were gray, cold and unyielding, as they returned her gaze. The line of his mouth was set, not frowning or smiling, but a mouth and face that revealed nothing. She saw that his face was cut with lines of age and experience like cuts of a knife in a wooden handle, to reveal some primitive counting process.

She did not speak. The silence lay between them like an invitation. She walked across the debris of the room to the tall windows and swung them out to catch the breath of cool evening.

She turned again and looked at him.

"This is about Manning," Devereaux said at last.

"I see. And you—who are you?" Her voice was as cold as his was flat, as unyielding.

"That doesn't matter."

"Of course it does. How did you get in here?"

"I came in through the front door."

"And the concierge?"

"She saw my identification. CID." Inexplicably, the wintry face altered to a smile.

"Are you from CID?"

"No."

"I didn't think so. You're an American."

"Manning. He was here before he was killed, he was supposed to have met you."

"How do you know that?"

"Madame Clermont." The accent was flat; no attempt was made to alter the broad American interpretation of the French he spoke. "He met you at four in the afternoon and he was killed the next morning and his body was dumped in the Seine. He had been with you and then he was killed. Does that suggest any reasonable line of questioning?"

She sat down in a brown chair across the room from him. The lights in the front room remained off. The fading light of day illuminated the shambles of the room in shades of purple; it might have been a battlefield in miniature. Across the dim room, each could see the shape of the other. And their eyes: they could see their eyes clearly, even in the half-light. Jeanne stared at him, and it seemed the color of her eyes changed from moment to moment, green to gray to deep blue and back through the narrow spectrum.

"Who are you?" she said.

"Devereaux," he said. "But it doesn't matter. I knew him."

"William? When did you know him?"

"After the first time."

"The first time?"

194

"Nineteen sixty-eight."

"Where are you from?"

"Did you kill him?"

Silence again. She stared at him for a moment before speaking. "No. I would not kill him."

"No matter what?" Again the winter-hard smile, the unyielding probe of the flat, surging voice. Like a knife repeatedly stabbing, again and again, without anger and without mercy.

"You have no right to question me."

"It's not a matter of rights. You knew about Manning, didn't you? Who told you?"

"William was a journalist from—"

"Don't say that," Devereaux interrupted. "It's a lie, and we can't start from that base. You knew what Manning was."

"Did you find out what I was from destroying my room?"

"Nothing is destroyed."

"Well, what did you learn in my possessions?"

"Your possessions are meticulous. As though you didn't exist. No souvenirs, no keepsakes. Everything has been stripped from your things, as though you did not exist."

"I do not need possessions," she said. "Not to know that I exist."

"Manning was a spy. He came to spy on you."

She did not blink; she stared at him.

"You knew that."

"Who are you?"

"I gave you a name and it doesn't mean anything. I knew Manning a long time ago."

"And me," she said.

They paused.

She said, "I'm sorry he's dead."

"Yes. Well. That's over," Devereaux said.

No, she thought. I am not sorry he is dead. I am broken by it, but there will not be tears or grief or the horror of revealing these things to a stranger.

"When they found him, he carried something," Devereaux said.

"How do you know what he carried?"

"I took it from a policeman. From a man who said he was a policeman. It was a photograph, an old picture taken when he was a lot younger. He must have taken it from your rooms when he searched them. It was a souvenir." The last words were uttered with an ironic tone, as though the word "souvenir" was meant in both the English and French senses of a keepsake and a remembrance of a past event.

"I don't understand you," she said quietly.

"He black-bagged your apartment, he must have. It was standard procedure. It must be where he got the photograph."

She was perfectly still; her eyes revealed nothing, not the soul and not the grief behind them. She stared at her own thoughts: William!

He took out the photograph and handed it to her. She held it and looked at it in the dim light. They were standing together before the Tuileries. He seemed so awkward, bantering with the photographer, the monkey of a photographer who had danced around them and complimented her with extravagance.

All those years, she thought with a sudden rush of sadness. It was as though all her memories were dying colored leaves on the branches of a maple tree and now blown away by the first chill wind of autumn.

She touched the edges of the photograph to frame it better in memory, to control the grief rising in her. She must not look at it. Firmly, she gave it back to him.

"Manning was a fool." His voice came harshly to her thoughts.

"Why would you say that?"

"When he left you in 1968, he was in love with you. He nearly quit the game. He talked about you, he sounded like a child when he talked about you. He told me he had loved you and betrayed you. And so they sent him back again to do the same job fifteen years later. Only now he didn't get the chance to betray you."

"I loved him."

Devereaux waited for her to speak again, but her statement had surprised them both to silence. She had never thought she would tell that to anyone. Her grief was for herself, but now this stranger had pulled it from her and displayed it.

"When did you know him?" she said when she thought her voice would not betray her.

"In Saigon. After he was here."

"And what did he say?"

"What I told you."

"You were his friend."

"No. Not a friend. He wanted to tell me, he wanted to tell someone." Devereaux's voice altered; it was softer now, it was as though he were understanding something for the first time. "You can't tell anyone. You're in the Section, you don't have friends, everything you do is done in secret. You lie, and you close up your life like closing up rooms of a house after you use them. He had to tell me, but I wasn't his friend."

"But you're here," she said.

"I was sent here."

"But why?"

"To find out what happened to Manning."

"Only that?"

"Yes," Devereaux said.

"You told me that he couldn't tell anyone," Jeanne said. "You described yourself."

Devereaux stared at her. "No. Not myself. I just understood him."

"Because you could never tell anyone," Jeanne said.

"He was not my friend." Devereaux got up and went to the French windows and looked down at the narrow length of rue Mazarine. "We were in a bar in Saigon and got drunk. He felt remorse about you. It wasn't his fault, it was the Section. He was too young for the job, too much of a romantic. They should have known he would have fallen in love with you."

"What should he have done?"

He turned, surprised. "Quit," Devereaux said. "He should have gotten out. Then."

She smiled. "And come back to me? And gotten me out of prison? And married me, made me an honest woman? And lived happily ever after?"

Devereaux now was silent.

"Who is romantic, Monsieur Devereaux?" Her voice was suddenly weary. "I was in their hands, there was nothing he could have done."

"So he did the next best thing," Devereaux said. "He suffered and came back after fifteen years to martyr himself."

"To betray me again, you said it."

"No. Not this time. I think I understand that now. It wouldn't have happened again." He said it softly.

"That is your romance," she said.

"No. But you were willing to use him this time, weren't you?"

"Yes. That's part of it. It had to be done. I didn't ask him to come back."

"And you set him up to kill him."

"No. Not William. Just to say that means you don't understand."

"Who are you, Jeanne?"

"I cannot say. Not now."

"You must."

"I work for the government of France."

"Manning wasn't killed because of that," Devereaux said.

"That's too cruel of you to say."

"Nothing is cruel except death."

"What do you want?"

"I want you to tell me about you. And Manning."

"Do you want my grief then? Do you want tears?" She stood up and walked over to him. He saw her eyes had changed again in the light, that they were the green of a rain forest, and they were damp with tears. "You see, I can cry and I can grieve if you want to see my humiliation. I can tell you that I loved William, but why would you want to know these things?"

"To know why he was killed." The same dogged words returned to Devereaux. He stared at her tears but he did not move away from her.

"I don't know. That is part of the grief as well. I don't know who killed him or why."

"I—"

Devereaux never finished.

The door of the apartment burst open and three men rushed into the front room. Each was armed with an Uzi submachine gun, fed with large, ugly banana clips of bullets, the murderous black barrels sweeping the room.

The three men wore ski masks and black sweaters and black trousers.

There was no sound; they came around the two of them and pointed the gun barrels at them.

Devereaux did not move, but Jeanne Clermont whirled, her eyes wide, regarding the gunmen with fear and contempt. "What is this? Why have—"

"Shut up, Jeanne Clermont. Traitor."

"Who is this one?"

"That's all right; I know."

"Who are you?" Jeanne Clermont said.

The first one—a larger man with a large head hidden beneath the mask—struck her with the tip of the gun barrel. The barrel crashed against her cheek and drew blood. She fell, one ankle twisting beneath her as her heels dug into the carpeting.

"What do we do with this one? Shoot him?"

"Shut up, Georges."

The middle gunman pulled out a wide roll of white tape. "Open," he said in rough French to Devereaux. Devereaux continued to stare at him, his hands held loosely at his side; he was deciding.

And then the third man slipped the pistol out of his belt.

"Open," the middle gunman said again, prodding Devereaux with the gun at his chest.

Devereaux opened his mouth and the tape was lashed across his opened lips, pushing against his tongue. They wound the tape around his head twice as he stood still. The tape bit against his lips and forced his tongue back into his throat; he felt like gagging.

They grabbed his hands and wound the tape around his wrists behind him. The first gunman was on his knees, repeating the procedure with Jeanne Clermont. She did not struggle. Blood congealed on her darkening cheek.

"We go downstairs to the courtyard in back, and when we push you in the car, you get down," the middle gunman said. "And if you give us a hard time, we'll break your face open. You understand, bitch? And you?"

Devereaux felt the gunman behind him prod the gun in his back, urging him forward. The first gunman grabbed Jeanne Clermont by the arm and shoved her along to the door. They were pushed along down the stairs to the main floor, where a fourth gunman waited with an Uzi trained on the frightened concierge.

Out the back way into the court. A gray Citroën, quite large. Devereaux stared at the license plate for a moment and then was hurled into the back of the car, his head forced down between the seat cushion and the back of the front seat. A moment later, he felt shoes against his face; he could smell them. A moment more and he heard a muffled cry from Jeanne Clermont, shoved in behind him. More feet, and then they pulled bags over their heads. He could not breathe for a moment, but forced himself to remain calm. Slowly, he experimented with breathing; slowly, breath came, stale and difficult, as though he were trying to breathe in a small box of a room.

Again he heard a muffled cry from Jeanne Clermont, but he could not see her. He could feel her body pressed against his.

The car started up and lurched into the street.

28

Fairfax

She had dreamed of Leo when she slept. Leo had been far away, down a broad valley full of spring flowers in the mountains. The mountains brooded in gray clouds behind them, but here it was all light. Perhaps it was morning. She could smell the flowers in the freshness of the damp breeze that blew down from the mountains. Leo was walking toward a cabin hidden down in the valley near the base of the foothills. It was so beautiful, she had thought in her dream, it was the first day of their lives together.

The zipper opened the front of the tent and awakened her. Reality pressed against her.

"Damn you, damn you!"

Bill Andrews reached into the darkness of the tent and grabbed her hair and pulled her. She felt herself being lifted up, pain pricking at her scalp.

Mrs. Neumann heard the lock snap, and then she was outside the tent, the chain still around her right wrist but the other end of the chain now held by Bill Andrews.

She blinked her eyes and looked around her, feeling slightly dizzy from the brightness of the room and the sudden sense of open space. She stumbled on her bare feet. And then she saw the pistol in Bill Andrew's hand.

"You gave Marge the wrong code," he said. His face was white with fury, as though all the blood had drained to his trembling fingers, tightly clutching both the chain and the pistol. "You tricked us and now Marge is trapped—I've waited for an hour for her. I know they've got her. They've got her because of you, you stupid cow, you stupid fucking bitch!"

Mrs. Neumann stared steadily at him. She kept blinking her eyes, and the brightness that had blinded her began to fade. She was in a laundry room in a basement. A white washer and dryer sat on a ledge; in a corner of the room she saw the top of a submersible sump pump. An electric box of gray metal on one wall. Pipes. A washer tub. Ordinary and horrible. There was no window in the room.

"What kind of a code did you give her?"

"What a couple of amateurs," she snapped. She had made her peace with her fear. She still felt afraid, but she knew it was a temporary condition. In a little while, perhaps in the next moment, Bill Andrews would kill her. The thought of her own death terrified her, but the thought of not seeing Leo ever again terrified her more.

She would not be afraid.

"What are you? Spies? Revolutionaries? Or do you just get paid by the KGB so you can keep living your middle-class lives?"

"I'm going to kill you."

"Yes." She talked to keep away the fear; she would not plead with him. She tried to fix her eye on the electrical box. Gray. Metal. Box. Wall. "But it doesn't matter. They've got you."

"So what? They can't do anything in time. There's no time left. Thirty-six hours and it will all be over."

"God, I despise you. How could you work for them?"

"Not them, for my country, for peace."

"You're a traitor, a goddamn traitor."

"People like you are never going to understand."

"I understand what you are."

"Get down. I'm going to kill you. Get down on your knees."

"Go to hell."

But he pulled the chain abruptly and she stumbled on the cold cement floor and fell, scraping her knees. She struggled up.

"You can go to hell!" she cried out.

He raised the black gun barrel, and she closed her eyes. She thought of a prayer, the only prayer she had ever known:

> Now I lay me down to sleep
> I pray the Lord, my soul to keep . . .

A child's prayer. She saw a macramé holder in the window of memory. There was snow on the ground, it was a wheat field in winter, and on the wall was a copy of the prayer lettered above a soft portrait of a child on its knees at bedside, praying with eyes closed.

> If I should die before I wake,
> I pray the Lord my soul to take.

The shot filled the hollow silence of the basement, and then she felt a body striking her.

She opened her eyes and screamed as Bill Andrews crumpled forward and his heavy body toppled on her kneeling form.

The entry door was open and two men with drawn pistols were framed in it. They were impossibly young, she thought. Too young.

"Are you all right?"

They pulled the dead body from her, and one tenderly lifted her to her feet, and she realized she was not going to die. Not now.

That was when Mrs. Neumann felt it was appropriate to faint, and let her weight sink gently into the strong arms of the two young men who held her.

29
Village des Deux Eglises

Calle stared down at the wide village street from the window of his room. He had arrived in darkness the night before. He had worn a medal from the war and they thought he was a pensioner, come to the village for the celebration. No one asked him questions; everyone treated him well. The concierge had brought him a bowl of soup and a bottle of wine and some rough country bread. He had slept well on the soft mattress in the small, clean room.

Below the window, the street was festooned with flags. There were flags of the French interwined with the striped flag of the British. The flags were all new, and their colors sparkled in the sun.

The village was marking the anniversary of the liberation. It had come at precisely 4:45 P.M. on the day of the Normandy Invasion, D day, June 6, 1944. The British troops had fought with a small, forlorn pocket of Germans on the western outskirts of the Village des Deux Eglises in the early part of the afternoon, but the battle had been turned when six members of the Maquis—elements of the underground resistance unit—circled behind the German nest and killed a dozen troops with hand grenades. The British had been received with kisses and tears; there had been a mass in the new church the next morning, and the bells had been rung for the first time since the Occupation began. The "new" church was five hundred years old; the second church, the "old" church, was actually the remains of an abbey that had existed when the English still owned this piece of France. After the English had been driven from Normandy, the French burned it down and killed the English abbot there.

Calle had liked that part of the story when he heard it the first time. "Perhaps the French will not be charitable to the English again," he had said, smiling his yellow-toothed smile. Tomorrow afternoon, at approximately the time when the English had liberated the tiny Normandy village, the president of France would receive in formal welcome the representatives of the thinning remains of the British army unit that had taken part in the operation. It was not a great fête, but the mayor of the village and several powerful councillors in Paris had prevailed upon the president to take part. After all, the village had been a spearhead of socialist sentiments, even in bad times.

By his own tradition, the president took part each spring in a memorial walk through a part of Normandy where the Underground had fought the Nazis and helped pave the way—with information and with key acts of sabotage—for the invasion by the Allies. At last, the president had agreed.

And the members of La Compagnie Rouge could begin their plan.

The bomb that would blow up the president and the members of the 9th British army taking part in the ceremony had been secreted three days before in the sewer that ran beneath the high street. The small detonation device had been pushed into the walls of the sewer, with the gelignite recast on the walls of bricks.

Calle would push the transmitter lever at the appropriate moment from his window perch in the Hôtel du Bois Anglais. Everything that could be done had been done.

He had received a signal to proceed from the farmhouse near Tours to the village twenty-four hours before. There had been certain changes in the plan along the way, and the latest event had not been expected—Jeanne Clermont had been kidnapped after it was revealed she was a traitor.

"What are you going to do with her?"

Calle had spoken over the phone to the man he had never seen. He was simply called "Three," which had no significance at all. Calle had spoken to him a hundred times and had drawn a mental portrait of the other man: He was a native, a Parisian in fact, by the sound of his accent. He was an older man because the voice sounded heavy and raspy at times, as though he had a cold or as though he had smoked too many Gauloises over the years.

Three had replied: "Eliminate her as soon as you have acted. Madame Clermont will be of some use to us after all. As will the American agent, Devereaux."

"How?"

"Madame Clermont, a loyal servant of the government, will be killed as part of the larger conspiracy that will include the attempt to kill Marchais and to kill Mitterand. And we will have Devereaux to present to the Palace of Justice, protesting his innocence all the while."

"Another American agent."

"Yes," Three had said. "We are all ready for the afternoon of June sixth."

Calle had traveled from the farmhouse, then up the broad, hilly range of the west to lonely Normandy, stuck out in the face of the North Atlantic ocean in the west of France, a region isolated by language and tradition and even sympathy from the capital. The Normans, at times, seemed more English than French, even though they thought of themselves as neither.

There was a knock at the door.

Calle pulled himself out of the chair by the window and went to the wooden door and opened it. The concierge smiled at him.

"Would you like café au lait? And some eggs, fresh this morning?"

"Madame," Calle said, bowing deeply.

"I could bring them to you," the old woman said. "It is so good that so many of you have come to our celebration."

"I could not miss it," Calle said. "I am an old soldier and all I have are memories of glory." He exaggerated the final words as only French permits, and the sounds of the words brought tears to the eyes of the old woman.

"God bless you," she said. "Will you join us then?"

"Yes, madame," Calle replied, again inclining his head in a slight bow.

"God bless you."

Yes, he thought, closing the door behind her. God will bless us tomorrow.

He smiled as he thought of the black transmitter resting in the cardboard suitcase under his bed.

30
Paris

Le Coq struck her again. He had struck her a dozen times in the past three hours. She had not broken, she had not wept. But she could not keep from crying out at the blows. When the police had tortured her fifteen years before, she had held out for a long time before she was reduced to humiliating tears, to begging for their mercy. But she had cried out from the first at the pain of the blows.

She tried to remember that early time as she sat on the chair and stared at Le Coq. She tried to remember her hatred for the policemen who had tortured her. She tried to keep the knifepoint of hatred in front of her so that the pain she felt would be turned back into hatred for her captor.

Devereaux was manacled to the hot-water pipe that ran along the baseboard near the far wall. They were in some sort of large loft room. The windows were closed and covered with dirty curtains. It was still dark. They had been held for nine hours. Le Coq had reminded her of the time because he had said she had only so many more hours of life left to her.

They had fastened manacles to her hands and then to the back of the wooden chair in which she sat.

"In a little while, traitor, you won't have to worry about your transgressions. You will be transformed into a heroine of the revolution despite yourself. God, I hate you!"

Le Coq's twisted face, scarred by the long, livid streak of the knife that had cut through his eye and disfigured him, spoke more eloquently than his words.

"Are you so pathetic, Le Coq, that you taunt me?" Her voice was controlled and even. "I'm not afraid of you—"

"Be quiet!" he shouted, slapping her again. Her eyes were both blackened, her face was bruised.

"I'm not afraid of you," she finished the sentence. "Any of you, cowards."

There was a single light in the room at the far end, near the door. Le Coq had been one of the four terrorists who had raided the apartment building on rue Mazarine.

Devereaux had not spoken at all. Twice Le Coq had questioned him, along with the big Algerian named Bourgaine. They had shouted at him and danced around him like threatening African warriors, full of curses and dire predictions. But he had not spoken, and when Bourgaine had worked him over with quiet efficiency, he had not even cried out. Le Coq had stopped the beating after Devereaux lost consciousness.

"We can't mark him, we're going to need him later," Le Coq had warned Bourgaine.

"I could kill him," Bourgaine said simply, as though he were describing a skill.

"No. We'll kill Jeanne, but Three warned us—"

"Who is Three?"

"Never ask," Le Coq had responded.

Now the Algerian had gone for food and Le Coq was alone with the two of them. He had concentrated his hatred on Jeanne Clermont for the past hour. A river of vile threats and black images had flown in his words to her, but she would not be affected by them. She sat upright, her hands behind her back pressing against the corners of the wooden chair.

Devereaux had watched the little drama in silence. It was as though they had both forgotten him, the unseen audience in the dark shadows at the edge of the room.

He had listened to Le Coq, to Jeanne Clermont, to the Algerian, and he had begun to understand it all in the past few hours. There was a terror cell and she had penetrated it and betrayed it for her government, but somehow they had discovered the penetration before she could be taken to safety.

And the events planned by the terrorists would still take place; only the details of the plan had been altered.

One detail was her death.

One detail was keeping him alive.

The manacle was tight around his wrist and the chain was short, less than four inches. The pipe was cold. He had known what he would do from the moment they had chained him, from the moment they had left him alone. He had known but waited because he wanted them to reveal themselves.

So Jeanne Clermont had been used again, beaten by the terrorists, screamed at, all for time, all for information.

"Do you know how we're going to kill you? We're going to blow your face off. That's all. You wonder why I kept hitting you in the face? Because it doesn't matter about your face, it doesn't matter how bad you look, when the American kills you your face will be destroyed."

Le Coq looked across at Devereaux for the first time in half an hour. Devereaux remained motionless, squatting on the bare floor, his arm down to the pipe. He could sit on the floor or lie down, but he could not stand upright; the pipe he was chained to was scarcely five inches from the wooden flooring.

"How do you like that, Mr. Devereaux?" Le Coq spoke English with a heavy German accent. "Do you like the plan?"

"And then what?"

"Then we will arrange to have you taken to the police, just like that."

"It doesn't sound very interesting."

"An American agent, hunted by the CID, and then you kill a member of the government? Why doesn't that sound interesting?"

"Because it can't be all of the plan," Devereaux said.

Le Coq laughed. "You'll see, you'll see."

Yes, Devereaux thought with utter calmness. It was just as well to do it now. At least Le Coq knew enough of the plan to make it worthwhile.

"More than you'll see, you one-eyed baboon," Devereaux said.

Le Coq made a little sound that was half-rage, half a scream. He rose and crossed the room to Devereaux and kicked him.

Devereaux reached behind the ankle and pulled Le Coq down suddenly, his head striking the floor. In a moment, Devereaux had the copper wire weapon from his wrist wound around Le Coq's neck. Blood seeped at the point where the wire bit into the flesh.

Devereaux's knee pressed against Le Coq's back, forcing his neck into the wire.

"You see," Devereaux said. "Now the keys."

Le Coq reached behind him and pushed the key chain to him.

Devereaux held the garroting wire wrapped in the manacled hand. His legs ached in the awkward position. Le Coq made gagging noises.

He unlocked the manacles after two tries with wrong keys. He suddenly rose, dumping Le Coq's body heavily on the floor in front of him.

Le Coq, relieved of pressure, turned, snarling like a trapped animal, his teeth bared, hissing.

Devereaux stepped inside his arms and crushed his nose with a single downward stroke of his half-clenched fist. Le Coq fell to the floor again, his face covered with blood.

Devereaux picked up the Uzi submachine gun next to the chair and checked the clip. He unsnapped the safety and then turned to Jeanne Clermont. He walked to her, knelt, opened her manacles.

She pulled her arms in front of her and rubbed her wrists until the blood began to tingle. Her cheeks were bruised, the blood swelling hideously beneath her pale skin. Her eyes were blackened, and one eye was nearly shut. She gazed at him for a moment.

He thought her face, despite the beating, gave him a sense of sad calm. He thought she was beautiful; for a moment, he understood everything that Manning must have felt for her.

"I don't know what I can do," she said slowly. Her voice was soft but still firm. "I don't even think I can get up. I'm dizzy."

He waited beside her.

"Yes," she said after a moment. "If you will give me your arm."

She rose, and he led her to the window. She looked down at the darkened street.

"Do you know where we are?" Devereaux asked.

She smiled then. "Absurd."

He waited.

"Versailles. Can you imagine the irony of this?"

"It has possibilities."

She looked at him. "I was to be protected," she said. "I was to be taken to a safehouse."

"Never trust a government."

He smiled then, a smile that matched the cool irony in his words.

"I suppose you're right. I always thought that." She looked down the darkened street. "Terrorists at Versailles."

"Just terrorists without a government," Devereaux said. "Versailles was never the symbol of orderly democracy, was it?"

"Louis the Fourteenth moved the court here and invited the Revolution a hundred years later," she said. "Why would the terrorists.have this place?"

"Maybe it was the only place for rent," Devereaux said. "Let me take you to the couch. We have to wait for the Algerian."

"Why?"

"Because I'm not finished with Le Coq," Devereaux said.

"You can leave this to the police, to—"

"No. Not now."

She tottered to the chair on unsteady feet; he felt the weight of her body next to him. He moved the couch to the far side of the room, away from the door. He went back to Le Coq, groaning on the floor, and pulled his frail body up. He put Le Coq in the chair and fastened him to the manacles that had bound Jeanne a moment before.

He picked up the remains of the tape roll on the floor and carried it over to Le Coq.

"Now you open," Devereaux said.

Le Coq bared his teeth, and Devereaux shoved the roll in his mouth and then fastened it with a handkerchief.

"This is the way this is going to work, Le Coq," he said quietly, his face next to the other's ear. "When Bourgaine comes back in a moment, I'm going to kill him."

Le Coq's eye went wide.

"After I kill him, I'm going to ask you a few things. If you answer correctly, I won't kill you; if you don't, I'll kill you as well."

Le Coq struggled in the chair.

"No. Sit still." Devereaux was close, his voice low, soothing. "Sit still and watch and think about what I've told you."

Devereaux got up and went to the door and waited on the other side. In one hand, he held the Uzi. The other hand formed an open palm, fingers tight together.

"What are you going to do?" Jeanne Clermont said from the shadows.

But Devereaux did not speak to her.

They waited in silence for a long time. Light began to form outside the single window.

Devereaux's face was haggard, yet calm.

The door opened and Bourgaine stepped inside. He saw Le Coq in the chair and stood still for a half-second, unable to comprehend the scene, to understand where the danger would come from.

A fatal moment.

Devereaux stepped from behind the door and slammed his opened palm heel up into the other man's nose at the bridge, driving splinters of bone backward into the brain cavity. The blow could work only with absolute confidence and an unerring sense of force and placement. Devereaux had not hesitated.

Bourgaine's eyes were wide, not in pain but in wonder, as though he were already seeing eternity.

He was dead as his big body crumpled to the floor. There was no blood, no evidence that Bourgaine had been killed.

Devereaux closed the door slowly and heard the locks snap shut. He walked across the room to the window and looked out. He came back to the chair where Le Coq sat. He untied the handkerchief and pulled the tape roll out of his mouth.

"You killed him," Le Coq said and gagged. Across the room, in shadows, Jeanne Clermont watched the two men with horror framed in her blue eyes.

"I told you that," Devereaux said tonelessly. "Now tell me what you know."

"I won't be a traitor, I won't betray—"

Devereaux sat down in the chair across from Le Coq. His eyes appeared sad, as though Le Coq had failed a reading lesson.

"Yes. It's not so bad to betray when the pain becomes intense enough. You'll betray everything, with pain or without."

"Jeanne!" His voice suddenly caught in his throat. "Jeanne! He can't kill me!"

Devereaux stared at his face.

He did not look behind him.

For a long time, Jeanne Clermont stared at Le Coq. She saw the face of the victim that she had been. She did not feel her wounds, she did not feel her pain in that moment; in that moment, she felt all the pain in all the prisoners.

So I must be the villain as well, she thought. I must betray, I must torture, I must be as villainous as they.

My God, she thought, we are all monsters. Why don't You have mercy on us? Let us die, at least.

She stared at the thin, wretched face of the terrorist. She felt only pity for him.

Devereaux leaned forward and struck Le Coq on the eye.

Le Coq blinked. The eye turned red and watered. Tears formed and fell down his cheek.

"How can you permit this? Jeanne! Madame!"

She said nothing, but there were tears in her own eyes as well. She saw his fear, felt his pain, felt his despair. All the pity for all the victims welled in her; it was almost a pain in her. She felt her heart would burst.

Devereaux struck him in the good eye again and there was a small bloody cut above the socket, on a ridge with the eyebrow. Blood dripped down, into the red of the single staring frightened eye.

"Now tell me," Devereaux said.

"My God," Le Coq cried in tears and pain. "Don't blind me, don't blind me!"

"Tell me," Devereaux said quietly, sitting still on the wooden chair opposite Le Coq.

And, in terror and pain and tears, Le Coq began, slowly, in a broken voice, to tell him everything that he knew about La Compagnie Rouge.

31

Moscow

General Garishenko crossed the Boulevard of the Cuban Revolution, which was little more than a wide alley, and continued along Petrovsky Avenue. He was of a rank and importance to demand limousine service to his apartment each day, but now, in the good weather, he preferred to walk. The walk to Frunze War College each morning was his only time alone in the day, until he returned home at night to Katharin. In some ways, it counted as the only time when he felt alone with himself, a sort of precious privacy descending like a curtain over his thoughts, shielding them from the constant, vigilant eyes of others.

But for the past three blocks even this time of isolation had been intruded upon.

He had been aware of the black Ziv limousine waiting at the junction of Petrovsky Avenue and V. I. Stavsky Street.

In the shop windows, he saw the reflection of the limousine as it crept behind him.

It was absurd, Garishenko thought: an official car in Moscow following him, yet the occupants were making no secret of their presence even as they seemed reluctant to act further. What was he supposed to do?

The car annoyed him. He felt the freedom of the daily walk shattered by the intrusion of its existence.

In the middle of the block, he stopped and checked the reflection of the following car in the window of a butcher shop that Garishenko had noticed was always closed. This time, he turned and stared back at the car and waited for it with his hands on his hips.

Like a reluctant child called back to the scene of a childish misdemeanor, the black limousine crept slowly along and finally edged to the curb next to General Garishenko. He walked to the car and opened the back door.

"Get in, Comrade General."

Garishenko recognized him. He had been at the secret conference three days before; he was a powerful man inside the Committee for State Security.

General Garishenko climbed into the padded softness of the limousine and sat down heavily next to the other man. He felt the edge of fear, as he always did when summoned to speak with an agent of the KGB. The other man smelled of cologne; his face was shrunken and white, his body was bloated like the body of a dead fish washed along the shoreline. General Garishenko realized he smelled not only the overpowering odor of the cologne but another smell, one of corruption, coming from the vast body next to him.

Garishenko waited as the car pulled from the curb and picked up speed. The glass partition between the driver and the passenger compartment was closed.

"Do you recognize me?"

"Yes, Comrade Belushka."

"That's good. I was at the secret meeting with Gogol three days ago."

"Yes, Comrade."

"What do you think of the plan of the apparatchiks?"

Garishenko stared at the sick, old face next to him.

"I know nothing of it."

"Comrade, please. I understand your caution, but there is no time for it." The old man turned to the window and stared vacantly at the empty street flashing by. "No time," he said again, absently, as though speaking to himself. In a moment, he turned back to General Garishenko.

"You know who I am, you know I am in the Committee."

"Yes."

"I know many things," the old man began. "Secrets. My life has been full of secrets."

Garishenko waited.

"I know about the way that Naya was tampered with. I know even about Tinkertoy in Washington. You see, I was in Washington until this spring."

"What has this to do with me?"

"Comrade General, your caution is admirable but misplaced. There is a time to speak with honesty and force. You are still young, and so you still watch your step so that you will not muddy your boots in the thaw. But I do not care about those things anymore." Again, the old man paused. A smile creased the pale, translucent features. "I am dying."

"Comrade—"

"What did you think of this plan, this Shattered Eye? Eh? Do you understand the implications of it?"

Garishenko nodded but did not speak. Even the nod was a betrayal of himself, but the old man had somehow extracted the truth from him.

"It is a dance of death," Belushka said. "We will trick the Americans to the point of war while we steal Western Europe from them, and then expect them, in their good sense, to step back from the brink. What utter madness."

"It is not for me to say," Garishenko said.

"Not for you? Are you a soldier? Look around you. Do you wish to see Moscow obliterated, to see the world in ruins because we have deluded ourselves?"

"I am a soldier," Garishenko repeated. "I follow my orders."

"You protested the game because it was rigged against you. I can tell you, the computer in Washington has been rigged as well. We have unleashed terrorists on both sides of the world and they are war dogs; they cannot be controlled. What if the Americans will not lose France or Western Europe? Then can we call the terrorists back? Can we say, 'Only this much and no more'? Madness. What was the final order you gave Naya in the war game?"

"I can't—"

"Yes. You must. The final response."

Garishenko stared at the old man, who fixed him with watery eyes. The old man placed his white, skeletal hand on his sleeve. "What was the final response?"

"A nuclear attack."

"Yes. Against Russia."

"Yes."

"And what did Naya do with your entry?"

"It was rejected."

"Yes," the old man said. "Not valid."

"Yes."

"Do you think it was not valid?"

"No."

"Gogol fixed the game. He has deluded everyone. Even the first secretary. They think there will be no war."

"But you think there will be war."

"I don't want to risk it. Not for this. In twenty years we will have all of Europe in our orbit. The West declines. There is industry in Europe but they have no oil or gas. We have the resources and we will draw them to us. But this stroke, this sudden rash act to compress the process of twenty years into a single day—madness."

"But what can you do?"

"Call it down."

"What?"

"Call it down. Gogol said the Americans have tapped into the computer at the War College. Then let us send them a message."

Garishenko stared at him.

"You see."

And Belushka pulled out the plastic-covered plan of the Shattered Eye that Garishenko had seen at the secret meeting three days ago.

"How did you obtain that?"

"Everything can be obtained," Belushka said. "What I need to obtain now is access to Naya."

"But you can't enter the building, you—"

"How have the Americans tapped the computer?"

"I don't know."

"Can they do it through ordinary phone lines?"

"Yes. It's possible. If they know the access."

"Then what is the access?" Belushka said.

"If I give you my code, you—"

"No. Not *your* code, Comrade General." The old man smiled, the lips pulled back from the teeth, and the smile was not unpleasant.

"Who?"

"Comrade General Warnov, I think. Yes. Warnov is a posturing fool. He has access to the computer but he cannot use it because he does not understand the computer. He will not even be able to explain how the plain got into the computer."

"Comrade Belushka, I don't—"

"Of course you do." The voice was mild. "You know all about General Warnov. You know everything about Naya."

"General—"

"In ten minutes you will be in a classroom instructing twenty-one senior-grade field officers. You will be with them for three hours. They will all testify to that. For those three hours, General Warnov will be with a whore I have provided him at his dacha outside the capital." Belushka smiled. "In those three hours, some-one will enter Naya and outline the plan of the Shattered Eye."

"But, Comrade, what if it doesn't work? What if the Americans do not—"

"Do not what? Every American base has been on alert for more than a month. They are constantly monitoring Naya. They have seen the war game and they have concluded that we are about to attack Western Europe. Why would they not monitor the plan for the Shattered Eye?"

"This is almost an act of betrayal to . . ."

"To what? To Russia? What is the real betrayal? Those who have deluded the first secretary into thinking the Americans will not go to war over this? Or you? You have shown them the truth and they choose not to believe it. What will be the point of being vindicated when Russia is destroyed and the world is in flames? I am going to die very soon; I do not want Russia to die."

"I must have time to think," Garishenko said, staring at the corpselike face.

"No. There is no time. Not for you or me or for Russia. You know that. To delay means they will have succeeded. And then, the day after tomorrow or the next day, when we are committed to war, then you will say, 'I had the time.'"

"But you could obtain the access."

"Yes. In a week. Perhaps in five days. But I do not have time either."

The car stopped. They were at a curb next to the old cemetery a block south of the college. The trees in the cemetery were full of leaves. A warm, humid breeze blew gently across the grounds.

Garishenko sat for a moment and stared at the cemetery. He smelled the sweet cologne, smelled the corruption. He sat and thought, in silence, as he watched the trees rustle in the gentle wind.

32 ___
Paris

Herbert Quizon sat at the wooden table in the little kitchen of his apartment on the boulevard Richard-Lenoir and ate his breakfast. He always ate the croissants dry, now and then dipping a flaky piece into his steaming cup of café au lait. Everything about the breakfast had rituals connected to it: He made the coffee in the same way, he steamed the cream at the same time, he purchased his croissants the night before from the same pâtisserie, he read yesterday afternoon's copy of *Le Monde*. Herbert Quizon was a man of habits carefully acquired, carefully adhered to.

The night before, Simeon had given him an envelope full of colorful franc notes. It was for the information about Devereaux. He wondered what would happen to Devereaux now.

The death of Manning had shocked him. He had passed along the information about Manning's possible dereliction in his assignment simply because Simeon had expressed such a strong interest in Madame Clermont and her workings inside the government. It was impossible to understand all the nuances of French politics, even for one who had spent most of his adult life in the capital city; it was utterly impossible to begin to understand the secret motives of the agents of the Deuxième Bureau. But when he had read of Manning's death in *Le Monde,* he knew that Simeon had killed him. The shock had worn off, of course; death was an old friend to the aged. He had genuinely liked Manning, even if Manning, like so many other young men, made himself a bit of a fool over a woman. It was too bad about Manning.

Still, one made compromises in life.

He tasted the last of the croissant and wondered if he should eat another. The companion croissant sat under the glass bell that served as a pastry freshener on the counter. He thought about the second croissant with the satisfied idleness of a man of leisure who can afford his leisure. Simeon's arrangement had been a good one, and except for the episode with Manning, nothing bad had come of it. He had certainly not betrayed his country, in any case.

216

He rose and went to the counter and lifted the glass bell and reached for the croissant. Then he heard the buzzer at his front door.

He put down the bell and went back through the bright yellow kitchen to the foyer and opened the door.

He saw the woman first.

Then the gun.

She was battered; her face was covered with bruises. One eye was nearly closed. She stared at him for a moment and then staggered forward, into the foyer.

Devereaux had the pistol in hand.

Quizon had never met Devereaux but he knew of him; this was the man.

"Who are you?"

"Be quiet," Devereaux said, his voice low and flat. He spoke English, and the words carried a peculiar menace. Quizon's world of words was French, and the English words intruded like burglars.

Jeanne walked across the tiled floor to the front room and sat down heavily on the couch. She leaned her head back against the couch; her arms dropped wearily at her sides.

"I want bandages and water and ointment."

Quizon stared at Devereaux. "Who are you to come in here and—"

"But you know who I am, don't you, Quizon?"

"I don't understand what you're saying." Quizon's own English was polite and a bit haughty, as though learned in an English boarding school. It was no match for the rougher, lower-voiced words of Devereaux.

"Get me what I asked for."

Quizon turned. He thought of the telephone, but the apartment was too small; they would hear him. He had a feeling that Devereaux had guessed the game, that he would not be allowed to live.

He took a laundered sheet from the towel chest and filled a small pan with cool water. He had only tincture of iodine for an antiseptic. He carried them into the front room and put them down on a low table in front of Jeanne Clermont. He knew it was Jeanne Clermont; he guessed everything that had happened to them. But why had they come here?

There was gauze as well as tape in the medicine cabinet in the bathroom. After a few minutes of delicate work, Jeanne was bandaged. It did not improve the look of her face; the bruises would remain for days.

"You should take her to a hospital," Quizon said. "Why did you come here?"

Devereaux sat down on the couch next to Jeanne Clermont and stared at Quizon pacing back and forth, slowly, on the far side of the room.

"I could call the hospital, get an ambulance," Quizon said.

"Sit down."

Quizon sat down.

"Tell me about Manning."

Quizon's eyes widened. He stared at the gray-eyed man across the room. Panic clutched at his throat like the feeling of Simeon's heavy hand.

"I . . ."

"Tell me."

"You know. I was the station man. Manning was my agent. I acted as control on the scene."

"Tell me about how he died."

"But I sent the report back to Hanley and—"

"Quizon, I know what you are."

Silence crept between them like a jungle animal; it waited on its haunches; it seemed to breathe, but there was no sound.

"I never knew that Manning would be killed," Quizon said at last.

"Who did you talk to?"

"I can't tell you, he would—"

"No, Quizon. All other threats are not valid. Only my threat. Now." The voice was reasonable but without mercy, the voice of a patient adult explaining the absolute rules to a child.

"He forced me to share information," Quizon said. "He would have expelled me from the country, they knew about me."

"Who is he?"

"Inspector Jules Simeon."

"He was supposed to protect me," Jeanne Clermont said. "Last night. Before they came. The Deuxième Bureau was supposed to take me to a safehouse."

"What happened?" Quizon said.

"How long did you work for him?" Devereaux said, overriding both of them.

"You don't understand. He wasn't an enemy. He knew about me, he knew about the Section."

"How long?"

"You see, he was in charge of the antiterror bureau. He gave me good information."

"What did he pay you?"

"It wasn't the money. At first." Quizon looked up with something like indignity. "I served the Section and what was I paid?"

Devereaux waited.

"Madame Clermont, I knew William in 1968. I was his control then, when I was still an active correspondent. I am sorry he is dead."

"Because you killed him," she said. "You little man. You killed him without any reason."

"They . . . Simeon wanted him but he was going to quit the mission, I knew it. He was wavering. He told me he couldn't betray you . . . ."

"Damn you," she said, so softly that the curse carried a weight beyond the mere words.

"This is the safest place for the moment," Devereaux said. "For us but not for you. Simeon is blown now and so are you. At the least, they'll send you back to the United States. At the worst, they'll charge you with murder."

"I didn't kill him, I only told Simeon . . ."

"Why, Quizon?"

"You don't understand. I lived here all those years, I couldn't leave Paris. I don't have anyone, I never married, I don't have any relatives . . . All my life is here in this city, don't you see? Madame? You're a Parisienne. What if you were forbidden to ever see this city again, to walk in the streets, to dine in the brasseries by the river?"

There were tears in the old eyes; his hands were trembling. "Don't you see how horrible it was? And until now, it was nothing important. I didn't have much information for him, I never—"

"You gave him Manning," Devereaux said. "You gave him Manning from the beginning, and then you gave him Manning's life."

Quizon stared at the merciless face before him. "Are you going to kill me?"

"No." Quietly. "Someone will, someone will come up behind you when you don't expect it and kill you. But I won't kill you. In less than two hours, they'll have you, Quizon. If you left now, you could get a flight to London. You might be safe there for a little while."

"But I'm not a rich man, how would I get money? Everything I have is in this apartment, everything I . . ."

"I don't know."

"In a little while, it would be safe again, I could come back."

"I don't have any say on that."

Quizon turned to her. "Madame. Madame Clermont? I've given you the killer of your lover, please, I assure you I never knew he . . . Madame, would you allow me to return when it is safe?"

Jeanne Clermont stared at the man for a long moment. Beneath the battered skin, her eyes were clear still, her soul shifting in shades of blue and green and gray. Devereaux stared at her, but it was as though she did not see him, did not see the other man. And when she spoke, her voice was distant:

"Yes. You can return. You don't need to be part of this. Not anymore."

Quizon began to babble his thanks, but she stared him to silence. He rushed around the apartment slamming drawers and packing a small brown leather valise. They sat in silence as he prepared to leave. They waited without speaking to each other or looking at each other.

The sullen morning light flooded the bright front room. There was a threat of rain in the lowering clouds that obscured the steeples of the city. The feeling of the city was close and muggy.

Quizon left, and they did not speak for a long time still, waiting, listening to the rumbles of the first few sounds of thunder.

Then Jeanne Clermont spoke.

"What will you do?"

"I don't know. I don't know what I have. Everything is part of everything else."

"But you guessed," she said. "About William and about Quizon."

"It was logical, the only thing that made any sense. And now it makes more sense about Simeon. What is the antiterror bureau?"

"It's devoted to investigations of terror groups operating inside the country." She smiled with bitterness. "And so, of course, the man in charge of the bureau could control the terror groups as well."

"The man called Three. Simeon."

"But all of this is so shadowy. Le Coq didn't know who Three was; Simeon merely did what he was expected to do, even in turning Quizon. There's no evidence he killed William at all."

"Except that we know he did," Devereaux said.

"Yes," Jeanne Clermont said. She stared again, not at the room but at the past, the sad remembrance of William Manning on that last night. He would not have betrayal her again, she thought—though she would have used him. He loved her finally, and so he was killed. Everything turned in on itself. She saw his horrified face as he had watched her while she told him of her tortures at the hands of the police in 1968. She had returned his love, wounding him as he had hurt her; if she had not loved him, she would not have bothered to wound him. Their love must be equal, she thought; now it was even between them, a placid sea after the storms of hurt and betrayed.

And he had left the apartment in the last hour of his life and she had not even watched him leave, she had been so tired.

And then he was dead and there would be no more betrayals or lies or pledges, no more chances to hurt or even to heal the wounds they had caused each other.

"What will you do now?" Jeanne said in a distant voice.

"Report."

She sighed, so softly that she might have intended to make no sound at all. "All of these games," she said. "Little games and the deaths we caused. And it came down to nothing at the end."

He stared at her as though he fathomed the melancholy in her laconic words. "What will you do about Quizon?"

"What should I do?"

"You don't want revenge?"

"Should I? Should I seek to kill everyone who has wounded me or who has insulted me or all those who killed William?"

Devereaux waited; there were more words to be said.

"I sought revenge once before, against a policeman. There was no satisfaction to it, only more pain, only the burden of another's suffering." She plucked at her soiled dress, distracting her hands so she could concentrate on her words. "Yes. I will do the petty thing, the little cruelty to Quizon, because I am still human. He loves Paris; he has lived here nearly all of his life. But he will never return to this city. Never." Words without fire, like the sentence handed down by a judge who must kill the man accused.

"I feel so tired," she said. "It is as though I have lived all my life and now I am old and tired and waiting for death."

"Simeon must have tapped Quizon, broken into his transmissions back to the Section," Devereaux said.

"Why does it concern you?"

"Simeon concerns me now. What he knew and what he was able to do with it."

"What are you going to do?"

Devereaux looked at her. "Rest now," he said, his voice soft again. "If there's a safe place in Paris away from Simeon, it must be here."

"What are you going to do?"

"Make a report," he said.

"And then?"

"Rest," he said, because he would not tell her all that would follow.

33

Washington, D.C.

"What do you make of this?"

The president of the United States turned to the man who was his national security adviser and waited for a reply. But the adviser seemed reluctant to speak at all. The others in the situations room were silent; the adviser carried weight in the meeting because he had expressed no opinion yet, because he had taken no side.

It was one minute past four in the morning of June 6.

Oddly, though the bright room was filled with clocks detailing the time in every time zone of the world, the room had a timeless quality to it. It would always be a room at the raw edge of morning, before dawn. The room was off the corridor that connected the basements of the White House and the ornate, old Executive Office Building across the way.

The president had been summoned out of a sound sleep. The national security adviser, who had been making a speech in Kansas City, had been flown back by special air force jet at midnight.

The matter was extraordinary, and the complexity of it had not lessened the sense of urgency that permeated the room. On a giant projection behind the president was a portrait of the earth taken by camera from two satellites—one at the north pole and one at the south. The twin globes were crossed with lines marking latitude and longitude as well as the zones. Depending on which projector was used, the photograph served as a map marking the spots of the American armed forces in the world, the Soviet forces, the forces of ten other countries deemed important enough to be fed into the computer scan.

Now the map showed all the forces of Europe arrayed against each other. Europe had been the focus of the debate for the past two hours.

"I think there is too much information," the national security adviser said at last. "And too much of it stands alone."

The secretary of state smiled at this, but no one else in the room joined him, and the secretary realized at last that the adviser had not intended a joke.

"What do you mean?"

"Two days ago, the Central Intelligence Agency received solid information that troop maneuvers by the Warsaw Pact along the south border of Poland were in fact preparations for a direct invasion of Western Europe. We put the boys on the front line first on yellow alert and, twenty-four hours ago, on red alert. NATO has been informed, the French liaison has been clued in." The adviser paused to light a cigar. Though the president did not smoke and no one smoked in his presence, the adviser was an exception. He was a man who spoke little, but each word carried weight with the president.

"Now the CIA tells us they have received details of a plan supposedly out of the Soviet war college computer that explains the whole thing is a hoax, set up to lure us into a warlike feint, and that the president of France is going to be targeted for assassination by terrorists. I mean, what the hell is the truth of the thing?"

"Exactly," the CIA director replied. He had been uncomfortable for the length of the meeting. It was the job of the agency to gather information and to evaluate it, and yet the information contradicted itself. Which was the truth? "I don't understand still how our alerts can be transformed into an act of war. If the president of France is assassinated, how would that connect with us?"

"We notified the French," the president said.

"Yes, sir," the CIA director replied. "That was three hours ago. But the French have their own way of looking at things. They said that their security was adequate for the president."

"Damn them," the president said. "Nobody's security is that good."

"The trouble comes back to the information again," the adviser said. "There's too much of it. And we don't have any third point of the problem to verify one or the other. We've got two legs of a tripod and the damned thing keeps falling over."

"I think we should not stand down from the red alert," the chairman of the Joint Chiefs of Staff interjected again. He had maintained the same simple point throughout the meeting, to the annoyance of the president. "If anything, we ought to gear it up to Complex One."

Complex One was the code for the beginning of the three-stage process that could lead to nuclear confrontation. Complex One had been called only once in the past eight years.

"I don't think so," the president said. "And I don't think the French are convinced. They have their own intelligence, and they haven't had a whiff of any sort of 'conspiracy' such as we describe. They didn't believe us when R Section came up with that Tinker-toy information about troop movements on the Polish border leading up to an invasion last spring."

"You can cry wolf only so often," the adviser said. "Tinkertoy was wrong, or at least R Section was wrong. Now maybe the CIA is wrong as well. Maybe everything we've been getting is wrong. We're beginning to look like a bunch of fools."

"Staying on alert is a reasonable precaution until this matter gets cleared up, one way or another," the chairman of the Joint Chiefs said. He was a large man with a large man's gestures. His uniform was the only piece of color in the room.

"I agree," said Admiral Galloway. The director of R Section, by tradition, sat across the table from the director of Central Intelligence. They were old adversaries, but in this, Galloway had said nothing. Tinkertoy had been fouled, in Galloway's eloquent nautical phrase. The discovery of saboteurs working inside computer analysis at the Section had cast R Section into an uncomfortable role.

"The trouble began with R Section," the CIA director said pointedly. "We kept getting these false starts from them and we kept passing them on, just like a bunch of fools. We put NATO on alert twice in the spring and nothing happened, and now we're passing along this stuff about Mitterand getting hit and they don't believe us. In fact, I wonder what we should believe about any of this information."

"It's your information," the adviser said with sarcasm.

"Yes, sir. And normally we would take the time to do evaluation and analysis. But this is an urgent matter. Something is going on in Moscow. There are factions at war there, and I think they're both trying to give us signals."

"Should I call the first secretary?" the president asked.

"What's the point of it? Maybe both sides are right, maybe they're both working the same side of the street. If there isn't going to be an invasion, then we just call down the alert. Why do they think we would be boxed in by them?"

"Maybe they don't," the adviser said. "Maybe they think we'll be too smart for them and do nothing. If only we could get a third leg on this, if we could only get some sense of perspective."

For a moment, they all sat in silence, staring with 4 A.M. eyes at each other, sick of the words and sick of the endless circle of the problem. Nothing could be resolved and yet they had to resolve the matter in a couple of hours. It was already June 6; at any moment they might hear of invasion or assassination and it would be resolved by other events.

The door at the far end of the windowless underground room opened and a Marine guard appeared, rifle in hand.

"Gentlemen," the Marine said, as though announcing a guest at a party. "I have received from post three an urgent request by the assistant director for operations of Section R to be admitted."

Galloway turned in his chair and stared at the Marine. The others looked at Galloway.

"Who's that?" the president said.

"Hanley. One of my . . . assistants. I don't know what—"

"Send him down," the president said.

The Marine closed the door.

"What the hell does he want?" Galloway said aloud, and realized it was not the appropriate question for the director of the Section to ask.

"You're in charge, Galloway," the adviser said. "What operation have you got relating to this?"

"Nothing, sir, nothing. We're just trying to clean up Tinkertoy, get back in business, I—"

The door opened, and Hanley walked into the large room and stared at the powers assembled at the long table. For a moment, he looked around, from face to face, and then they realized he was looking for a place to stand.

The chairman of the Joint Chiefs shoved his chair closer to the director of Central Intelligence and a place was made at the table. Hanley stepped to the table and stared at Galloway for a moment and then looked at the president.

"We received information twenty minutes ago," Hanley began. "From one of our agents. He was operating in Paris."

"Quizon," Galloway blurted, though it was a breach of security.

"No. I'm afraid it's more complicated than that," Hanley began slowly. "You see, it was all related finally to what was wrong with Tinkertoy, how the bad information got into the computer, who fed it, and what the source was. It was largely coming through Quizon, that was our station man in Paris and—"

"What the hell are you talking about, Hanley? We're not interested in Tinkertoy right now," Galloway snarled.

Hanley blinked at him and began again in his mild voice. "Sir. The plot against President Mitterand is confirmed. Most of the elements of what the CIA has gathered have been confirmed—"

"Not by that goddamn computer," Galloway said loudly.

"Be quiet, Admiral," the national security adviser said softly. "Tell us what you have, Mr. Hanley."

"Sir, it started with one of our agents, called November—"

"I fired his ass six months ago, I got rid of him," Galloway said loudly.

"Admiral," the adviser said.

"One of our men was killed in Paris a month ago. He had been investigating the information that was causing us trouble in Tinkertoy. I didn't trust the computer; something was rotten in the Section. So I got someone from the outside. I called in November."

"You did *what?* You did *what?*" Galloway's face went a deep shade of red.

"Admiral!" The adviser turned sharply to the old man. "Will you kindly shut up!"

Even the president glared at the director of R Section.

"November has put it together. At this moment, through a . . . liaison . . . he has contacted the French government directly. The plot to kill Mitterand was scheduled for three forty-five this afternoon, Paris time, that would be in . . . yes . . . about four and a half hours from now."

"How can you be sure?"

"Because he penetrated the terrorists. La Compagnie Rouge it's called. That means Red Company in French," Hanley said with typical pedantry. "We were aware of the existence of a terror

226

group in that country, but we never pinned down much information about them. Now I can understand why."

"What is confirmed?" the president said.

"This terror group was working under the direction of a man named Simeon, though we don't have exact proof of that yet. He was code-named 'Three' and none of the terrorists knew his identity, but November is convinced that he is this Simeon. And that Simeon killed our agent at Paris and turned our permanent station man there. And everything that November gives us from his end about the misinformation fed to Tinkertoy is generally confirmed by our woman in charge of computer analysis."

"The one who was kidnapped," the security adviser said.

"Yes," Hanley said, staring at the mild man with the large cigar. "We were set up, and so was the CIA."

The director of Central Intelligence began to protest, but the security adviser held up his hand. "How, Mr. Hanley?"

"Tinkertoy was programmed to make us disbelieve it, to send out false trails and clues, to use bad information to confuse the Allies. The same thing was supposed to be done with British Intelligence, sir, but a human factor intervened. One of the British agents decided to go free-lance with the disinformation he had stolen from a Russians plant—"

"I don't follow this. How does it relate to Paris, to these war games?" The president's frankly perplexed look was shared by others at the table.

"Sir, we have all relied on our computers for analysis of the information we feed into them. But as Mrs. Neumann always told me, 'Garbage in and garbage out.' We had been too clever. We had tapped into the Russians, we had agents everywhere. So the Russians decided to let us get a lot of information from them. Garbage. False information. And then they had a plant at Tinkertoy—this Margaret Andrews—and she began to change around the real information we had so that the garbage tended to be supported by what we had previously thought was solid stuff."

"How long did this go on?"

"More than a year."

"And no one suspected."

Hanley stared straight at Galloway. "No, sir. Until our agent was killed in Paris. Everything was unraveling, I thought. November was out of the Section, he had been let go, so I undertook to call him in."

"You didn't clear this with anyone."

"No, sir."

"Why? Admiral Galloway was your superior officer."

"Yes, sir."

The adviser stared at him for a long time and then at Galloway. When he spoke, his voice shattered the silence like a window breaking in the night. "And what did your November man find?"

"The terrorists. And the man behind them. The reason we never learned about La Compagnie Rouge was that this Simeon was with the Deuxième Bureau in the capacity of chief of counterintelligence operations for the interior zone, in the antiterror bureau. Now and then he would scoop up a fish, but he was actually the man who permitted the terror cells to operate. And he, in turn, is run by Moscow."

"But how could he find out all that?"

"He was abducted by the terrorists twelve hours ago. He escaped, and he helped save the life of . . . the government liaison who had been working on the same mission for the Mitterand government."

"And if the assassinations part of it is right," the director of Central Intelligence said, "then the rest of this Shattered Eye plan must be right as well. If we can trust November."

"We have no reason not to," Hanley said calmly. "He doesn't know anything about the Shattered Eye. He's only passing along the information he obtained."

"The third leg of the tripod," the national security adviser said. "But how can they expect to lure us into a war position, then have us step down from it?"

"Sir, perhaps it was a calculation. A computer risk proposition. As we do with the Board of National Estimates."

"My God," the president said. "Are they mad?"

Hanley stared from face to face at the table. No one spoke, but their morning faces, red-eyed and sallow, with dry lips and shaking hands, contemplated the nature of the Soviet risk.

"They thought we would walk away from Western Europe," the president said.

"They intended to use November and other agents to place the blame of the assassinations on the CIA and on us," Hanley said.

"Now wait—" the CIA director began.

"Do you have agents traveling with the president of France now?"

"Yes. Well, we always—"

228

"That's the way it was going to work," Hanley said. "You see, Simeon—this person from the Deuxième Bureau—was in the position to make the arrests. He could feed into the investigation and put the finger on the Langley operatives inside the French government."

"It's so complicated, but it would have worked," the adviser said. "Who do you suppose put us on to this Soviet plan? Inside Moscow, I mean?"

"I don't know. It was just a computer, just something we picked up that we never expected to pick up."

"And if Hanley hadn't sent this November to Paris, we wouldn't have believed it," the adviser said.

For a moment, the last remark of the adviser sank into silence. No one looked at the others. It was absurd but it was perfectly true: Hanley had broken the rules and taken an outside man and contracted a little job because he didn't trust the security of his Section anymore. And at the last minute, the outside man had gotten the truth. And somewhere in the paranoid heart of Moscow someone had anonymously transmitted a copy of the plan called Shattered Eye in the vague hope that it would signal the West to step back from the brink of war.

"Everything depended on that computer," the chairman of the Joint Chiefs said at last.

"No," Hanley replied with a quiet voice. "It all depended on the human factor in the end."

34 __
Paris

The world did not take unusual notice of the events of June 6 because there was nothing unusual in them. In a hundred places across Europe and in the British Isles, a dwindling number of those who remembered the war gathered at little celebrations to mark another anniversary of D day of 1944, the invasion of Europe by the Allies.

At the American facilities in the east of England, an open house was held and local residents of the villages of Suffolk were invited to share American beer and American coffee and American cakes and listen to American speeches on the long-standing friendship and alliance between the peoples of Britain and the United States. Because it rained that day in Anglia, attendance at the American festivities was not as high as the public information office had predicted; it was all to be blamed on the rain finally.

An unusual meeting of the National Security Council held in the situations room of the White House was not noted by the press for the simple reason that the press was never told of it.

The president of France decided, at the last minute, not to attend the ceremonies that had been planned to honor the fighters of the Résistance in the little Normandy Village des Deux Eglises. Nor was anyone aware of the arrest of a Basque terrorist named Mano Calle, who was in a hotel in that village. Only the concierge in the hotel noticed the exit of Monsieur Calle, surrounded by four security men from the Deuxième Bureau; she noted to her husband that the men, who had shown the proper identification, appeared to be nothing more than Corsicans. She did not like Coriscans at all and did not consider them French.

The Deuxième Bureau had no reason to publicize the roundup of several suspected terrorists operating in Paris or in the château country outside of Tours; it certainly had no reason to reveal that a plastic bomb had been found in the sewer beneath the main street of the Village des Deux Eglises.

And despite an examination of the terrorists that was both brutal and efficient, no evidence could be found to link their activities except through the man who was known as "Three" but whom none of them had ever seen. And so there was no reason at all to charge Jules Simeon, a respected veteran officer of the antiterror bureau who had performed brilliantly in arranging the arrests of the terror gangs.

In fact, nothing happened on the sixth of June or on the days that followed.

In the Soviet Union, it was noted in *Pravda* that a respected member of the inner circle of the party named V. I. Belushka had succumbed to the ravages of cancer and that his body would be buried in the little cemetery outside the walls of the Kremlin. But it was not noted in *Pravda* that Lieutenant General A. R. Warnov had been arrested and tried in secret court on charges of espionage and treason. Or that General Alexei Ilyich Garishenko, after a long night of excessive drinking, had apparently committed suicide by flinging himself out of the ninth-floor window of his apartment on October Revolution Street.

Slowly, in the weeks that followed the extraordinary, mundane events of the sixth of June, a gradual shake-up in the staffing of R Section was completed. It included a stripping and reprogramming of Tinkertoy as well as the administration of new loyalty test background checks on the staff of the computer analysis division of the Section. As part of the shake-up of the Section, the president reluctantly accepted the resignation of Admiral Thomas M. Galloway, the director of the intelligence division.

Nothing at all had happened; nothing appeared out of order; even a close examination by historians would not have detected anything unusual in the workings of the official world of Washington or Moscow or even Paris.

Without any explanation at all, Acting Director Hanley of R Section reinstated a field agent who bore the code name "November." He was put back on staff and salary, retroactive to his apparent resignation the previous January. The files involved in the "resignation" were altered, both on paper and in the maw of the computer Tinkertoy. Where they could not be altered, they were destroyed.

And a woman named Jeanne Clermont, who had been attached to the Ministry for Internal Reforms in the government of François Mitterand, resigned her post on June 11 without any explanation. It was rumored, of course, that she had accused Simeon of being the man called Three who headed the terror squads operating on French soil. The accusation could not be proved, and the old guard within the Deuxième Bureau had rallied around Simeon; Madame Clermont, in any case, was an outsider in the government, a radical, a passing member of an aberrant regime. Mitterand would step down one day and so would his radical friends—so the old guard agreed—but the structure of the government of France would remain. And they were certain they were the structure.

Jules Simeon had been touched by the respect of his friends within the government. He had not panicked in the bad week of accusations and charges that followed the arrests of the terrorists. He was a simple man, he explained, and not the first policeman ever accused of working in concert with the enemies of the law. His record was blameless, his decorations many, his loyalty previously unquestioned.

Mitterand's principal political advisers urged him not to act

231

against Simeon; "Be patient, he is neutralized in any case," they counseled, and the cautious Socialist, who had endured years of compromise to become the president of France, listened to their counsel.

So Jules Simeon remained untouched by all the events that had not happened on the sixth of June. He even continued as the chief of the antiterror bureau, though he realized his future actions would be monitored closely by his enemies. It did not trouble him.

The Americans, of course, operating on the information provided by November, protested to the Deuxième Bureau, to no avail. It was no secret that the Bureau maintained a cold and jealous distance from the American agencies, an aloofness that reached back to the early 1970s, when French ports served as the prime gateways for the heroin traffic to America and the Americans accused the French of doing nothing to stop the trade.

Simeon had been brilliant. He professed outrage at the charges of the Americans and Madame Clermont. He pointed out that he had served France with honor for twenty-five years and that he had helped break the back of the terrorist plot against President Mitterand.

If it was a charade, then all the participants had agreed to take the charade very seriously.

In Moscow, Gogol saved his job. He pointed out to his superiors within the KGB that the plan for the Shattered Eye had failed not because of any intrinsic weakness but because of the traitorous acts of Warnov, who fed the plan into the computer called Naya, which all sides knew was tapped by the Americans. To the relief of the bureaucrats who ran the KGB and reported to the bureaucrats on the Central Committee, Gogol was exonerated with a reprimand. After all, the bureaucracy had to look to itself; it was the State, in any case. And Gogol, carefully, began to plan reestablishment of the terror network in France. In time, it might even be possible to use Simeon again.

Jeanne Clermont emerged from the English bookshop across the narrow street. She stared at the café where she had seen William Manning on that damp, fog-shrouded morning. She crossed the street and entered the café and saw him, sitting at the table, watching her. This time, she was not startled, as she had been when she first saw Manning; it was as though she expected him.

She sat down next to him at the table and nodded when he

ordered her a café au lait. His own coffee sat cold and still and milky in his cup. He ordered from the waiter in an accentless French that was nonetheless perfectly clear, perfectly at home. Each word surged relentlessly into the next word he spoke. His voice was remorseless and flat and calm.

"Why did you resign?" Devereaux asked at last.

"Because there was nothing else to do. If Simeon is the beast, then I have failed."

"It's never a matter of winning," Devereaux said.

"How did you know I would come here?"

"I read his reports."

"William."

"He noted everything in detail."

"Why did you come here?"

"To speak to you."

"Is there anything more to say?"

"About Simeon."

"You have made your reports and I have made my mine, but the government—even this government—is like all governments." She realized the words sounded bitter to her ear; would he understand the nuances in her voice?

His eyes held hers: cold, gray eyes that captured, made still, the changing light in them.

"Why did you think it would be different?"

"Because I had to believe that. What is the worth of my life if everything that I believed in was not so?"

He said nothing.

She sipped the coffee, tasting the mixed sweetness and bitterness.

"There is nothing that can be done now," she said at last. It was a statement but her tone had framed it as a question.

"For what purpose?" he said. "Revenge?"

"I thought I was beyond revenge."

"Then why should anything be done?"

"Because he still exists."

"No," Devereaux said. "That's not the reason. Because he killed Manning."

She stared at him for a moment before she spoke again. "Yes. He killed William."

"Almost certainly," Devereaux said. "It's the only thing that makes sense."

"And you can do nothing?"

He did not speak for a long moment. His eyes rested on her face. His large hands lay flat on the little table between them.

"Do you want me to kill him?" Devereaux asked at last.

She closed her eyes as though in pain. When she opened them, he sat still.

"Would you?"

"Yes."

"Why?"

"Because I can do it," Devereaux said. "It is what I can do."

"Is it such a little thing?"

"Is it a little thing to ask me?"

Again, she closed her eyes as though to hide herself, like a child who imagines herself invisible when her eyes are shut.

But he waited for her.

"No. I can't ask that. I don't want that. I do not want his death."

"Not for revenge? Not for Manning?"

"No." And then she understood what she would do; it was as though the weight in her had been lifted. "No. I can't kill him, not at all; I won't regret Simeon's death too. One grief is enough. To remember that William is dead is more than I can bear."

"Then what will you do?" Devereaux said.

But now she could not tell him.

35
Versailles

Simeon groaned beneath the coverlet and turned in the bed, but the ringing of the telephone would not cease. He opened his eyes at last and blinked in the darkness of the bedroom: What time was it? Who would call him at this hour?

He groped for the telephone on the nightstand at the side of the ornate oak bed. The room was clammy and cold. Outside, in the half-light of a gloomy dawn, rain fell straight down in sheets on the old city. It had been a moody June, full of rain and sudden thunderstorms, oppressive with long, steamy days of muggy weather beneath ever-present gray clouds.

Simeon grunted his hello.

It was not common to receive a call in his apartment. Few people had his number, and it was changed every five weeks in any case. Fewer still at the Bureau would disturb him at this ungodly hour.

It was a woman's voice.

"I want to meet you."

He waited; he did not speak; his breathing sounded heavy to himself. The gray windows were streaked with rain.

"Will you meet me?"

"I have nothing to say to you, madame."

"You know me."

"I know your voice."

"Then will you meet me?"

"No, madame; I do not see the profit of that." He held the ornate receiver in his hand; his mind was racing. The line was not bugged although she could tap the line; but for what purpose? She had been discredited in the government, she had resigned and placed herself beyond the pale of respectable radicalism again. What did she want of him?

Except revenge.

"I will meet you anyplace," she said. Her voice was dull, even strange; but Simeon thought it must be the connection. It was merely the storm.

"We have nothing to say to each other, madame," Simeon said at last. No, it was better not to be involved with her. If she proved a problem, much later, he could deal with her quietly.

"Your son, David," she said.

For the first time since the breakup of the terror network, Simeon felt a momentary pang of fear. But he said nothing; he was a hard man in a hard service, and he would not speak his fear.

"He is at Rouen," she said.

"Madame Clermont, you threaten me?"

"Yes."

"What have you done?"

"Nothing. I want you, Simeon, only you. But I will do what I have to do to get you."

"Are you insane?"

Now she waited.

"Madame?"

But only silence lay between them.

He thought then of David, working alone at Rouen; he was not part of any of this. If Simeon loved—and Simeon was certain he had loved in his life—then he loved David.

"What do you want?"

"I want to see you," she continued patiently. "I want you to explain to me why you killed William."

"I did not, madame."

"But I know you did. I am not in the government now, monsieur. I am not a court. I do not need proofs and bits of evidence. It only remains for me to be convinced that you killed him, and I am convinced."

He listened, but heard only the crackling on the telephone line.

She was a terrorist still, he thought then; what act of terror would be beyond her? She was an enemy of the State.

Simeon thought those things without any contradiction in conscience. He had never confused his duties to France and his requirements as the paid contractor for the Soviet Union. One did not threaten the other. If he became moderately wealthy in his dual roles, then it was no more than what he deserved.

But Madame Clermont was out of control now.

"Where will you have me meet you, madame?" he said at last. He waited for the trap she would spring—a room on some obscure street, a place where she could gain the advantage over him.

"Should we meet at Versailles?"

"What?"

"At eleven this morning, in the garden. Do you know the place by the Grand Trianon? I will wait for you there alone."

"Why do you choose that place?"

"But you favor Versailles, monsieur." The voice was flat but not without irony. "A place for your paid terrorists. A place for kings, it's all the same. Government and terror are part of the same village."

He did not understand anything she said. He thought of the gardens in his mind's eye. There would be no trap. The gardens were open, he could approach her alone and determine that she was alone. After all, he was the chief of the antiterror bureau and she had proven to him that she was a terrorist. It would not be so difficult. His moment of fear was past. He was certain again.

Versailles was a dreary suburb of Paris, sleepy in its habits, existing off the tourists who poured through in the hundreds of thousands to see the great palace and grounds erected by the Sun

King, Louis the Fourteenth. Louis had chosen Versailles to escape from the mad dictates of the Paris mob, which had always cowed French kings. He had constructed a carefully balanced world at Versailles where the tensions of court society were exactly matched; it was an artificial world in a palace where Louis stood at the head of all events. And the artificial world had endured until those same raging Parisian mobs killed Louis's grandson and stormed the palace and grounds. The palace and the vast formal gardens beyond remained a peculiar landmark of power—of kings and mobs.

None of these ironies occurred to Simeon as he pulled up at the edge of the gardens behind the vast palace buildings.

It was shortly before eleven and it was still raining. The rain slanted across the legion-perfect rows of formally cut trees in the immense gardens.

The gardens were separated by two great canals that intersected and formed a cross. At the right edge of the transverse of the cross was the piazza that led to the Grand and Petit Trianons, the little palaces on the grounds constructed as places for kings to tryst with their lovers. The piazza was approached by stone steps that led up from the "little" canal, so called because it was smaller than the upright of the cross of water called the Grand Canal.

He crossed the grounds slowly beneath the umbrellas of the trees. Here the grass did not grow and the ground was not so wet. For three hundred years the stately trees had grown according to the plan of a king.

Simeon felt for the Walther PPK in his pocket. It was a very precise pistol and Simeon was a very good shot with it. He understood what he would do. If Madame Clermont was ignored, she would strike at him, perhaps with an act of terror against his son or himself. She could not be ignored.

Simeon, during the long drive from the capital, had thought the matter over and decided that Madame Clermont was mad.

Devereaux had made a reservation on the Concorde for his return to Washington. Despite the rain, Devereaux had been assured by the woman at Air France that the flight of Concorde for Washington would leave as scheduled that afternoon.

Now he finished packing his single bag in the small hotel room and again considered the rain falling relentlessly beyond his window. He felt vaguely unsettled, as though there had been no resolution to the problem presented to him by Hanley on that flight to JFK airport.

"But there are no solutions," Hanley had told him once. "There are only little moments when you can lift your head up out of the mud and see that you are still surrounded by mud."

The speech by Hanley on the transatlantic line had amused Devereaux. "Your new power has changed your way of talking."

"No," Hanley had said then. "I always thought these things, you know."

The bag was closed on the rumpled bed. Devereaux slipped on his soiled raincoat. It was just after ten in the morning; he would have plenty of time to get to de Gaulle airport.

There was a knock at the door.

He opened it, and the concierge of the small hotel stood before him. She wore a perpetual frown, but Devereaux ignored it; it was the professional frown of the Parisian in service.

"Monsieur Devereaux," she said. "This message was to be given to you at ten o'clock."

She handed him an envelope.

He glanced at it but did not open it. "When?"

"What, monsieur?"

"When were you given the message?"

"This morning. About eight hours. A woman—"

But he knew then. He closed the door and turned and opened the message.

IF YOU WILL GO TO THE PLAZA AT THE GRAND TRIANON AT NOON, YOU WILL FIND YOUR EVIDENCE AGAINST SIMEON.

JEANNE

Ten minutes later, Devereaux was in the lobby of the small hotel without his bag in hand. "I think I will stay another night," he said to the desk assistant. "Will you tell me where is the Grand Trianon?"

"Do you mean at Versailles?" she asked. "I don't know of any bistro that—"

Versailles, Devereaux thought. He understood then. At noon it would be resolved.

From a distance along the canal, despite the pelting rain, Simeon saw her standing alone at the stone railing of the piazza. She watched him advance alone toward her.

It was just eleven.

Jeanne Clermont wore a tan coat but she was bareheaded against the elements. Her light brown hair was streaked with rain and matted against her face. The wounds inflicted upon her by Le Coq and the other terrorists had mostly healed. Drawing closer, Simeon saw that her eyes were extraordinarily clear, as though they revealed all her thoughts and all her secrets.

He touched the cold stock of the Walther PPK in the pocket of his trench coat. He felt the burden of the rain soaking into the heavy fabric.

There was no one around her. His eyes had carefully swept the formal woods as he walked alone in the rain across the transverse of the watery cross. Not even the gardeners employed by the State to keep Versailles as a monument were out in the rain. Lightning broke across the foul-tempered sky, and thunder rumbled through the woods.

She had chosen such a day, he thought then; a day when they would be alone, when she could lure him to this open place and kill him.

He stopped at the bottom of the stone stairs that led up to the square.

"Madame Clermont, I have come," he said, smiling still in his vaguely comic way. His eyes glittered beneath the brim of his trilby hat, stained dark by the rain.

"And alone, as I am," she said without tone.

"What did you wish?"

"I want to know why you killed William."

He produced the pistol with a single smooth movement of his right hand. He did not look at the weapon but at her. But she did not flinch at the sight of the gun; it was as though she had expected this.

"Do you so love to die, madame? To suffer for your lover?" The comic voice drawled slowly over the ironic words.

"I betrayed him," she said.

"To return his own betrayal of you fifteen years ago, madame," Simeon said. "It was a fair exchange."

"It is not something you would understand."

"You must die now, madame," he said gravely.

"Yes."

Simeon stared at her in the rain, in the midst of the reminders of an empire and another age. A vague uneasiness came over him. "Why do you choose to die?"

239

"Because I choose not to live," Jeanne Clermont said. "I am surrounded by death." Her voice was low, speaking to him from her own grave. "I have died and died again with my husband and with my lover and with those whom I betrayed. My death will be an answered prayer."

"If it was only death you wanted, madame, you should have taken your life."

But she shook her head slowly back and forth; the rain on her cheeks glistened like tears, but her eyes were calm; she was not distraught.

"Then if your prayers are not answered by God, I shall answer them for you." He smiled at her.

"Why did you kill William?"

"Don't you understand even that?" he said.

She waited.

"He would not betray you, madame, not again. And that made him too dangerous."

She groaned then, a groan from her own grave, a sound muted by the thunder rumbling across the vast gardens.

Simeon fired then. He was very close and the shot was very sure. Jeanne Clermont fell behind the balustrade and her body slumped in the folds of the raincoat on the stone floor of the piazza.

She did not move. Simeon started up the steps toward her fallen body. He did not see the man behind him, running along the gravel path of the little canal, who now stopped and removed a black object from his raincoat.

Simeon only heard the shot.

He turned in the rain and fired instinctively at the other man, who was nearly one hundred and fifty feet away, obscured by the rain and the gloomy morning light.

They fired again, at the same time, and stood still.

And again.

The fourth shot struck Simeon full in the chest, and he was flung back by the force of the bullet. His chest felt crushed beneath the force of the slug. He grasped at the slippery stone of the balustrade and then lurched forward. He could not breathe. He took another step down the staircase and felt his fingers slipping off the railing. He raised his pistol, but he could not find the strength to fire it. He looked down, once, and saw that his chest was soaked in blood and rain.

And then he tumbled down the steps to the base of the walk

that led back to the Grand Canal. He was dead as he struck the ground.

36 ___
Paris

The sweltering day had descended to a cool, refreshing evening. The last of the sun lingered in the glow of the buildings that formed the sheltered sides of the place Dauphine on the Ile de la Cité.

They sat at the same table at the Rose de France where she and William had met fifteen years before and where they had dined again during their last spring. The last spring of his life; the last spring of her love.

She was much older now, it seemed to Devereaux. Her eyes no longer changed in the fading light; her eyes revealed nothing of her. Everything seemed hidden in her, as though all the moments of grief and tragedy had finally built a wall inside her that could no longer permit the windows of her eyes to let light within.

Jeanne Clermont had nearly died, they said at the hospital. It was a miracle that she had survived Simeon's bullet.

The president of France had been chagrined by the events of that morning in the gardens of Versailles. *Le Canard Enchaîné,* the irreverent Paris weekly, had revealed the secret role of Madame Clermont in the breakup of the terror network. The president of France and the director of the Deuxième Bureau suspected the information in the newspapers had come from certain American sources, but there was nothing to be done, and so they gave Madame Clermont a medal and asked her, on behalf of her country, to say nothing more to the press. She listened and agreed when they asked her to agree; she recovered from her wounds despite her wishes.

She could not tell them that she had intended to die on June 19; she could not speak to them of William; she could not tell them that she regretted that Devereaux had come too soon, or that he had saved her life when she did not want it saved.

Devereaux had remained.

He had come to her, in her rooms on the rue Mazarine, after

241

her release from the hospital. For a long time he had sat with her, in the afternoons, as the warm winds of July stirred the dust in the parks of the old city and obscured the heavy sunlight that seemed to oppress the place. Paris was a city of springs and autumns, a city of intense emotions in the seasons. The oppression of summer and the cold, stabbing heart of winter were only endured, like growing old or growing out of love.

"I wish you had not come too soon," she had said once to him, but her voice had been gentle, as though she had forgiven him for saving her life.

Another time she said to him, "Everyone is condemned to die." They had sat in the half-darkness of her front room; she had stared vacantly out the tall windows at the roofs of Paris. "But only a few are condemned to live after the time when death would be preferred."

She did not speak often when he came to see her. Sometimes she would greet him at the door and then return to her chair by the window and it would be as though he were not there at all. Jeanne could not explain the sense of melancholy that had descended on her. It colored her days. At night, when she lay awake in the darkness of the room, listening to the city boom in life beyond her open windows, she would think of Manning as he left her that morning. She would think she had heard the shots that took his life.

Jeanne Clermont had grown thin and grown old.

The proprietor of the Rose de France had made a nervous joke about her thinness. He had insisted on serving her his special veal, and he had been comically disappointed when she barely ate it. He spoke to her several times, but she would stare at him for a moment after he finished the words, as though trying to understand what he had said. Her responses were polite and laconic.

The dishes were cleared. Only wine remained on the table between them. She stared at her glass for a long time before she spoke to him.

"You knew that William would take me to this place?"

"Yes."

"How many lives ago was that? It seems so long ago."

"Jeanne."

She stared at him then, at his gray eyes, at the lines cut deep in the rock of the winter face. He seemed to reflect the coldness in her, as though this melancholy had been transferred to his own features.

242

"There is nothing to be said," Jeanne Clermont replied. " 'Every joke that's possible has long ago been made.' Do you know that? An Englishman said that. It becomes so absurd; it must be someone's joke, don't you think? Perhaps God's."

"You survived," Devereaux said. "It is the only important thing."

"I wanted to arrange my own death but I could not; I can only arrange the deaths of others, it seems."

"That is self-pity," he said.

"Should I not pity myself then?" She paused and picked up the glass of wine. The light caught the dark red of the liquid. She tasted it; it was warm against her tongue. She put down the glass and held it. "You place all on your survival. A simple philosophy because you think there is nothing beyond this place, beyond our bodies or this little square. A simple faith, to believe nothing. It is comforting to think that death merely ends life."

"You wanted to die," he said.

"To see God and understand the joke at last. I wanted to laugh with Him."

"Manning knew what he was doing, that someday here or in Saigon or in any of the places he might have been killed."

She said nothing. She stared at him, but her eyes had become dull, without depth. The mirror of her soul that had been in them had been shattered and swept away like broken glass. "You see death as such a simple matter. You take death; you give it away."

Devereaux touched the stem of the glass before him but he did not pick it up. The shadows of the trees had crossed the walks; the restaurants were all lit gaily around the darkened square.

"Do you understand me?" she said at last.

"Yes."

She smiled at him. "You loved then? Are you wounded? Is existence pain? Do you yearn to die?"

"No. It is too easy to die."

"When I sleep, I dream of him; when I waken, I feel him next to me in the empty bed. In a little while, my memory of him will begin to fade, as it did the first time he left me; and I will become able to endure the pain of his parting from me and go on for as long as I must live. That is what I cannot bear, that I will even be able to forget him at times, that the pain will lessen, that before I die it will be as though he had not existed."

Now, for a moment, her eyes glistened with tears. In that

strong face, the dampness in her eyes seemed to betray her. "I long to be wounded each day by his memory; I want the thought of William to always cause me pain, to always think of him dead, to always think of him as he left me that morning. But memory is such a traitor. It will fade in time, the pain will lessen, and William will be someone I had known. Do you see? I don't want to forget him and yet I will, day by day, year by year. Don't you see? That is why I wished to die, while the pain of losing him was new to me."

Devereaux sat for a long time and stared at her haunting, darkly lovely face, at the shining eyes. In her he was reminded of his own life of betrayals, of promises made and denied, of acts of love and acts of hatred that faded equally in memory until they had become mere items in a catalog of his mind. Yes, he understood her.

The proprietor came out and looked at them and did not speak. He put the bill, facedown, on the table and waddled away.

Devereaux sighed. He reached in the pocket of his coat and pulled out a sheaf of franc notes and put them on the table. In the middle of the wad of notes was a photograph. He had forgotten the photograph.

He put it on the table, apart from the notes, and looked at her.

She stared at the photograph.

A young woman and a man standing at the entrance of the Tuileries on a day in spring, captured in an instant of memory by a chattering monkey of a photographer who danced around them and made her laugh, who was part of the day and the time.

She stared at the photograph until tears blurred her eyes and the photograph became only a vague whitish shape on the table. She felt the tears dropping from her eyes down her cheeks. When she wiped at them, finally, she felt the pain of her tears stinging her eyes. She wiped harshly at them with the back of her hand and drove the tears into her eyes.

And when she looked up, Devereaux was gone.

The evening had come so softly. The sounds of the city beyond this quiet park were muted. The warmth of the day lingered but the breeze of night was cool to her face, to the hot tears staining her cheeks.

Jeanne Clermont picked up the photograph and put it in the pocket of her dress and got up from the table, scraping the chair across the sidewalk.

It was as though Devereaux had only been an apparition, and yet, he had been there: There were two glasses of wine on the table, there were franc notes covering the white bill. And the photograph in her pocket. He had given her a souvenir to keep the pain of her memory of William Manning fresh for all the years left to her. He had understood her sorrow.

Jeanne Clermont slowly crossed the little street and walked in the park to the opening between the banks of buildings that led to the Pont Neuf over the Seine. Beneath the trees, an old man with an accordion played a sweet and sentimental song for a young couple sitting together at a table before another café. She remembered the words of the song and repeated them to herself in a whisper.

She would remember.

Begun in Paris, May 1980
Finished in Chicago, February 1982